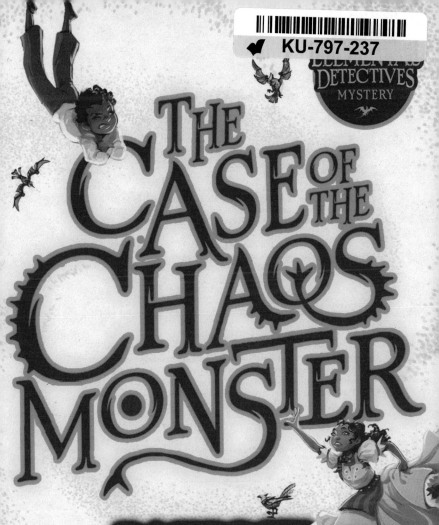

ELEMENTAL
DETECTIVES
MYSTERY

THE CASE OF THE CHAOS MONSTER

PATRICE LAWRENCE

ILLUSTRATED BY PAUL KELLAM,
MARILYN ESTHER CHEE AND LUKE ASHFORTH

SCHOLASTIC

Published in the UK by Scholastic, 2023
1 London Bridge, London, SE1 9BG
Scholastic Ireland, 89E Lagan Road, Dublin Industrial Estate,
Glasnevin, Dublin, D11 HP5F

SCHOLASTIC and associated logos are trademarks and/or
registered trademarks of Scholastic Inc.

Text © Patrice Lawrence, 2023
Cover illustration by Paul Kellam © Scholastic, 2023
Map illustration by Luke Ashforth © Scholastic, 2023
Inside illustrations by Marilyn Esther Chee © Scholastic, 2023

The right of Patrice Lawrence to be identified
as the author of this work has been asserted by them
under the Copyright, Designs and Patents Act 1988.

ISBN 978 0702 31563 3

A CIP catalogue record for this book is available from the British Library.

Printed and bound in Great Britain by Clays Ltd, Elcograf S.p.A
Paper made from wood grown in sustainable forests
and other controlled sources.

MIX
Paper | Supporting
responsible forestry
FSC® C018072

1 3 5 7 9 10 8 6 4 2

www.scholastic.co.uk

TO THE MAKERS OF
MUSICAL MAGIC

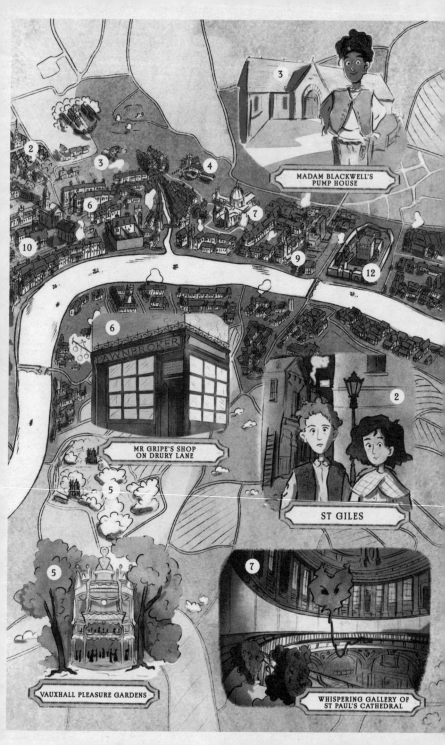

MADAM BLACKWELL'S PUMP HOUSE

MR GRIPE'S SHOP ON DRURY LANE

ST GILES

VAUXHALL PLEASURE GARDENS

WHISPERING GALLERY OF ST PAUL'S CATHEDRAL

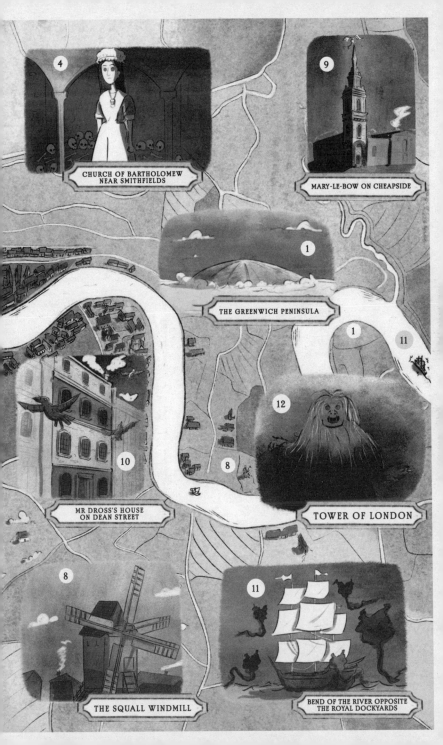

4 CHURCH OF BARTHOLOMEW NEAR SMITHFIELDS

9 MARY-LE-BOW ON CHEAPSIDE

1 THE GREENWICH PENINSULA

10 MR DROSS'S HOUSE ON DEAN STREET

12 TOWER OF LONDON

8 THE SQUALL WINDMILL

11 BEND OF THE RIVER OPPOSITE THE ROYAL DOCKYARDS

THE STOWAWAY

No one could see the stowaway unless it wanted them to. It was a Fumi, an elemental spirit made of air. It could draw in smoke and other vapours to give itself a shape. Then, it had a short thin body like a matchstick and a head like a blacksmith's anvil. The Fumis in Salzburg, where it lived, chose this shape as it gave their faces a strong jaw, just like the Solid human rulers of their empire. The Fumi's eyes, when it wanted to have eyes, were simple holes in the smokiness, its mouth a twist of darkness. But it could also be completely invisible, with only the faint scents of mashed malt and fried chicken giving away its presence.

1

The stowaway was forbidden from leaving Salzburg. The Fumi Elders said that it was too young. They promised – well, said "perhaps" – that in a century or so, if it showed enough skill, it could join the Fumi Sail Bloaters that powered the empire's sailing ships across the oceans with a supernatural power. That way it would see more of the world.

But the stowaway didn't want to wait a hundred years. And it certainly didn't want to be a Sail Bloater and take soldiers to fight wars. The stowaway loved music. It wanted to be a Music Weaver. It wanted to waft through the city's churches and concert halls and, one day, even the court of the Holy Roman Empire, lifting and smoothing and widening the music, drawing it into every nook and corner, making it perfect for every listener.

The Music Weavers only took the best apprentices. The stowaway had been given one chance to show them what it could do. Its magic had been too strong and too eager. It had almost blown a double bass out of the interview room window, along with the musician playing it. The trumpets had exploded in the Royal Court's music room two miles from there and the choir in the Salzburg Cathedral had fainted away. The stowaway had been told to never return.

But perhaps … perhaps there were other places

where it could work with music. But how could it learn about them? And even more importantly, how could it reach them?

And then, suddenly it was in luck.

The stowaway had been watching a particular family for a while now. They were a family full of music. Sometimes, when the little boy and his older sister were practising their instruments, it would let the harmonies rock it backwards and forwards until it felt like it was part of the music itself. When it was feeling furious with the Elders, it would drift towards the family's apartment hoping for music to soothe it.

Then, the stowaway heard them talk about leaving Salzburg to travel. They talked about it for months, but at last everything was packed – clothes, instruments, pen and paper for composing music and writing letters.

At the last moment, the Fumi stowed itself next to the tin ballerina in a small wooden music box. The girl in the family loved this music box. When she opened the lid, the ballerina twirled and a tune tinkled. She made a special pouch to carry it and wrapped the music box over and over again in a scarf before burying it in a case. Shut tight in the music box, the stowaway dissolved into the red velvet lining that cradled the ballerina and slept.

When the stowaway woke up, they were no longer

travelling. This was so exciting! Salzburg and the bad-tempered Elders must be far away now. All it had to do was wait patiently for someone to open the music box so it could look around. Surely there were Music Weavers here that it could make friends with. Perhaps it could practise its magic and go back and impress the Elders.

It waited. Where was the girl? Why hadn't she opened the music box?

The stowaway longed to see outside. It wouldn't hurt to puff out just a little, would it? The box would open just a tiny bit, enough for it to peer through. One quick look…

It loosened itself from the folds of the velvet and drew itself together. Then…

Puff!

The lid flew back and the ballerina shot upright then fell. The box croaked a couple of notes and creaked to a stop.

What … what had the stowaway done?

A door opened and the girl ran towards the music box, gasping as she saw how the ballerina had toppled sideways.

"Who did this?" she cried. "Who broke my music box?"

Tears poured down her face. The stowaway was

heartbroken. It hadn't meant to break anything, especially something so precious.

The girl's mother said, "Don't worry, Nannerl. There must be someone in London who can mend it for you."

No, the stowaway thought. *I broke it! I will mend it.*

It tried and it tried, but it couldn't fix the tiny metal cogs and hammers that made the sounds. Music made from just metal and wood didn't respond to its magic. Music Weavers wove their magic where Solid humans sang and played their instruments. For years, they studied the vibrations of the human voice box and the thousands of ways that hands, feet and lips created rhythm and harmonies. Human music was the only music that they understood, and they understood it well.

The stowaway had learned something of this when it had studied for the apprenticeship. It knew what it had to do. If it couldn't mend the hammers and cogs, it would find some real music, some human music and draw just a little of it away. If this was a *music* box, couldn't it hold all types of music? All it needed was the stowaway to waft music into it.

The stowaway crept away from the music box and pressed itself against the window. It was light outside and, not too far away, a bugle was sounding. That was where the stowaway would go first. Fixing the music box should be easy and take no time at all.

THE DOMEDARY RISES

A young soldier called Owen was very surprised when his bugle exploded. He'd been sitting on a small stool in Soho Square practising a new tune. It was a song he had written himself about the time that London had fallen under an enchanted sleep. He had decided that he would sing each verse then blast the bugle in the chorus very loudly.

Wake up! Wake up! (Bugle blast.)

Wake up! Wake up! (Bugle blast.)

Wake up! Wake up! (Very long bugle blast.)

He'd realized that it was best to keep the words of the chorus simple so that anyone could join in.

Owen was very proud of his bugle. He'd been the first in his regiment to be given one. It had been difficult to play in the beginning. It was just coiled brass with a mouthpiece at one end and a trumpety shape at the other. Gradually, he'd learned the bugle's secrets. He had to breathe through his mouth so he could make the notes longer. He had to shape his lips, tight and slack, tight and slack, for high and low notes. He had to play slowly.

Owen had heard that there was a child called Wolfgang Mozart living not far from Soho Square who was so talented at composing and playing music that he was going to meet King George and Queen Charlotte. Owen held up his bugle so the sun made its polished brass glow. He was sure that this so-called child genius could never play the bugle as well as him. He started his preparation. He screwed up his face then relaxed it again, opened his mouth and closed it. He puckered his lips then made himself yawn, pushing the air out of his lungs as hard as he could before breathing in deeply.

A little girl selling flowers passed him and snickered. Owen didn't care if he looked strange. Today was going to be a good day. This was the best song that he had ever written. If he chose his spot carefully and played his best, he was sure that his hat would be full of coin by sunset. He smiled to himself and stood up.

It was time for the whole of London to hear Owen's talent. He puckered his lips again and fitted them to the mouthpiece. He breathed in through his mouth and blew. The first note was pure music. So was the second. He would finish the introduction and start singing his song. Just one last note and—

Silence.

The note should have bloomed like a tulip and spread across the square. Owen narrowed his eyes, jammed his lips into the mouthpiece and blew with all his might. The bugle trembled as if the music was unwinding inside, then shook so hard it felt like it was trying to wriggle away from him.

What was happening? Owen gripped the bugle tighter.

But suddenly, there was nothing to grip. The bugle *had* shaken itself free from his hands. It bounced across the grass and landed upright, balancing on its mouthpiece. Owen was about to reach for it, but with a squeal and a note so high that all the local dogs started barking, the bugle exploded into slivers and shards of shining metal. They rose into the air, shimmered like a halo, then dropped to the ground.

Owen surveyed the debris. Only the mouthpiece remained undamaged. He picked it up and stared at it. Was his tune so excellent that it had burst the instrument?

"Wake up! Wake up!" he sang quietly.

Or at least, he sang the first "wake up". The second seemed to blow away from him. He tried humming, but the first notes faded away and wouldn't return.

Where had his music gone?

A few miles to the east on the Greenwich peninsula, a shiver rippled across the River Thames. Mr Potter and his son, Adrian, were returning with a passenger from the Isle of Dogs. The boat rocked against the tide and took father and son past their mooring.

"This isn't right," Mr Potter muttered, punting the boat back towards the shore. "Something has upset the river."

"Over there!" Adrian pointed towards Blackwall Reach. "Father! Look!"

"What is it?" their passenger asked.

He was a miserable man in a strange red hat and matching shabby long coat. He looked like he hadn't eaten for a while and smelled as if his clothes had never been properly dried. He clutched a bulging sack full of strange sounds; it ticked as if it was full of clocks and trilled like birds.

Just where the river bent to the east, an immense curved white shell broke the surface. A long spindly orange leg rose beneath it, followed by more legs than

Adrian could count. But why *was* he counting? This must be a dream. It couldn't be true!

The morning light seemed to crackle around the beast before it tottered and sank back into the river. Mr Potter shouted a plea to God to save them from peril.

"What … what…?" Adrian's voice trembled. "What was that?"

Mr Potter buried his face in his hands. "I … I think that's the Domedary," he said. "I thought – I hoped – that I would never see this aberration in my lifetime."

"It's real?" Adrian still hoped that his eyes had tricked him.

"It's real, my boy," Mr Potter said. "It's been silent since Cromwell's time, when it rose up and sank the City Marshall's best galleons – all the crew on them too."

Adrian was shocked to see tears seeping through his father's shaking fingers. His own hands shook as he tied the rope to the mooring post.

"We must leave the river if the Domedary's woken," Mr Potter said. "No, Adrian, we must leave London altogether. No one is safe. That monster will hunt down and destroy what has awoken it. Everything else will be crushed in its wake."

"What has woken it?" the passenger asked. He was still staring eastwards.

"Legend is that London's music keeps it sleeping," Mr Potter said. "It stirred before when Cromwell closed the theatres and stopped the singing in the taverns. The Domedary needs proper London music, the music of the streets, the music of the river, the music that makes folk sing and dance for joy."

Adrian was confused. "But there's music now, Father! I don't understand!"

Mr Potter puckered his mouth and began to whistle. Adrian recognized the tune; it was "The Elfin Knight", his favourite. He was about to tell his father that there was nothing wrong with the music when he felt a light breeze across his face. The song was cut short while his father still blew the air from his lips. Adrian tried to sing, but he was three words in before the words and tune seemed to gust away from him.

"It *is* gone!" Adrian said desperately.

They sat in silence while the boat rocked to and fro.

"Our only hope is that the monster looks weak," Mr Potter said. "It can barely stand. If it gains strength, it will surely kill us all."

"Unless London's music returns," Adrian said, though he still did not understand how music could be lost.

The passenger chuckled.

Mr Potter glared at him. "This is no time to be laughing, Mr Dross!"

"I have to disagree," Mr Dross said. "I have just learned of a furious monster that is controlled by music, a monster that could destroy London itself. That makes me very happy indeed."

MADAM AND THE MISSES
BLACKWELLS' WELL

Marisee Blackwell watched her grandmother paint the new sign and grinned. Grandma finished the last "S" with a flourish and stood up. She rubbed her back and winced.

"I should have done this a long time ago," Grandma said.

Marisee kissed Grandma's cheek. "I don't think I was ready then."

But Marisee certainly was now. The new sign stated in very large black letters:

Madam Blackwell and the Misses Blackwells' Medicinal Waters.
The Cure for Dry, Sore and Irritated Eyes.

Misses Blackwell! *Misses!* One of those "Misses" was her, Miss Marisee Blackwell! The other, of course, was Mama. If – when – she came home, Mama would see that she hadn't been forgotten, even if Marisee sometimes felt that Mama had forgotten her. There'd been no word from her since she'd left London when Marisee was too small to remember her.

But Marisee wouldn't think about that. Today was a day to celebrate, because now everybody would know the Blackwell Well was hers too. She really wished Robert could be here to see it. He'd know exactly what this meant to her.

Marisee's grandmother, Madam Mary-Ay Blackwell, was the Keeper of London's Wells. She was at the beck and call of the Chads, London's elemental water spirits, smoothing their leader's feuds with the other elementals. Marisee had always known about the Chads, but until recently, she knew much less about the others. The air spirits were called Fumis. They wanted to waft above London's rooftops but all the stinking smoke from the chimneys and factories was weighing them down. The

Fumis hated the fire spirits, the Dragons. Both blamed the other for starting the Great Fire of London in 1666. The Dragons mostly kept to the City of London, the part of London within the old Roman walls. It was where the merchants traded and the Lord Mayor lived, not far from the Bank of England. Marisee knew from grim experience that the Dragons did not always look like dragons...

The last elementals were the Magogs, the earth spirits. No one knew much about them apart from the fact that their rulers, the giants, Gog and Magog, were asleep at the bottom of the Thames. There had once been a war between the elementals which had left London empty of humans – or Solids, as the elementals called them – for a while. No one wanted that to happen again, so the Lord Mayor, Richard Whittington, had written his long, long Articles about how the London elementals should behave. It was also a truce and the Chads, the Dragons, the Fumis and a representative for the Magogs had signed it, promising to keep the peace.

They had kept the peace. Just about. But as far as Marisee knew, the Chads, the Fumis and the Dragons still hated each other.

Madam Blackwell also toured the wells, springs and rivers of London, taking the Chads' complaints about pollution and being diverted or covered up to the Lord

Mayor of London. The Lord Mayor changed every year, so Grandma always felt that she was starting over again. She'd been complaining about getting tired for a long time, but it was only since the enchanted sleep that she had truly allowed Marisee to help her. Now it was official, in writing.

And Marisee even had her own Chads to care for.

She ran back into the kitchen and grabbed a handful of jars, stoppers and labels. She'd bring some water back for Grandma to check. They were especially interested in the River Fleet. It was getting so dirty and smelly that more and more of it was being covered over. But it also had a new Chad spirit, a child who'd once been a foundling called Sally Blake. She was now called Sally Fleet, a new kind of Chad, who was happy to care for an underground river instead of an overground one. Grandma and Marisee had actually seen Sally Fleet first emerge from a pile of mud. Grandma had never seen a Chad "born" before and wanted to know as much as she could about her.

And Marisee liked visiting Sally Fleet. She was the only Chad who seemed anywhere close to her in age. There were others who looked young, but had been around for centuries and behaved like that. Everything seemed so new to Sally – and Marisee loved being her guide. She gave her grandma another quick kiss and raced across the field to the village, the flasks jangling in her basket. Mr Glace, the butcher, was driving down to London to check over some cattle at Smithfield Market. He'd agreed to take Marisee as a passenger in his cart.

The road was bumpy. Mr Glace talked for the whole journey, not pausing for any reply. It was mostly a long complaint about his baby not sleeping because no one could sing them a lullaby. Marisee nodded when she thought it was expected but was busy concentrating hard on not falling off her seat. Slate, the horse pulling the cart, seemed to speed up and slow down for no reason at all. Marisee was relieved when she could jump off by the church of St Bartholomew near Smithfield.

Marisee ran down the worn stone steps to the crypt. She was so used to the pile of old bones in the corner that she barely noticed them now. It was here that her friend, Robert Strong, had been tricked into betraying her by the Shepherdess. Marisee was standing right where he'd crumpled to the stone floor. She'd never forget the thud as his body had hit the ground and the sick helplessness when she'd thought he was dead.

Robert wasn't dead, or not that she knew of, but it sometimes felt that way. She hadn't seen him since that morning. Just as London was waking up from the enchanted sleep and everything had seemed full of hope again, they'd had to leave each other. He'd been so guilty and upset about giving the Shepherdess the power to destroy London. Grandma had comforted him, but Marisee wasn't convinced that Robert had really believed that he was forgiven. They'd never had a chance to talk about what had happened.

That was six months ago. Six months! She'd cheered when Grandma had told her that he'd run away from the awful Hibberts, hoping that he'd make his way to Grandma's house. But he hadn't. Grandma believed that it was better for Robert to stay hidden and wouldn't let Marisee look for him. She said that there were spies everywhere and vicious men prowled London's streets, capturing anyone they believed had escaped from enslavement. They collected a reward before forcing the kidnapped people on to ships to the plantations in the West Indies.

No news was good news, Grandma insisted. But sometimes, it felt hard for Marisee to be happy when she thought of Robert. He must be so lonely, struggling every day to find enough to eat. She knew that there could be terrible consequences if he came to see her and was caught, but still, did he ever wonder about her or was he too busy trying to stay alive? If he could read or write, he might have sent her a note just to let her know that he was safe. Surely there must be some way to see each other soon.

But now, she must carry out her duties. Marisee counted three paving stones west from the door, then three stones south. The Foundling Hospital, where Sally Fleet had lived as a human child, had registered her as baby number 33. That was why they'd chosen this stone. Marisee stood on it and scuffed her heel twice against the left edge. She waited then scuffed her heel again.

"Are you here?" she hissed.

A spark of silver flew out from the stone, crackled across its surface and skittered into the space around the edges. The silver washed back until the whole slab was covered.

Marisee held her breath and closed her eyes. She hated this bit. There was a loud grumble and a flash so bright that she could see it through her closed eyelids. Then she was plunging. It only lasted a couple of seconds but enough to feel that her skeleton and skin were down in the tunnel and her insides still above in the crypt. Sally Fleet had yet to finesse her magic.

Sally was waiting for her. She looked like a girl of thirteen with straight dark hair and pale skin. Her eyes were all brown with no pupils and Marisee noticed that her fingernails had grown wide and flat-edged, as if easier to slice away the earth in the underground river channels. She still wore the uniform of a foundling girl – brown drugget dress, black boots and a pristine white apron and bonnet. The metal tag around her neck was engraved with the number 33; the figures glowed with a silver light.

"Was I better this time?" Sally asked.

Marisee swallowed hard. Her insides and outsides were back where they should be. She gave a weak smile. "Definitely better." She checked the empty flasks in her basket. "And none broken."

Sally grinned and looped her arm through Marisee's. Although she – almost – looked like a human girl and moved her feet like she was taking steps, she glided like a stream and smelled of damp earth and old puddles.

"Auntie Turnmill wants to see you," she said. "She's with the lost things."

Sally pulled Marisee down a long tunnel until it widened out into the size of a room. This was where the River Fleet held some of its secrets. Marisee skirted the skeletons of old boats and nooks filled with tatty wigs, chair legs and every variety of tools. She ducked beneath the long poles that leaned against a corner as if a sedan chair had been dropped into the river and the chair and box had rotted away and headed towards the woman standing on the millstone in the middle of the room.

This was Turnmill Brook, an ancient water spirit who remembered when the River Fleet had been clean and strong, its powerful watermills grinding wheat into flour. She was also Marisee's favourite Chad. Perhaps it was because Marisee couldn't remember her own mother and Turnmill was everything a mother should be. She was brave, didn't take nonsense from people who tried to order her around and was very loyal to Madam Blackwell. She could also speak to horses, something that Marisee greatly wished that Turnmill would teach her.

Turnmill wore a waistcoat and breeches, and her hair was braided and twisted into a coil that was held in place by shards of pottery. A large wild boar circled her, grunting. Its eyes were small and hard. Its thick tusks curved upwards, tapering into sharp tips. Its body was crossed with scars. He was the river spirit keeping an eye on the Fleet Ditch.

"Good afternoon, Marisee," the boar said. His voice was rich and smooth.

Marisee jumped. "Um… Good afternoon, Ditch."

According to Turnmill Brook, Ditch spoke eighty-three different languages and could swear in many more, but in Marisee's experience he rarely did more than grunt.

"I'm trying to teach him manners," Turnmill said.

Ditch grunted back at her.

Turnmill stepped off the millstone and hugged Marisee. For a moment, Marisee felt engulfed in a swift, fresh current and her head filled with the crack of wheat grain crushed between giant wheels. When Turnmill released her, it passed.

"Where are you going today?" Turnmill asked.

"Staple Inn and Clement Danes," Marisee said. "To see if the springs have anything to tell Grandma."

"Excellent," Turnmill said. "Though I've heard some worrying news from Effra that you should pass on to Madam Blackwell."

"Effra?" Marisee was suddenly very interested. "From south of the river?"

Turnmill nodded.

"Has she seen something strange?" Marisee said. "Perhaps I should go and talk to her."

The thought was exciting. Marisee hadn't met Effra yet. She had never even crossed Westminster Bridge. Maybe it was time that she did.

"Not seen something. More felt it." Turnmill looked thoughtful. "We've all felt it, though it is gentler this side of the Thames. There are so many people and buildings it can hide the real feel of London. But something *is* out of balance. The Thames moves in an unusual way and London sounds hollow. At Sadler's Wells last night, their sweetest soprano suddenly croaked like a frog and fell silent. The band put down their instruments and stopped playing." She gave Marisee a knowing smile. "I know you're curious, but if you want to find out more, you don't have to talk to Effra. Go and ask Sadler. He's closer to home."

Marisee smiled back. Sadler, the fox-like Chad who guarded Sadler's Wells, was well known to the Blackwells; he'd guarded Madam Blackwell's house during the enchanted sleep.

"He's not far from Grandma," Marisee said. "So he can go there himself with his news. Effra's much further away. Sometimes she must feel forgotten and…"

Turnmill's voice was serious. "Anyone would think that you're looking for a new adventure, Marisee."

"No!" Marisee didn't even sound convincing to herself. She liked helping Grandma more, but there'd been something … special … about racing through London with Robert and saving the city from the enchanted sleep. "And not without Robert," she added.

"Well, here's some more news for Madam Blackwell," Turnmill said. "The Lambeth Springs told Effra that there was a commotion in the Pleasure Gardens in Vauxhall last night. Have you heard of the Pleasure Gardens?"

"Yes!" Marisee was outraged. Hadn't everybody? It was *the* place to go and be seen! Where the best-dressed people strolled beneath strings of beautiful-coloured lights listening to wonderful musicians.

"The organist was five notes into Mr Handel's 'The Cuckoo and the Nightingale'," Turnmill said, "when two organ valves exploded and a pedal whirled through the air, hitting the organist on the nose. Mr Tyers, the Gardens' proprietor, claimed that the bellows were at fault, but the Lambeth Springs disagree. They said that the orchestra looked like they were fighting their instruments. One moment there were harmonies, the next discord, then nothing. Effra's going there tonight to see if anything else happens. If Madam Blackwell agrees, perhaps you can visit Effra tomorrow to find out more."

Tomorrow? How could she wait until tomorrow now that she knew this? She'd be too worried that something might take place in Vauxhall that she should know about straight away. Last year, Grandma had kept a big secret from her that had made it harder to stop the enchanted sleep. It could be dangerous to wait. Marisee had to visit the Gardens tonight. Tomorrow could be too late.

Turnmill eyed her suspiciously. "I mean it, Marisee," she said. "You can go and meet Effra tomorrow. Who knows what could happen at the Gardens tonight?"

Exactly! That's why Marisee wanted to be there! But she said, "Of course, Turnmill. I can go tomorrow."

She hoped that river spirits couldn't actually read minds.

It took a long time for Marisee to visit everyone on her list. Sally Fleet insisted on coming with her and had so many questions about every new thing that she saw. Marisee introduced her to some of the quieter Chads that cared for the smaller springs. Many had been underground for as long as they could remember and none of the big rivers had ever talked to them. They had so much to say! Marisee tried to listen and make notes about their worries, but in her mind she was already crossing Westminster Bridge and walking west on the south side of the Thames towards Vauxhall Pleasure Gardens.

At last, Marisee found herself standing back in the crypt, holding her filled water flasks and with a head full of things to tell Grandma. But did she really want to go back to Clerkenwell straight away? She knew she should. Grandma would be worried if she wasn't home soon. It wasn't long until twilight and the road to Clerkenwell was dark and dangerous.

But on the other hand, here she was, already in London, and Vauxhall wasn't *that* far away. She wouldn't have to stay in the Gardens for long. If anything happened, she'd be able to give Grandma a proper account. Grandma might not go south of the river, but if Effra thought that there was danger, then Grandma should know about it to make sure that the springs and rivers were safe.

No one wanted another magical disaster to creep up on London, did they?

No. They didn't.

Marisee hid her flasks behind the pile of bones and set off. The streets were so busy. Soldiers were emerging well-fed from chop houses. Ladies and their maids browsed the draper shops. Street sellers offered everything from shoe polishing to rhubarb, and so many tired and dusty folk were begging for money. Carts of fruit and vegetables clattered along the narrow street towards the market stalls at Covent Garden. Everything seemed as it should, but Turnmill *was* right. Something felt strange.

Marisee sped up as she reached Whitehall – not far to Westminster Bridge now. And there it was, its many arches stretching across a river so wide that it really could be the sea. She had been with Grandma to Southwark before, on the south side of London Bridge, but the land beyond Westminster Bridge was like a new country. Excitement bubbled in her stomach as if she *was* embarking on a new adventure. But it wasn't *really* an adventure. All she was doing was finding out information for Grandma.

All *you're doing?* The tiny thought prickled at her. *Be*

honest, Marisee! Are you sure you're not looking for another adventure? She sighed to herself. She hated to admit it, but being Grandma's assistant *was* a little bit more boring than she'd expected, especially after she'd got used to jumping down the wells. She spent a lot of time listening to Chads complain, or collecting water or, even worse, collecting money from grumpy rich customers who wanted the Blackwells' healing water without paying for it.

But at the same time, she didn't want to have another adventure without Robert. He made her feel brave even when she was frightened. She ran along the bridge, not stopping until she reached halfway. The sun was setting, softening the hard shape of Westminster Hall to the west. The Thames curved to the east so she couldn't see the new Blackfriars Bridge or beyond that London Bridge and the Tower of London. In the north, the steeples and bell-towers of churches pierced the sky. Boats jostled each other on the river below, galleons and barges and wherries ferrying passengers between the north and south banks. A schooner was being nudged eastwards on the tide until it turned the bend in the river and disappeared.

Was the river really moving the wrong way? How could Marisee tell? Hopefully, she'd meet Effra, who'd explain it all to her.

As Marisee left Westminster Bridge, twilight

seemed to come quickly. Greyness faded into black. Why hadn't she thought of bringing a lantern? Beyond the road, it was mostly marshes; no glowing shop windows or street lamps. Marisee jumped. Did that shadow just move? This would be a perfect spot for highwaymen and footpads, waiting to pounce on their rich victims. She hurried on. A carriage rushed past her, lurching slightly on the uneven road. Its rear lights grew smaller and smaller until she was alone again. There was just silence and deepening darkness, but at least no highwaymen had leaped out to attack.

Still, Marisee wasn't so sure if this was such a good idea after all.

A bush rustled and a big dark shape scuttled along the verge. Marisee stopped still. Her heart was banging like a soldier's drum. Suddenly, she felt very alone and very frightened. She wished that Robert could magically appear by her side. She wanted to be brave.

The shape moved again, darting across the path in front of her. Marisee caught sight of a large, bulbous abdomen, many legs, a jewel-like glint of … eyes?

Too many eyes.

THE CAPTURE-CREATURE

Robert Strong sat at the table with the book, pen and ink in front of him, and a shard beast lurking in the corner behind him. Nothing about the shard beast was soft. It leaned against a wall, eyeing him, even though Robert couldn't actually see any eyes. The beast was shaped like a wave, the tip curved over into what could be a head, but there was nothing resembling a face. Its body was covered in thousands of glass needles that jangled together when it moved. Robert knew that it could shoot those needles at its enemies. Its three legs seemed to be made of clay, with bright red kerchiefs tied around the knees. Its feet, if indeed it had feet, were hidden inside black leather boots. They flapped open, the eyelets empty of laces, but that didn't slow the shard beast down at all.

"Ignore it and concentrate!" Emma tapped the abandoned book. "It took me ages to get Steeple to steal this for me. You of all people should be used to strange beings."

Yes, that was true. Last year, Robert had met Marisee Blackwell, the Well Keeper's granddaughter, when London had fallen into the enchanted sleep. He and Marisee had survived a riddling dragon, a plague monster in a lake in Hyde Park and the vengeful supernatural Shepherdess who had wanted to trap people in their happiest dreams. There had even been a tithe-master wearing a coat of live swans who lived in a tunnel near the Foundling Hospital. He demanded payment of a tenth of something precious from anyone who wished to pass through his tunnels. He'd taken a tenth of Robert's memories, including every treasured memory Robert had of his older brother, Zeke. It hurt to know that such an important part of Robert's life had been forgotten. Perhaps the tithe-master had been the worst monster of them all.

Robert wished that Marisee was here with him. It didn't seem right to be near magical monsters without her. And he wanted her to know that he was safe and well, even if he was bored from being hidden in this parlour for so long. Maybe he could write her a letter, but who would deliver it to her all the way in Clerkenwell? He wished so hard that he could. Imagine seeing trees again, and grass and the sun and the sky. He'd only been out once in six months and that hadn't ended well, and with notices in the coffee shops advertising a reward for his capture, it was still dangerous for him to leave. Marisee and her grandma had felt like a real family to him, but just like his family in Barbados, he was forced to be apart from them. The law said that he was a runaway slave. It would cause terrible trouble for Madam Blackwell if he was found at her home.

"And don't forget," Emma was saying, "the shard beasts were here before you were."

That was also true. Robert was the newest member of the Red Guard Gang of St Giles. He had been born enslaved on the Hibberts's cocoa plantation in Barbados, until Lord Hibbert had sent Robert to serve his wife in London. As London woke from its enchanted sleep, Robert had returned to the Hibberts's mansion in Bloomsbury because it had seemed too dangerous to run away. Lord Hibbert had been waiting, newly back from the West Indies. He'd told Robert with great delight that he'd sold him to another plantation owner and he would be shipped away. Robert had known that would mean a certain early death. He'd turned and fled.

It was a chase that still made Robert tighten with fear when he thought about it. He had raced out of the Hibberts's kitchen and through the stables.

"A guinea to whoever catches that boy!" Lord Hibbert had yelled.

The stable hands had dropped their brooms and harnesses and bales of hay and joined the chase. Robert was exhausted from the past days' adventures, but he found new strength. He would *not* be sent back to work to his death on a plantation. He raced through Bloomsbury Square and past St George's Church, glancing up at the steeple where only the day before, the statues had stepped down from their high roost on to the street in front of him.

London was still muted, as if the blanket of enchanted sleep had not been fully thrown aside. A couple of hackney carriages were weaving uncertainly along the road and Robert dashed in front of them. Neither of the drivers noticed him.

"Stop him! He's a thief!"

The shout came from Benjamin, one of the Hibberts's grooms. He seemed more awake than the others, his arms pumping as he ran. A stockinged foot was stuck out in front of Robert, but Robert saw and leaped over it.

"Oh, no, you don't!" The well-dressed servant who'd tried to trip him made a grab for Robert's wrist.

Robert twisted away, pelting across the road and through a narrow alleyway between two houses. He emerged into a small yard hung with drying bed linen, pushing through the lines of damp, heavy sheets. He hoped so hard that there was a gate on the other side.

"I *will* catch you!" Benjamin called. "But if you come quietly, I'll share the guinea with you!"

Robert saw Benjamin's black-booted feet as the groom weaved his way through the laundry. He *was* catching up. Robert pushed onwards, feeling slightly guilty about the dark smudges he was leaving on the sheets as he swiped them aside. He ducked beneath a pair of lace pillowcases and found himself staring at a wall. It was as tall as him, made from old, jagged bricks. There was no gate.

"Or maybe I won't be willing to share." Benjamin had swept the pillowcases aside so hard that one of them flopped on to the muddy ground. He called back. "Found him!"

A cheer had sounded from behind the sheets, mixed with laughter and taunts and the chasers' hands had slapped aside the linen.

Benjamin grinned. "You've got nowhere to go but on that boat!"

Robert was suddenly filled with rage. If it hadn't been for him and Marisee stopping the Shepherdess, Benjamin and every single one of those grooms would still be withering away in their sleep. The rage burned through Robert. He sprang towards the wall, his fingertips grabbing at its crumbling top edge. He found purchase on a spike of broken brick and hauled himself over. He dropped to the other side without checking what he'd be landing in first. It was soft and smelled appalling.

"The first one of you who helps me over gets half my guinea!" Benjamin yelled from the other side.

Robert heard boots scrabbling against brick. He forced himself up and ran onwards. The street was narrow; a small group of children who'd been playing together stopped to watch him pass. If anyone followed him, the children would certainly know which way to point them.

He came to a junction with a wider street, paused for breath, then hurtled across, plunging into a lane of tumbledown houses, risking a look back. He didn't see anyone. It was barely a lane, more an alleyway, starved of light because of the overhanging gables. The ground beneath him was pitted and puddled with … Robert wasn't sure what and did not want to know. There was no other person about, though Robert heard people stirring behind the doors and windows – the murmur of voices, a baby crying, the clank of a spoon against a pot, and from somewhere deep inside the tangle of alleyways, a rooster crowing.

Something bounced off Robert's head, clipping his scalp and rattling on to the ground. It was a small stone. Robert rubbed his head and looked up. A child was sprawled along a beam that crossed from one rooftop to the attic window in the house opposite. As his and the child's eyes met, a sack dropped over Robert's head and a muscular arm gripped him, pinning his own arms to his sides. Robert had known straight away that it wasn't Benjamin. Benjamin was strong from years of carrying around heavy buckets and horse tackle, but still slight. Robert felt almost a wild-animal strength in his captor. The coarse hair beneath their sleeve poked through Robert's shirt into his skin. As Robert tried to wriggle free, he was engulfed in a reek of ancient dust, raw meat and stagnant water.

"I need you whole, little boy," a voice rumbled into Robert's ear. "But if you try to escape, I might have to do a little bit of hurt to you."

Then his captor growled with anger and Robert was released so quickly he fell to the ground. He whipped the bag from his head then wished he hadn't. He'd only seen his captor from the back. They wore white leather breeches that fell loose to below their knees. Robert glimpsed white stockings and boots trimmed with fur. The shoulders beneath the long, tattered jacket were wide and the captor's thick, grey hair curled out from beneath a pale knitted cap, on to the jacket collar.

But it was not only his captor that filled Robert with terror. It was the beast that stood in front of his captor in that narrow alley. It was made from glass. Even in the gloom, Robert sensed the sharpness of the quills that covered its body. At first he'd thought the third leg was a strange shadow, but then it had moved separately from the others, bending while the two front legs reared up. The red kerchiefs tied around where its knees should be, had strangely made Robert want to laugh, but then he'd heard a rattle behind him. A second glass creature was waiting there.

"You can stay and watch or you can follow me."

The voice came from the child who'd been sprawled across the beam. They looked around eleven years old – only a couple of years younger than Robert himself. Their hair was tucked into a red-and-black Scot's bonnet cap, and a red kerchief, like the ones worn by the glass monsters, was knotted round their neck.

Suddenly, the child roughly pushed Robert aside just as the glass monster behind him charged. It felt like the air around Robert had been pierced a thousand times as glass quills shot through the alley.

"This way!"

The child darted into an open doorway and up a flight of wooden steps. Robert quickly followed, pushing against his exhaustion. He'd been tired from running, and all the previous day's injuries had started to burn. His arms and legs were clenched by cramps. His head felt light too, as if he would faint if he tried to think too hard.

The first flight of stairs took them into an attic. It was crowded, as if at least two families, with their children, were living there. Robert shivered. He had seen an attic like this a few days before in a dream, guided there by the Shepherdess. He'd felt so sorry for the families that had fallen under the Shepherdess's spell. But he'd fallen under her spell too. He'd betrayed his friend, Marisee, by giving the Shepherdess what she'd asked for – a golden box she believed contained the power to create a new London. Now these families were waking. Some were drowsy and confused, while others laughed, sharing meals of bread and apples. They waved at the child and stared at Robert with curiosity as he followed the child through a small hatch door that looked like a cupboard. It led on to a narrow roof ledge.

Carefully, he copied the child, edging his way along the ledge, then scrambling up a rope tied around a chimney stack on the opposite roof. He stepped across the gap without looking down and eased himself up the cracked tiles, before squeezing through a barely open window. It was another attic room, empty apart from a large bed and an old man in a white sleeping cap snoring beneath a blanket. They crept out of the bedroom, then down, down, down the stairs into a pitch-black cellar. Robert had heard wood scraping across ground.

"Hold out your hand!" the child instructed.

Robert obeyed. His fingers had been grasped gently.

"Be careful. We're going down some steps."

"Into a tunnel?"

"Yes."

Robert had found himself in many tunnels recently. He'd been swept along one, borne in a fast-flowing stream by a water spirit. He'd trudged through others that had taken him beneath crumbling buildings. He had found new clothes and boots in another, just before he and Marisee had met the tithe-master...

"Is there anyone else down here?" he asked.

"No one knows about it apart from the Red Guard Gang."

"The Red Guard Gang?"

"Shut the hatch, will you?" the child said. "And save your questions 'til later."

Robert reached for the door above him and pulled it down. The darkness became darker and he felt sealed inside it. The child bobbed away and Robert nearly tripped. He steadied himself and took a cautious step forward until he sensed the edge of the stairway beneath his foot.

"Better keep to the right," the child said.

"Why?"

"Because there's nothing at all on the left."

He counted nine steps before his foot jolted down on to flat ground. Then, the child quickly let go of his hand.

"It's low here," they said. "You'll need to crawl."

Robert couldn't have seen less if his eyes had been closed. His heart was beating so hard, he'd been sure that the tunnel had shaken. Then light had streamed in the other end as another hatch opened. He climbed up into the room where he found himself now. The child shook their hair free from the cap. She was a girl.

"You're safe here," she said.

She glanced over to the corner. A third glass monster was crouched there, its body hunched tight as if waiting to spring at him.

"But if you want to stay," the girl said, "you have to pay."

THE RED GUARD GANG

Robert sometimes found it hard to remember that Emma, who was now patiently teaching him how to read and write, was the same girl who'd stood glowering at him demanding payment. He knew now that there were three shard beasts all together. They could be told apart by their feet. One wore black boots that flapped open with no laces. Robert supposed that they would have great difficulty tying them. One sported black shoes with a large silver buckle and the other, unlaced brown boots.

"Aren't other people who live here curious about them?" he'd once asked Emma.

"I reckon that St Giles folk have always known that dreams and real life can mix together," she'd replied. "Do you ever have those dreams where you go to sleep hungry and dream of a feast that filled you up like it was proper food?"

Robert nodded.

"Me too," Emma said. "It's like getting a good meal while you're still asleep. Before the enchanted sleep, we just enjoyed the dreams without thinking too hard about them. The shard beasts don't hurt the St Giles folk, so they've decided not to think too hard about them neither. And anyway, most folk have bigger worries."

An hour or so after Emma had brought him to the gang's den, the rest of the Red Guards had filed in. There were six of them, though now he knew that the members came and went, depending on whether the constables were out searching for them. Emma was twelve. Her mother was a lady's maid, but she'd been raised by an aunt. When her aunt died, she was left homeless. Turpin and Duval were two young brothers, who only ever spoke to each other. Their eyes had widened when they'd seen Robert, and Duval had reached out to touch him before Turpin pulled his brother away. Garnet couldn't be more than six. She wore a dark green bonnet that she refused to take off and kept a cloth doll tucked in her belt. She followed Robert around and was always full of questions. It made his heart hurt – she reminded him of his youngest sister.

The other two Red Guards were older than Robert. Steeple was a thin boy with a quick smile and a soot-smeared face. The gang leader, Spindrift, didn't know exactly when he'd been born. Like Robert, Spindrift was small compared to some boys his age, but Robert had known instantly that he was strong. All of them wore clothes that had been mended many times and red kerchiefs tied around their necks or heads, apart from Spindrift, who wore his as a band around his hat. That morning, the brim had been pulled deliberately low so that Robert could see little of his face. He'd been grasping a plain wooden staff that was polished to a shine.

He'd tapped the staff on the ground. "Who are you and why is the capture-creature looking for you?"

Capture-creature? The name felt right. It had never said Robert's name, but he knew that it had come for him. If the shard beasts hadn't charged, the creature would have succeeded.

"I've never seen it before," Robert said. "I don't know what it is."

But whatever it was called, it was wild and powerful. He was glad that the windows were boarded up. He'd hate to glance out and see it there, looking back at him.

"*We* call it the capture-creature because that's what it does," Spindrift said. "It hunts people and captures them. What it calls itself…" Spindrift shrugged. "No one's asked it, though there are rumours."

"Rumours?" Robert said.

Spindrift looked him up and down. "All of us here fear being caught. There are prisoners younger than us that get sent to the gallows. But none of us has had the capture-creature trailing them. Why do you?"

Robert swallowed hard and said nothing. The only person who'd want him that badly was Lord Hibbert.

"I ran away," he said.

"Haven't we all?" Steeple laughed.

Spindrift didn't laugh. "You have to earn your keep here," he said. "If you don't pay us, you'll be back on those streets and when the capture-creature finds you – 'cause it will find you – you can ask it about the rumours yourself." Spindrift held out his hand. "We don't give free board. How are you going to pay your way?"

"Look at his clothes," Steeple said. "He's just a foundling boy. He ain't got nothing."

Garnet tugged at the hem of Robert's coarse brown jacket. "What's it like at the Foundling Hospital?" she asked, excited. "Do you get food every day? Do they sell you to pirates?"

44

"He's no foundling," Spindrift said quietly. "*I think
he can pay now.*"

Robert couldn't see Spindrift's eyes, but he felt the
strength of his stare. He looked around him. The room
must have been a parlour once. There was a fireplace –
the hearth clean with a full scuttle of coal next to it. A
table beneath the bricked-up window was piled with
blankets and pillows. A tattered travelling trunk was
pushed against a wall. This place was a hundred times
better than the Hibberts's kitchen, where he'd slept in a
cold, hard corner.

Did he want to give them the only valuable thing
he owned to stay here? Or did he want to take his chance
on the streets with Benjamin and the capture-creature?

Robert had reached deep into his pocket and pulled
out a golden box. A few hours before, he'd believed that
this box could destroy London as he knew it. He'd given it
to the Shepherdess and betrayed the people he'd cared for.
Luckily, the box had been empty and Marisee Blackwell's
grandma had given it to him as a present that morning.
She'd said that gold was always useful in London. He
hadn't expected it to be useful so soon. The gang gasped,
and even Spindrift stepped forward to stare at it.

"You steal this?" Spindrift asked.

"It's mine," Robert said. "It was a gift."

"Are you a prince?" Garnet asked. "Only princes have gold!"

Spindrift plucked it from Robert's palm and held it close to his eyes. He flicked open the hinged lid. The others craned forward.

"It's empty," Robert said.

Spindrift nodded and tapped the lid shut. "It looks like proper gold. And there's something about it…"

The gold box had once held London's magical founding elements – air, fire, water and earth. The Shepherdess had wanted the box because she believed it contained all the ingredients to create a new London that she could control. Unbeknown to Robert and Marisee, Madam Blackwell had already secretly removed the elements, but perhaps Spindrift felt a shadow of that power.

"I declare this gold box is Red Guard property," he said.

Steeple cheered. "That's going to be worth a pocket full of guineas! Who's ready for a good hot dinner? Every day for a year?"

Duval and Turpin looked at each other. "We are!" they said together.

Spindrift handed the box back to Robert. The rest of the gang muttered, confused, until Spindrift slammed the staff back down.

"But it will remain in the care of…?" He looked over at Robert. "What's your name?"

"Robert, Robert Strong."

"It will stay with Mr Strong."

"What?" Steeple looked unhappy. "You made me empty my pockets the minute I stepped through the hatch. And I never saw none of it again, neither."

"Because most of what you had in there was dirt, Steeple." Emma laughed.

Steeple did not.

Spindrift sighed. "If *you* want to carry that gold box on you, you can. But think about it, Steeple. What will *you* say to a magistrate when they search your pockets and find it? I don't think they're going to believe that it was a present from your ma. Do you?"

Steeple shrugged his shoulders and his quick smile returned. "Fair enough."

"And we can't leave it here," Spindrift said. "Not when we're all out. So it stays with Robert for the moment. This is something special and it needs a special plan. Are we in agreement?"

"Yes!" Steeple slapped Robert on the back. "Welcome to the Red Guard Gang. I'll show you the ropes so *you* don't get caught by the constables neither."

Spindrift turned back to Robert. "You're here on two

conditions," he said. "You always remember that the gold box is your payment to us. And second, you don't betray no Red Guard nor babble our business to outsiders, ever."

"No," Robert said. "I won't."

How could he babble anything to anyone? His friends and family were all so far away.

At first, Robert had thought that he'd only be here for a few weeks while he worked out what to do next, but a week after he'd arrived, Emma told him that she'd seen a notice in a coffee house offering a reward for Robert's return.

Steeple had been polishing his boots with an old rag. "How much?"

Emma glared at him, then whispered in Robert's ear. "Six guineas. You must be really precious to them."

"Precious?" He laughed. "You take care of precious things. You don't work them until they break."

Emma gave him a serious nod. "I hadn't thought of it like that. But perhaps you'd better stay here for a little while longer."

It wasn't like he had anywhere to go, and this wasn't so bad. There was no Lady Hibbert, for a start. Turpin and Duval were experts at grabbing fruit falling from wagons and the occasional pasty from a stall-holder that was looking the wrong way. So although food wasn't plentiful, there *was* food.

Emma had been taught to read and write from an old Bible by her aunt. Robert persuaded her to teach him and during their first lesson, she told him about the gang.

"There's been a Red Guard Gang for a long, long time," she'd said. "It's for the ones like us who haven't got family."

"I have a mother and sisters," Robert had said. And a brother who he could barely remember.

"Not in London, you don't," Emma said. "Turpin and Duval came from a workhouse in Exeter. It took them two months to walk to London because they thought they'd find their fortune here. Spindrift found our boys soaked through and starving by Glasshouse Yard and brought them back. Garnet had three brothers and two more sisters when her ma married her stepdad. He used to take her out begging, then he said she'd got too old for folks to feel sorry for her. One day he just walked off and left her outside a grocer on the Strand. It was me who found her."

Robert glanced over at Garnet, who was sitting on the floor by Steeple, helping him patch the knees on some worn black breeches.

"Did she have the doll with her then?"

Emma smiled. "No. Spindrift made it for her." She nodded towards Steeple. "And him…"

"I can tell my own story." Steeple grinned and stretched. "I was a climbing boy. I got sold to a chimney sweep when I was smaller than Garnet." He poked her and she laughed. "I was supposed to get food and clothes but didn't get much of neither. When one of the other boys died, I decided I wasn't going to be the next one pulled dead out of the flue. I'd already heard about the Red Guards. I just waited around St Giles long enough for 'em to find me."

"And what about the glass … the…?" Robert had had no idea what to call the beasts then.

"The shard beasts?" Emma laughed. "You should have seen your face in the alley!" She pulled a terrified expression. "Though the first time I saw one, I passed right out. You were lucky they were there. Me and Spindrift didn't catch the magic sleep; I suppose because neither of us have got anyone who loved us enough to come back in our dreams. So we took turns keeping watch. I saw the capture-creature and tried to warn you when I threw that stone, but it was too late. I don't think the shard beasts were trying to protect you. They just love a good fight."

"Where did they come from?"

"I reckon it was that earthquake in Fleet Street," Steeple said. "The one that happened a few years before I was born."

Garnet dropped the breeches she was trying to darn. "What's an earthquake?"

"It's when the whole world shakes." Steeple picked her up under her arms and bounced her around the room. She shrieked in delight.

"I think the shard beasts are made of clay and glass," Emma said. "And ... and..." She looked embarrassed.

"And magic?" Robert offered.

"Yes, magic," she'd said. "If you believe in that sort of thing."

"I do," he'd said.

Months later, Emma looked up as the hatch lifted and Spindrift climbed into the room followed by Turpin and Duval. They all wore so many jackets that Robert was surprised that they could fit through the gap.

As they shed their layers, their day's work was revealed – linen handkerchiefs plucked from secret pockets, a silk purse tucked beneath a shirt, a silver chain from inside Duval's shoe. Turpin opened a bag to show two muddy meat pasties and a few bruised plums.

"You found them in Covent Garden market, didn't you, Turpin?" Duval said.

Turpin nodded and grinned. He'd lost his baby teeth in the front and no new ones had grown in their place. It made him look very young.

"You found it," Spindrift said. "It's yours."

Duval nodded, carefully brushed the dirt from the pasty and took a big bite. He closed his eyes and smiled.

"It's mutton, Turpin," he said. "My favourite."

Turpin's grin widened and he followed his brother into a corner of the room. They beckoned to Garnet, who ran over to join them. She sank her teeth into a plum and sighed.

"They've earned their supper," Spindrift said. "Now it's time for the rest of us to earn ours."

"Are we going out?" Garnet leaped into the air, plum juice running down her chin. "Can I come with you?"

A look passed between Emma and Spindrift.

"Yes, we are going out," Spindrift said. "And yes, you can come with us."

Garnet cheered, almost choking on her fruit.

"Show me your gold again," Spindrift said to Robert.

Robert held out the gold box. It had never left him since that first day. He'd wondered if it had been forgotten, but now Spindrift took it from him and inspected it, then handed it back. He nodded towards the trunk.

"You'll be needing different breeches," he said.

Steeple grinned and threw back the trunk lid.

"Help yourself, Master Robert Strong!" Steeple said. "You're coming with us on another adventure!"

An adventure? Robert was finally leaving the den again?

The trunk was crammed with clothes, breeches, waistcoats and shirts, stolen bolts of wool and linen, wigs, shoes and stockings, hats, caps and bonnets, and a carefully wrapped grey silk dress.

Robert had seen inside the trunk a few times when the gang had been planning a special outing. They usually survived by pickpocketing and begging, but sometimes they'd steal from a shop. A gang member would have already studied the shop to check the merchandise and how easy it was to steal. Then they'd scrub the dirt from their faces – apart from Steeple. The soot was part of his skin now, so he'd lurk nearby as a lookout. Emma would distract the shopkeeper while two others would take the most valuable items they could carry.

Steeple held up a pair of dark blue velvet breeches with a grey woollen frock coat.

"These should fit," he said.

The breeches would certainly be too big around the waist and there were ragged holes around the coat cuffs. But after six months of wear and little chance to wash them, Robert's Foundling Hospital clothes were looking very old indeed. He was happy for a new outfit even if it reminded him of the uncomfortable uniform that Lady Hibbert had made him wear. If Robert was dressed like this, people might just presume he was a servant and not notice him. Though – his heart beat a little harder – he was sure that the capture-creature wouldn't be tricked so easily.

As far as Robert was aware, the capture-creature hadn't returned to St Giles. He hoped it was stalking someone else now.

"Mice have chewed at the coat," Emma was saying. "But if you tuck the cuffs over and sew on brocade, no one will notice."

"And you'll have to keep it buttoned," Spindrift said, "because we haven't got any spare shirts."

"Use this." Steeple held up a cream scarf. "Wrap it around your neck so no one can see what's underneath."

Robert took it. "Thank you."

"We're going to Mr Gripe on Russell Street near Drury Lane," Steeple said. "He's got a pawn shop. He used to be good for buying some of our … goods. But last time I took him a silver candlestick, he cheated me." He grinned. "It's time for revenge!"

The "adventure" was planned for just before sunset,

when the streets were shadowed but the lamps not yet lit. Even more importantly, it was when Mr Gripe sent his assistant to collect his supper from the chop house on Tavistock Street. The assistant liked to dawdle and watch the performers in Covent Garden. It was sometimes nearly twenty minutes before he returned.

The streets would be busy too, especially with folk heading towards the theatres and coffee houses. There'd be plenty of coaches for the Red Guard Gang to weave between and alleys to escape down.

"And some of them ladies' skirts are so wide I could hide right behind them," Steeple said.

While the others joked, Robert tried to steady his heart in time with his sewing. He'd carefully cut the brocade from a large waistcoat to add to his new jacket's collar and front. In and out the needle went, his blood thudding through his body at twice the speed.

In Spindrift's plan, he, Robert, was the decoy instead of Emma. He had to approach the counter and make a big show of producing his golden box. Once he had Mr Gripe's attention, Robert must be reluctant to hand it over for inspection, giving Steeple time to come and steal back the candlestick. Robert would not have to play-act not wanting to hand over the box. He'd almost died because of this box.

But what if Mr Gripe thought that Robert had stolen it? What if he locked Robert in the shop until he could be dragged to gaol? What if Lord Hibbert, or Benjamin or ... the capture-creature was waiting to seize Robert and send him back to the West Indies?

"Ouch!" Robert was sewing so quickly that he'd pricked himself with the needle. His heart raced on.

Steeple glanced over at him. "You still worried about getting caught?"

Robert nodded.

"I'll take care of you." Steeple smiled.

Robert wiped away the blood and finished sewing. He went behind the screen to change. The velvet felt good after the Foundling Hospital's rough drugget breeches and he liked the looseness of the too-big coat.

Spindrift and Emma changed too. Robert had seen them in costume before. The grey dress was too big for Emma, so she wore breeches and a waistcoat like Spindrift. Together they looked like the sons of a merchant. Steeple smeared more soot on his face, but not so much that he'd be arrested for trying to disguise himself. He carried a broom with him so he truly did look like a chimney sweep.

And that was it. It was time to go. Only Robert's second time out in six months. He was going on another adventure. Though it didn't feel like a proper adventure without Marisee. And hopefully it would end better than the last one with the Red Guard Gang.

THE EXPLODING
ORCHESTRA

Marisee stared at the dark shape with too many eyes.

"Welcome, Well Keeper's granddaughter." The creature's voice was like the crackle of salt on flames.

Marisee's banging heart slowed. Her fear ebbed away as her head filled with the swish of windmill sails blown in a brisk wind and the sharp tang of watercress. She could feel the slow flow of an old stream. She might not have been here before, but Lambeth was famous for its windmills and market gardens. This was not a monster; this creature was part of Lambeth itself. It was a Chad.

"Are you Effra?" Marisee whispered.

"I'm glad you know of me," Effra said. "Madam Blackwell rarely ventures south of the river, but we will not bear her a grudge. My cousin cares for a spring filling the timberyard wells on the river edge. She saw you and came to tell me. It would be disrespectful to let you travel unaccompanied."

The shadow became solid. A heavy round body, a head, eight bright eyes, eight long, thick legs. Effra's back was covered in hairs that trapped the silver in hundreds of bubbles like tiny lamps. Marisee really wished Turnmill had warned her that Effra took the form of an enormous spider. But then, of course, why would she? Marisee wasn't supposed to be meeting Effra tonight.

"Turnmill said that you've felt something wrong with the Thames," Marisee said.

Effra's eight eyes blinked one by one. "This morning it felt like I had been ... I think the closest feeling in your Solid world is 'kicked'. All the springs I've spoken to have felt it too."

"Kicked?"

"Or shoved. Or something similar," Effra said. "It wasn't pleasant. The Thames is weighed down by cargo and filth. It lets itself be pulled out to sea then pushed back again. We know those movements, but this morning it jolted and pushed against the tide." Effra stopped in front of Marisee, turning all eight jewel-eyes towards her. "I think something terrible is stirring beneath it."

Terrible? Marisee imagined the filthy river bubbling and something fearsome and relentless rising from it. Could she and Grandma fight something like that?

Marisee could see the distant glow of the Gardens ahead. It looked so peaceful and beautiful, as if nothing could ever disturb it.

"Was it here, in Vauxhall?" she asked.

"No, it was east, on the peninsula."

At least Marisee would be safe for the moment.

Effra scuttled to the side of the road as a carriage passed. The spider's silver dimmed until it was swallowed up in the shadows. The horses neighed loudly and the driver urged them on.

"Move, you silly beasts! There's nothing there but a girl!"

"Effra?" Marisee called. "Effra!" Had the Chad left her here?

"Chairmen," Effra whispered.

Marisee heard the footsteps then. The sedan chairmen passed with barely a look at Marisee, clutching the poles at the front and back of the box-like cabin where the passenger sat. A horse-drawn carriage or a cart was bumpy enough. This must be even worse!

When the chairmen were out of sight, Effra emerged, the bubble-like lamps blinking silver again.

"The creature that has woken is called a Domedary," Effra said. "It's a desolate, angry beast that knows nothing but destruction."

A year ago, Marisee would have laughed at the idea of an unknown monster asleep at the bottom of the river. But now she knew that there were many magical beasts hidden around London – and beneath the filthy water of the Thames a creature would be truly out of sight.

She glanced towards the river. This was not just any magical beast, though. It was one full of anger and destruction – and it had stirred. Perhaps ... perhaps it had only stirred once and would quieten again. Because if it didn't... Could London survive such an attack when it was still recovering from the Shepherdess's spell? And Marisee wasn't magical. What could *she* do?

"You say that it knows nothing but destruction?" she said, quietly. "How do you know?"

"It rose up in Cromwell's time," Effra replied. "But long, long before that I fought it. There were many giants here..."

"Giants?" Marisee said. "Like the Magogs? I always wondered how they ended up at the bottom of the Thames."

"It was Brutus of Troy," Effra said. "When he landed in Cornwall, many thousands of years ago, he fought the giants there and won. Only one giant was left alive. He was called Gogamagog. He was thrown from a cliff by Brutus's champion during a wrestling match. He split in two when he landed and became Gog and Magog. Brutus preserved the bodies in honey and sailed with them around the coast to what is now London."

"Why?" It seemed to Marisee like a lot of trouble.

"To show his power," Effra said. "If anyone challenged Brutus, he'd proclaim that he was the giant conqueror."

"How did the Magogs end up in the river?" Marisee asked.

"Brutus's reputation travelled before him," Effra said. "All who lived on these marshes prepared themselves for war – men, women and children; farmers, butchers, seamstresses and musicians. The mills barely turned and the crops were not fully harvested. Every musical instrument was laid aside in favour of bows, spears and slingshot."

The children were fighting too, Marisee thought.

Even those younger than her going to war knowing that they may die.

"Thames Rex was truly a king of rivers in those days," Effra continued. "Huge and powerful!"

Marisee tried hard to imagine the sluggish river she was so used to, raging back and forth to the sea.

"As Brutus's ship eased its way along the estuary," Effra said, "Thames must have felt the giants' presence. Or perhaps Gog and Magog spoke directly to the river; they were not truly dead, just stunned by the fall. Thames pushed and pulled at Brutus's ship until the hull split away and the giants fell from the hold into the muddy water. The thud was so great, mud splattered for miles around."

"And the monster woke up," Marisee finished.

"Yes," Effra said. "Perhaps it was already stirring when the humans stopped playing music. Perhaps Thames Rex deliberately nudged it awake. Perhaps the giants called to it. I think that it was all of those."

"And what happened?" Though Marisee wasn't sure that she really wanted to know.

Effra sighed. The silver lamps dimmed. "The children, women and men of the marshes fought bravely. We rivers and springs joined the battle when the monster came to shore, weaving between its legs with water surges and silver thread, trying to topple it. But the Domedary had no mercy. The sharpened barbs on its immense legs cut through our threads and shredded everything before it. It leaped into the air and trampled the ground flat." Effra's lights dimmed completely. "Few humans survived."

The shadows around Marisee seemed to grow darker and a cold breeze blew across from the river.

"What stopped it?" she asked, casting nervous glances towards the Thames.

"It was weary from fighting," Effra said. "It returned to the river to rest and feed. The human musicians composed songs to honour their dead and the Fumis blew the music across the water. Then, Thames Rex, perhaps feeling guilt for helping to rouse it, swept its waves from bank to bank. The humans and the elementals had made a lullaby to soothe it. The Domedary sank back to the riverbed and didn't stir again until Cromwell."

"He closed the theatres, didn't he?" Marisee asked.

"He did," Effra replied. "And he frowned on folk singing just for the joy of it. But the Lord Mayor ordered the tavern owners to ignore Cromwell's orders, especially those on the river's edge. For night after night, they were filled with musicians and dancers until the Lord Mayor was satisfied that the river was still."

Marisee shivered and squinted back down the dark path she'd travelled along. She thought of the children that had gone to fight the Domedary and never returned. There were so many more people in London now. Could they raise a proper army to defeat it? Or even better, could they find a way to stop it before it attacked again? If it was music that calmed it, what had happened? Though, wasn't that why she was going to Vauxhall, to find out?

Last night, musicians at Sadler's Wells and the Pleasure Gardens couldn't play their instruments. For some unknown reason, London's music was failing and the monster was rising. Perhaps she should return to Clerkenwell now and tell Grandma. How could she alone be a match for such a beast if it attacked?

But hadn't she been a match for the Shepherdess? She and Robert? Since she had come all this way, she should have a quick look. She was Miss Blackwell of Madam and the Misses Blackwells' wells. She was the granddaughter of the Keeper of London's Wells and would one day be the Keeper herself. If the Chads feared something, it was up to her to protect them.

Even against a river monster that destroys anything in its path?

Yes, she told herself. Or at least she had to try.

"We are nearly at the gate to the Pleasure Gardens," Effra said. "I will find you inside."

The bubbles of silver burst and fluttered away like dandelion fluff. Then Effra was gone.

The road had certainly become busier. Carriages were lining up, horses fretting as the passengers climbed down. Marisee pulled her jacket tighter. Her plain cotton work dress looked like rags compared to the swathes of silks and brocades that swirled around the fine ladies who dismounted from their carriages and stood for a moment under the lamplight to be admired.

She took a deep breath. *Their dresses may be fine*, she said to herself, *but I'm not here to be seen. I'm here because London might need me!*

She pulled herself upright, squared her shoulders and marched towards the entrance booth.

The ticket collector looked her up and down and lifted his nose into the air. "Do you have the entrance fee?" he asked, with a smirk.

"No, but…"

He waved her away, offering a more friendly smile to a group of women in elaborate gowns behind her. As they swished past Marisee, their mix of perfumes was so strong it made her eyes water.

She stepped forward again. "I just want to—"

"Mr Longoli!" the ticket seller exclaimed. Somehow, he managed to make way for the gentleman to enter and block Marisee at the same time.

She moved away from the ticket booth. Was there another way into the Gardens? Perhaps there was a river entrance or a secret tunnel, or even a bush she could scramble through without being seen. She should have asked Effra.

A woman behind Marisee screamed. Marisee spun around, heart beating hard again. Had the Domedary…? No. There was no sign of any monster.

The woman was trying to make her way out of a carriage, but the skirt of her dress was so wide that she was caught in the door. Someone inside the carriage was trying to squeeze the skirt through the narrow opening. Marisee was sure that she heard a snap as part of the skirt frame broke.

"You are ruining my dress, Polly!" the woman shrieked. "Absolutely ruining it!"

Two footmen were twisting and pulling the skirt from the outside. The woman was furious, with the footmen *and* Polly – though Marisee was surprised that there was room for Polly in the coach.

"I'm doing my best, ma'am," came Polly's muffled voice.

The woman was finally manoeuvred out of the carriage and stormed along the path to the ticket booth accompanied by Polly, her maid, who seemed to be struggling to hold back a smile. The woman's skirt swung from side to side from her waist. It was so wide, Marisee reckoned, that it could have hidden a small child.

A small child or … a thirteen-year-old Marisee if she was quick.

The woman and her maid halted by the ticket booth. The skirt blocked the whole path. The woman brandished a token at the ticket collector, still muttering insults at her maid. The ticket collector asked her a question which seemed to infuriate her even more. As she and her skirt swung to face them, Marisee crouched low, darting past them into the Gardens. Her movement must have caught Polly's eye, because Marisee glanced back to see her watching. The maid shrugged and smiled.

Marisee ran through a dark, gloomy tunnel and then… It was like she had stepped into the inside of a diamond. Everything was bright and light. The trees were strung with hundreds of glittering lamps which reminded her for a moment of Effra's silver bubbles. Before her was an elm-lined avenue with the glint of a gold statue at the end.

"Where should I go first?" she muttered to herself.

"Go home!" said a miserable-looking man in a strange red hat and shabby matching coat. He was carrying a sackcloth bag that twitched and ticked, like living clocks. "This place is full of wealthy villains!" He shook the bag. The things inside made a strange trilling sound. "They all want my genius but refuse to pay their debts! Soon, I will be ruined!"

He stalked off into the night.

"Oh, ignore him!" An elderly gentleman gave her a kind smile. He held an ear trumpet to his head. "That's Mr Dross, the automata maker. He wishes to replace nature with machines." He shook his head. "No machine could ever replace the child genius Wolfgang Mozart."

"Who?" Marisee asked.

"You have not heard of the child prodigy?" The gentleman's bushy eyebrows shot upwards. "He visited yesterday with his sister, but the organ was damaged after just a few notes and the musicians were too troubled to play. Young Mozart is returning this evening. I believe that he will play the very compositions he will perform for King George and Queen Charlotte." The gentleman clapped his hands with happiness. "But we … *we* … have been permitted a preview." He pointed to a row of trees. "The orchestra is through there, in the Grove. Make sure that you can see and hear everything! This will be a night that you will never forget!" He walked towards the Grove, still smiling.

Now she was here, Marisee could hardly believe it. She was actually inside the famous Vauxhall Pleasure Gardens! She wanted to run up and down the avenues and peer between the trees to see the statues and pavilions and supper rooms. She checked herself. She wasn't here to do that; an ancient monster had stirred in the Thames. She needed to gather as much information as she could to report back to Grandma. Then they could plan what to do next.

She thought of the Domedary and Effra's tale of death and destruction. Marisee had seen no sign of it from Westminster Bridge, but she wouldn't linger.

She followed the path into the Grove. It was so beautiful that she gasped. She couldn't dream in her sleep like other people – no Well Keeper could – but she imagined that this must be what good dreams were like. There were two tall buildings in front of her, both with many floors, joined by a bridge. One building had a lower floor of plain walls broken up by arches, with a high open-air gallery where people were already gathering. It was topped by a tower shaped like a squat belfry.

The other building must be the orchestra stand. It wasn't exactly round – it was many-sided and every side shone with hundreds of glass lamps – blue, golden, red, golden-white. They glowed in rows up and down the side of the building, or were draped like garlands and gathered into wreaths across the balconies. It was all topped by a cupola with gleaming pinnacles and finials, bathed with the rainbow of lights.

The musicians were assembled on a raised stage, splendid in red frock coats and black tricorns. Marisee counted around twenty of them. A child at the front of the stage was standing behind a harpsichord. He wasn't like the child musicians that Marisee knew, standing on street corners in tattered and worn clothes, singing or playing the hornpipe, begging for coin. This child was dressed very smartly indeed in a jacket and a ruffled shirt. He even wore a wig!

As the violinist raised his bow, whispers of excitement ran through the Grove.

"They're about to start!"

"See that boy? That's Mozart!"

So this was the Mozart child that the gentleman had told her about. The crowd suddenly seemed to grow denser and Marisee could barely see the musicians. She had to see everything, or else how could she tell Grandma about it? Everyone was taller than her, especially the women, who seemed to be teasing their hair into higher and higher styles. She stood on tiptoes. That didn't help. She tried to edge through the throng, but everyone just pushed closer together. She squirmed back through the crowd. Perhaps if she was further away she'd see better.

No, it wasn't better. There were just more people in front of her now. She leaned against a tree and sighed. Her hands rubbed against the rough elm bark as she looked around. All eyes were on the musicians.

She jumped up and grabbed the narrow branch above her. Her boots scrabbled against the tree trunk, tangling in her skirt. Something ripped. Marisee ignored it, clinging to the branch, walking her feet upwards to where the branch joined the trunk. She took a deep breath and hooked her heels one at a time over the branch. She imagined she must look a real sight, swinging upside down with her skirts flapping below her. She twisted herself around until she was lying along the branch, then gradually pushed herself upright so her back rested against the trunk and her legs dangled over the branch.

She let the breath out and wiped her forehead. That was not easy, but at least she had a better view.

Mozart seemed even younger from up here! Behind him, the violinist waved his bow, ready to start. The audience cheered and clapped.

The music uncurled in a delicate harmony. The

audience sighed with delight. The old man was right; Mozart was a talented musician. But suddenly, the cymbals jumped out of the player's hands, slammed together by themselves, and then shattered. The audience laughed as the musicians grasped at their hats. This must be part of the entertainment.

A breeze seemed to twist around the orchestra stage like a ball of twine. A cornet unfurled, as quick as a whip, until it dissolved into fragments of brass. The violinists continued to play, and it was one of the worst sounds that Marisee had ever heard. When the Fumi air spirits spoke English, their voices were a metallic screech. The violins sounded like a choir of Fumis with hiccups. The music blasted and squeaked, halted and hooted until it stopped.

Was this what had happened the previous evening? Here and at Sadler's Wells?

Young Mozart cast a confused look towards the musicians. The audience glanced uncertainly at each other.

"It is worse than last night," a woman standing beneath Marisee grumbled, rubbing at her ears.

There was another gust of wind and every key on the harpsichord flew into the air. Mozart shrieked. An older girl ran on to the stage, grabbed him and quickly bore him away just as the drums popped one by one, the skins curling like petals.

People were hurrying from the Grove now. Marisee spotted the kind elderly gentleman shaking his head as he left. Marisee had seen enough too. She had definitely heard enough. Something was taking music – only magic could do that. If London's music was gone, the Domedary could attack. It was time for her to return to Grandma.

"Marisee!" a voice hissed. "Marisee!"

"Effra?"

Marisee looked around. Were those Effra's bubbles of silver in the bush below or more lamps?

"Get out of here!" Effra ordered. "Straight away!"

"I am!"

Marisee was about to slither down from the tree when a wave of river water hit the Gardens, smashing the lamps and casting the Grove into gloom. There was a moment of silence before the world was filled with panicked shrieking. Men and women staggered to their feet, sliding in the mud. There was a rumble as the front of the orchestra stand fell away and more shrieks as the musicians raced across the bridge to the other building.

Marisee clung to the trunk, blinking away the stinging water. Her dress was soaked through, but it was the shock that was making her shiver. The wave did not just bring water. It brought the blades of oars and webs of rigging, old shoes and the ribs of shattered barrels. And it brought something even more terrible.

A long, thin orange leg stomped down in front of Marisee. It was taller than the orchestra building. Even in the half-darkness, she saw the barbs that spiralled around the leg. That was just one leg. There were many more.

This was it. This was the monster that Effra had called a desolate angry beast, destroying everything around it. Marisee felt her arms weaken. It was like the wave had washed away her courage. In the flickering light of the few lamps still burning, she could see people strewn across the gardens. Some lay completely still; others were groaning in pain. Shoes and fans and wigs were scattered across the grass among the debris from the river. And there, at the base of an elm tree, was an ear trumpet. It looked just like the kindly gentleman's. She hugged the tree tighter.

"No," she whispered. "Please don't be hurt."

Tears were prickling, but she was Marisee Blackwell! She'd helped to save London from an enchanted sleep! She couldn't just stay up a tree, crying. She started to straighten her shoulders.

A bellow shook the night. Another leg appeared, ending in a clawed foot that stamped down into the puddled ground in front of her, grinding the ear trumpet into the dirt. Marisee looked up to see a curved pale underbelly crusted with oyster shells. And there were more legs – eight, nine, ten. The knees buckled so the creature's body lowered. It was crab-like, with a hard white shell and no head that she could see. It moved unsteadily, as if it was unused to dry land. Now seeing it in front of her, Marisee understood. It *would* destroy everything. She clung to the tree, staring up at the monster, then down at the people lying in the mud. How could a thing like this possibly be beaten?

"Marisee!" Effra called again from below.

Marisee had to escape. *She* may not know what to do, but Grandma, Turnmill … someone would have an answer. She pushed herself against the bark, wishing she could be invisible. But she had to keep looking – she needed to see every detail of the Domedary. Even a tiny thing might help them work out how to defeat it. She made herself peer around the tree trunk.

The Domedary's underbelly split open, the oysters dropping away. The split became a mouth with two fangs, as sharp as swords. It lifted a leg and the elm tree next to Marisee shook as the barbs rattled down through the branches, splitting the trunk in two. The leg shot into the air again, a garland of broken lamps dangling from its clawed foot. It shrieked, as if in triumph.

The leg plummeted towards Marisee. Lamps shattered. Glass shards and candle stubs tumbled through the branches, then twigs and small branches, as the leg sliced the wood like it was soft dough. It was close, so close that Marisee saw the clawed foot curl and uncurl.

"Jump!" Effra's voice called. "I'll catch you!"

Silver threads darted around the base of the tree, forming a web.

"I'm coming, Effra!" Marisee called, though could Effra hear her quavering voice above the crash of trees and the people screaming?

She pushed herself away from the tree, but her hands slipped. Her head banged against the trunk as she tumbled down. The Domedary's leg followed her, the branches splitting apart with a sound like fireworks. Marisee was showered with wood and leaves.

"Effra?" Marisee shrieked as she fell.

But a dark, smoky wind was whirling around the tree and Marisee could see nothing at all.

MR GRIPE OF
DRURY LANE

Robert and the Red Guard Gang left by a door to the alley so that they didn't dirty their clothes climbing over roofs and through tunnels. All had cloaks wrapped around themselves to hide the costumes. Spindrift led, followed by Robert and Steeple, then Turpin and Duval, arm in arm, and Emma holding Garnet's hand at the rear. Garnet was chattering away, excited at being allowed out.

"And if there's any sign of trouble, we leave straight away," Spindrift had said, as he jammed the door shut. It was cleverly disguised to look boarded up and abandoned.

"So no trickery," he'd added. "I don't want to wave anyone goodbye at Tyburn gallows."

Steeple patted Robert's shoulder. "He worries too much. Everything will go as planned."

Robert hoped so. It was good to be out of that room, even if the rookery of St Giles was not a place for strangers to wander through. Magistrates would only enter if flanked by three or four soldiers armed with swords and pistols, and even then they couldn't be certain of their safety.

A young man in a bright red soldier's jacket pushed past Robert. He seemed to be holding the brass mouthpiece of a bugle.

"Was it me?" he muttered to himself. "Was it my song?"

Robert glanced back at him, but Spindrift urged them on. As they passed a tavern, a violin flew through the open window and landed by Robert's feet. It looked like it had already been stamped on.

A furious face appeared in the window. "That fiddle fixer in Soho! He's a liar and a villain! He just made it worse!" The face disappeared again.

Robert felt a poke in his back. It was Steeple

with his broom. "Best not to linger when there's trouble brewing!"

Robert stepped over the flattened violin. He needed to keep his mind calm for what was ahead. Spindrift had said that he must be confident but not arrogant. He must make Mr Gripe feel that he *could* believe that Robert truly owned the gold box even if the pawnbroker really questioned it. Robert had to be sure of his story. He was an African prince's page. The prince had fallen on hard times and needed a loan to help him pay his debts. Emma had written a letter explaining the situation that he was to hand to Mr Gripe. It was sealed in red wax engraved with the shape of a crown to look like an official stamp. Robert hoped that Mr Gripe studied the letter rather than him. As much as he wanted to leave the den, it was still a risk. If he was recognized he would be seized and enslaved again.

They left the tumbledown alleys of the rookery and were soon on the wide busy road heading towards Covent Garden. Robert tried to recognize the streets from six months ago, but when he thought about the chase, his stomach lurched in fear.

"Here we are," Emma said. "Drury Lane."

"The muffin man, the muffin man!" Garnet's song turned into a shriek.

"What a noise!" Steeple laughed.

"But I want to see the muffin man!" Garnet insisted. "Where's the muffin man?"

"Busy in his shop baking muffins," Steeple said. "But try not to be too noisy, Garnet. We don't want to draw attention."

Robert was secretly pleased that Steeple had quietened the little girl. He didn't like being surrounded by so many people. He tensed every time someone brushed against him in case that brush turned into a tight grasp and he was pulled away. He tried not to look into passing carriages in case he met the eyes of someone who recognized him. He scanned the sedan chairs for the Hibberts's coat of arms. He even studied the pedlars, looking for the furry boots of the capture-creature.

"And over there's Mr Gripe's shop," Steeple said.

Robert glanced down the short alley. It was a small shop, though the front was almost all window. The three gold balls hanging outside let everyone know its trade. If someone needed money, they could take a precious item to Mr Gripe. He would decide how much it was worth and lend them that sum. The item would be returned when the loan was paid back – *if* it could be paid back. If not, it would end up in the window, for sale. The stolen candlesticks and snuffboxes that Mr Gripe fenced for London's thieves were kept locked in a trunk in the back room, though Steeple had sworn that he'd seen his candlestick in the window.

They turned into the Covent Garden piazza. It was even busier here, people coming and going between the coffee shops and the market stalls. A crowd of people were arguing with a man standing on the steps of a theatre. From what Robert could hear, they wanted to go in but the manager had cancelled tonight's show because the orchestra couldn't play for some reason. Acrobats juggled knives outside the portico of the big church. Beggars threw themselves at the feet of the richly dressed people leaving their carriages. Duval and Turpin chattered to each other, casting sideways looks at the food stalls.

"It's strange," Emma said. "Usually there are musicians in every corner. The stall-holders complain because no one can hear them calling their wares."

Robert nodded, but he wasn't really paying attention. He was watching as Duval darted forward. A few apples had fallen from a handcart. He scooped them from the ground and hid them beneath his cloak. A moment later, Turpin and Garnet were crunching away.

Steeple tapped Robert's pocket. "Take your hand out. You're telling every pickpocket in Covent Garden that you've got riches in there."

"What if someone takes the box?" Robert said.

"I'll stand close to you," Steeple said. "Make sure they don't."

Garnet gasped as the acrobats flung the blades at each other, catching them by the handles when it seemed impossible. Robert tried to enjoy it, but he could only think of what lay ahead. What if Mr Gripe caught Steeple stealing? What if he'd seen the notices in the coffee shops offering a reward for Robert's capture? He'd heard of people throwing themselves from boats rather than returning to the plantations. Would he be prepared to go that far if he was caught?

Emma's voice made him jump. "Are you ready?" she whispered. "Spindrift's just seen the assistant leave. Gripe's alone."

Robert wasn't ready. He didn't want to do this. They hadn't even planned what to do if it went wrong – except run.

Steeple nudged him. "Don't worry. You'll be perfect!"

Robert tried to smile.

He took a deep breath and set off across the street. He let his cloak fall open so Mr Gripe could see his costume beneath – though hopefully he wouldn't look too carefully. The brocade down the front was rather crooked. Robert had to remember that he wasn't alone.

The rest of the gang would be right behind. And hadn't Emma been a decoy many times and survived to tell the tale? He just had to perform his role, refuse Mr Gripe's offer, then leave quickly when Steeple had stolen back the candlestick.

He crossed the road carefully, squared his shoulders and walked towards the shop. He paused to peer in the window where Mr Gripe displayed goods for sale. There was a pair of matching silver fob watches, with intricate patterns etched on each cover displayed next to dainty women's gloves. There was one silver candlestick; it looked plain and not especially valuable. Below that was a golden goblet on a low shelf, though perhaps it wasn't real gold. Robert could see silver through the tarnish. Even rich people came to Mr Gripe when they fell on hard times. A little of Robert's fear left him. His pretend predicament would not seem unusual.

The shop door opened. A tall man stood in the doorway. His chin had not met a barber's blade for some days and was covered in bristles. He wore no wig and his long hair was loose and tied back under a wide-brimmed felt hat. His eyes were pale, but sharp.

"Do you see anything that interests you, young sir?" he said. He seemed friendly but he didn't smile.

"I... I..." Robert coughed, hoping that his voice

would sound more confident. "I would like to conduct some business."

"Then you must come in." Mr Gripe held the door wide open. Once Robert was through, he closed it with a bang. Then he locked it. This … this wasn't the plan! How could the others come in if the door was locked? A small noise made it out of Robert's throat.

"Fear not," Mr Gripe said. "Until my assistant returns, I am by myself. I prefer to remain safe. So many thieves and hooligans walk these streets. Do you not agree?"

"Yes, sir." It was a croak, but better than nothing.

"And London streets can be dangerous for young gentlemen such as yourself," Mr Gripe said. "It would be a travesty if there was" – he looked thoughtful – "a case of mistaken identity and you were seized from the streets by some over-eager apprentice seeking a reward. Is that not so?"

Did that mean that Mr Gripe knew who Robert was? What was Robert supposed to do now? Spindrift had said that if there was any sign of trouble, they should give up. Robert had to get himself out of the shop and return to the den.

"I apologize for inconveniencing you, sir." Robert stayed by the door. "I have come to the wrong shop. If you will please let me leave now."

"This is the right shop." Mr Gripe moved back behind the counter, the front door key firmly in his grasp. "But let us see each other better." He opened a door behind him and for a moment, Robert was sure that he caught a familiar scent. It was wild and ancient, borne on an icy breeze. He made himself strain to see beyond the door, but there was just a small parlour with a fire burning in the hearth.

Mr Gripe returned carrying a lamp, and closed the door behind him. He raised his eyebrows.

"So what is your business, young man?"

That smell must have been Robert's imagination, although everything about this place made him want to run. He couldn't, though. Not until the door was unlocked. It was now almost fully dark outside. The lamp threw light over a ledger, a row of pens and bottles of ink, but beyond that was shadows. If he was to get out, he had to put some of the plan in action.

Words formed in Robert's mouth. *I'm an African prince.* No, that wasn't right. *I belong...* No! *I'm the servant of a...* Yes! That was it!

"I am the servant of an African prince that has found himself in trouble!" The words tumbled out so quickly, Robert wasn't sure if Mr Gripe could understand them.

Mr Gripe nodded. "Your esteemed master has sent you with an item or items to pledge?"

"Yes! He has!"

And Robert had the letter that Emma had written, explaining everything. Of course he had! He took it out and laid it on the counter. Mr Gripe smiled sympathetically but didn't touch it.

"Tell me yourself, what is the pledge, young sir?" he said.

Robert was supposed to take his time in withdrawing the box, but he was no longer a decoy. It was just him, Mr Gripe and a locked door. The sooner this was over, the better.

And it was there again, that smell, as if it was seeping beneath the parlour door. Wild and old, stagnant water and raw meat.

"Perhaps you would care to show me?" Mr Gripe said.

Robert's jaw worked.

"The item or items." Mr Gripe picked up a magnifier from his counter. "You must show me so that we can agree a value. If you are not content, you can leave with no obligation." Mr Gripe jangled the key before placing it on a hook behind the counter. "No obligation at all."

No obligation. That meant that Robert could

really walk out of here with the gold box. He just had to place it on the counter for Mr Gripe to inspect, decline the offer and leave through an unlocked door. He dipped his hand in his pocket. Then deeper. His fingernails scraped the seams. Robert's heart hammered. The box *had* been in his pocket while they were watching the acrobats. Steeple had been standing close to him to make sure…

But no, perhaps the box was in his left pocket. But even as Robert scrabbled desperately around for it, he knew that the box was gone.

"Is it a very small item?" Mr Gripe asked. "A nugget of gold? A miniature carving in ivory?"

"It's … it's … been taken." Robert patted his pockets, hoping against hope that it had returned. But they were still flat and empty.

Mr Gripe gently replaced his magnifier on the counter.

"Such a pity," he said. His lips moved. Perhaps it was a smile, but the semi-darkness made it a grimace.

Robert backed away towards the door.

"Please let me out and I'll return another time. You said 'no obligation'. I must be free to go now."

"Ah," Mr Gripe said. "Freedom. But that's not yours to claim, is it, Robert Hibbert?"

Outside, something hard slammed against the door. It sounded like Spindrift's staff.

"Robert!" Emma shouted. "Are you in there?"

Another slam. "Robert!" It was Garnet's high voice. "Robert!"

"Get away!" Mr Gripe shouted back. "Or I will call the constables! I know where you live, Master Spindrift!"

Robert started back towards the door. "It's a trap!" he yelled. "Leave!"

He took another step, then a hand grabbed the front of his jacket. He felt brocade rip away as he was swung around until he was face to face with it – the capture-creature. Its eyes were dark brown, all brown with no white. Its nose jutted forward like a snout. Its chin was square, its mouth thin until it opened revealing two long incisors rising from the lower jaw. Its skin was covered in thin, pale hair.

The hand that gripped Robert was covered with coarser hair, its nails so long they were almost claws. And that smell, it was so thick that it seemed to smear itself into Robert's skin. The capture-creature lifted Robert and clamped him under its arm like he was a bundle of cloth. The more Robert tried to wriggle free, the tighter the grip, until he could barely breathe.

The capture-creature kicked open the parlour door.

"Don't forget my three guineas," Mr Gripe called.

"We agreed two," the creature growled back. "Plus one for the sweep."

The sweep? No! Not Steeple, who'd stood so close to him in Covent Garden to stop other hands digging into Robert's pocket.

Steeple – whose own hand must have dipped into Robert's pocket and taken the box!

Steeple, who'd lied about the candlestick and must have made plans with Mr Gripe to betray Robert.

The capture-creature strode through the room and out of a back door into a small yard. Robert tried to gulp air into his tight chest.

"There's a boat in the dock, waiting." The creature shifted Robert's weight, squeezing him even tighter. "You're supposed to be the last piece of cargo. But they're going to be waiting a long time because I have you now and there is another place that I must deliver you."

"You're … you're not sending me back to the West Indies?" Robert gasped.

"Oh no," the capture-creature said. "There are different plans for you."

It thrust open a gate, stopped and sniffed the air. It was heavy with coal smoke and the greasy stink of cheap candles. The darkness seemed to spin around them, thinning like smoke.

"No!" the creature roared. "I owe you no favours!"

The spinning smoke, the thick soupy air, the pressure of the creature's arm squeezing Robert's ribs... Robert felt his eyes roll up and then there was no light at all.

WHISPERS IN THE GALLERY

Robert opened his eyes. He felt as if his skin was crooked and he needed to twist it around to fit properly. His thoughts were twisted up too. The capture-creature had disappeared. The dark street had disappeared. He was lying on a cold stone floor beneath a high, ornate dome. Where was he and how had he got here? He sat up stiffly. A scattering of burning candles showed a gallery sweeping around the inside curve of the dome. In front of him was a balustrade and beyond that ... he wouldn't look just yet.

He seemed to be a long way up so whatever was on the other side would be a long way down.

"Robert?"

He knew that voice! He turned round, slowly, in case it was a trick.

A girl was sitting on a bench behind him.

"Marisee?" he said. "Is it really you?"

The girl leaned forward. "And you, Robert?"

They stared at each other. The girl's face was mostly shadowed, but as she moved towards him, he saw two long scratches across her cheek. Her hair was matted with leaves and twigs, but he knew that if he looked closely, he'd see the stubbly patch where six months ago, the tithe-master had taken his payment from her – a tenth of her hair.

Marisee gave him a careful smile. He smiled back. Her smile widened. His smile widened even more. Suddenly, he felt much less alone. He'd truly wondered if he'd ever see her again, but she was right here.

"What … what are *you* doing here?" he said.

"I don't know!" She brushed a twig from her hair. "You?"

"I don't know either," he said. He shivered, remembering the capture-creature's wild animal strength. "But I'm glad I am here." *Wherever "here" is,* he thought.

He may not be truly safe, but for the moment he was free of that creature's grip.

And he was even more glad that Marisee was here too. Whatever was going to happen next, they'd face it together.

He forced his aching body up and on to the bench next to her. He tried to stretch, but his ribs throbbed. He winced.

"Are you hurt?" Marisee asked.

"Not really," he said. Close up, he could see that the scratches across her face were still bleeding. "You're hurt, though. What happened?"

"There was a monster." Marisee touched her face and blinked back tears. "It was going to kill me." She sniffed. "I thought I was going to die, Robert. The scratches will heal, but I don't think I'll ever forget that."

"Monster?" he said. Had the capture-creature taken Marisee too? "Was it wearing white leather breeches? Did it have long grey hair?"

Marisee looked confused. "No, Robert! It was enormous and—"

She seemed to run out of breath as the tears poured down her face. As well as the scratches, she was soaking wet and shaking. When he'd imagined them meeting again, it hadn't been like this. In his head, they'd be strolling through the water tunnels with Turnmill Brook or even eating ice cream in Hyde Park. But they were here, in this dark, unknown place. He'd been betrayed by someone he'd thought was a friend, and Marisee was so frightened and upset she could hardly talk. He took off his jacket and wrapped it around her shoulders.

"Thank you," she said.

"What happened?" he asked gently.

"It was…" Marisee shook her head. "It crushed the…" She wiped away tears. "It hurt the old man … the kind old man…"

Robert brushed invisible dust from his breeches. He wished he knew how to comfort her. He didn't even have a handkerchief. He tore the rest of the brocade from his jacket and offered it to her.

"Thank you." She sniffed again and wiped her eyes. "Sorry to ruin your outfit." She held up the brocade. "The first time I met you, Lady Hibbert made you dress like a prince. You're not… Have you returned to her?"

"No!" His voice echoed around the gallery. "I would never go back now! And I'd be happy if I never saw any of these clothes ever again."

Marisee nodded. For a moment, they were both lost in their own thoughts.

Robert looked around. He was sure that he could

hear talking – or whispering. He couldn't make out the words, but it was definitely there.

"Where are we?" he said. "Is there someone else here?"

"I think we're inside St Paul's Cathedral." Marisee frowned. "And yes, I can hear voices too."

The air was suddenly full of whispers as if the stone itself was spilling its secrets.

"Robert Strong. Marisee Blackwell." A dense smoky shape rose from the empty space beyond the balustrade. Its body was long and thin, its head shaped like a shovel. Two dark patches could be eyes. Its voice reminded Robert of the twist of a weathervane in the wind. He knew that sound! A wisp of smoke that moved when it talked. It was a Fumi, an air spirit.

"You have been brought before the Fumi Council of Elders," it said.

So he and Marisee had been summoned here by an elemental. He knew that most elementals distrusted Solids and would go to extreme lengths to avoid them. What could they want from him and Marisee?

As the Fumi spoke, a storm cloud rose from below the gallery towards the dome. It pulsed with the smell of the city – the hot pies of Covent Garden, the belching chimneys of St Giles rookery, barrels of wood ash in the laundry yards, soaking in rainwater to make lye. The pulsing slowed and the cloud split apart into separate Fumis. Robert counted ten. They all held their thin bodies straight and solid as if they were tied to poles. Threads of pale smoke curled around what could be their heads like magistrates' wigs. The dark lines of their mouths trembled; Robert realized that they were talking to each other. They spoke in gusts and flurries and little spots of colour that flicked around them. This was the sound he'd heard.

The whispers stopped. Robert and Marisee looked at each other. He saw his own worry mirrored on her face. But also, excitement prickled inside him. The Red Guard Gang had promised him an adventure. *This* could be the real adventure.

A Fumi drifted towards them. It had no white wig-like wisps about its head; it wasn't an Elder like the others.

"I will shape our words into Human English for your understanding," it said.

"*I do not need help!*" Another Fumi swooped towards them in a dark spike of mist. White smoke curled around its head. Its voice creaked like an old shop sign in the wind. "A favour for a favour! That was the agreement you made with us when we saved you from the sleepers."

It was true. A Fumi had helped them when Robert was captured by the plague monster. It was a deal that

Marisee had been forced to make to save Robert. The Fumis didn't care; they gave nothing for free.

"You want to claim your favour," Robert said.

The Fumi twisted and stilled. "It is time."

Marisee leaned forward. "So that's why you rescued me from the Domedary?" She sounded outraged. "Not because I might have been flattened?"

"Domedary?" the Fumi squealed and swooped back towards the others.

The Council talked amongst themselves, speckles of dark blue and orange scattering around them.

"I am sorry." Robert recognized the voice of the Fumi without the white wisps. "Not all Elders have knowledge of this evening's ... of the..." The Fumi turned back to the Council. Their voices rose again then fell. "Not all knew that the Domedary had risen again."

"The Domedary?" Robert looked at Marisee. "Is that what the monster's called?"

Marisee thrust back her shoulders. Robert remembered that she always did that when she was frightened; it was to make herself feel brave.

"It is a creature of the eastern reaches," the Fumi said. "From beneath the river out beyond the peninsula."

"A creature?" Marisee said. Robert could feel her

shaking again. "It's not a creature! It's a monster, an angry monster that destroys everything!" She wiped her eyes with the brocade again.

"Why has it left the river?" Robert asked.

"It's been woken up," Marisee said. "I know it sounds strange, but it needs London's music to keep it sleeping. I heard the story from Effra, a Chad who cares for a river in Lambeth. It must have risen because something's happened to the music."

Robert didn't understand. "How could something happen to music?"

But then he remembered the flattened violin that had flown through the window in St Giles and the theatre owners cancelling performances.

The Fumis were still huddled together, a cloud of dense smoke wound through with white.

The Fumi with the white tendrils swooped back, its head inches from Marisee's. "The matter is most urgent," it said. "You must find the music. The music will calm the monster. If the monster destroys London, we will be blamed for awakening it. Do this and only then is the favour returned."

Only then, Robert thought. This seemed like an immense favour.

Marisee turned to him. "I saw it happen in the

Pleasure Gardens. There was a gust of wind and the musicians' instruments exploded, just before..."

The Fumi suddenly seemed much bigger, wide and dark, the white smoke billowing around it like a poisoned cloud. The air was so heavy with the smell of London that Robert could barely breathe.

"A gust of wind!" it shrieked. "A gust of wind! How dare you blame this monster on us!"

"No," Marisee said. "It's just that I felt—"

"The Dragons want to blame us! They want to destroy us! *We* will not let that happen! *You* will not let that happen!" The Fumi coiled around Robert, the stinking smoke pressing against his skin. It lowered its voice. "We know what looks for you, Robert Strong. We saved you from the plague monster. Now your life is ours to give away. Find the music, or your life is forfeited."

Then it was gone. The whole Council was gone. The gallery was silent. Robert realized that he was shaking. He gripped the bench to hold his body still.

Marisee stood up and peered down into the cathedral below, then back at Robert. It was like the Fumis had taken the words with them. Neither of them seemed to know what to say.

Eventually, Marisee said, "What did the Fumi

mean when it said it knew what was looking for you? They didn't mean Lord Hibbert, did they?"

Robert didn't want to meet her eye. He didn't want to think about that creature again, how easily it had picked him up and carried him away. How he'd been sure that once it held him, he could never escape.

"Lord Hibbert sold me to his cousin," Robert said, "to work in a plantation in Jamaica."

"He *sold* you." Marisee's fists clenched. "But people can't be sold like ... like shoes."

"But they are," Robert said quietly. "Though you're right. Lord Hibbert will be looking for me, but the Fumis mean something else. I don't know what it really is, but it's called a capture-creature because that's what it does. It's almost human but wild too. It *had* caught me. It said that it had another place to deliver me to. I don't know what it meant. I'm only free because the Fumis brought me here."

"And if we don't find the music," Marisee said, "the Fumis will help that creature find you."

"Yes," Robert said. Though he wondered if it needed their help. It had found him twice already.

Marisee was shaking again, water from her dress dripping off the bench on to the floor.

"You need to go back to your grandma's," he said, "before you become ill."

"I can't stop thinking about the Pleasure Gardens." Marisee clutched her arms around herself. "The Domedary was screaming, Robert. It stamped down on the orchestra stand as if it was made of sand. I think… I think people died. We have to stop it."

"I know," he said. "But where do we begin?"

"We should return to Vauxhall," Marisee said, though she looked as if the Pleasure Gardens were the last place that she'd ever want to visit again. "There may be clues there."

"I don't mind going alo—" he started.

"Wait." Marisee lifted her hand. "Did you hear that?"

Robert hadn't heard anything.

Marisee pressed her ear against the wall. He did the same. The stones seemed to be whispering again.

"I think it's the way the gallery works," Robert said. "Sound can bend around with the wall."

Robert pressed his ear more firmly into the stone. The whispers sounded like Human English, but he couldn't quite catch the words.

Marisee scratched her head, dislodging a shower of leaves. "Is it something about a school? Look … for the school … on the popular cut?"

Robert concentrated hard. He'd heard the same. "Popular cut? What does that mean?"

This time the whisper came louder and sharper. "Talk to the Squall. Go north south to the Poplar Gut." Then the whisper sank so low that Robert had to flatten the side of his face against the wall to hear it. "Last human year, you saved me from the tithe-master, Robert Strong. I have paid back *my* favour. I can help you no more."

Robert thought he saw a pop of pink in the distance. Then silence.

"It was the Fumi you rescued from the jar," Marisee said.

"Yes," Robert said. "A favour for a favour, but this time it's one that worked for us."

NIGHT-TIME RIDERS

Marisee watched the candles in the whispering gallery snuff themselves out, leaving just those burning in a candelabra near a flight of stairs. She took a sneaky look at Robert. In the months since she'd seen him last, he'd changed but Marisee wasn't sure how. He was even wearing fine clothes like the first time she'd met him, and he obviously hated them as much as that time too. What *had* he been doing? Surely, there must have been some way that he could have got word to her to let her know that he was safe. She held back her frustration. She'd ask him for the full story when they had time.

At least he hadn't been starving. She was pleased about that. But he looked sad. His smile had been quick and guarded. Was it because of what had happened to him since she'd last seen him? Their lives must be so different. She could wander above and below London with her important new job, while he … who knows what he had to do to stay alive.

And then, of course, he had betrayed her and Grandma to the vengeful Shepherdess in the crypt. Marisee understood why he'd done it and had forgiven him. But had he forgiven himself? Did he trust her? And more importantly, did he believe that Marisee would ever trust *him* again? If they were about to embark on another adventure together, they *had* to trust each other.

Robert followed her down the spiral of steps, round and round, until finally it ended at a small door. They stepped out on to the floor of the cathedral. The gallery and the dome itself were far overhead, but she could see little in the dark. The only lamps burning were close to another door leading on to the street.

Marisee started towards it, but Robert waited in the shadows.

"What if … what if the capture-creature is waiting for me?" he said.

"I'll have a look," Marisee said, though she felt

a tremble of fear too. She peered outside. Warm light glowed from the windows of St Paul's Chapterhouse and the school on the edge of the churchyard. The churchyard itself was busy with people cutting through to the taverns along Ludgate Street or the houses down towards the river. For a moment, Marisee imagined the Domedary rising from behind those narrow streets, stamping on the homes like they were kindling. But nothing seemed strange, except... Just there, tucked inside the portico...

Turnmill stepped out from behind a pillar. "Marisee! I'm going to tell you from now that even a thousand sorrys won't make your grandmother forgive you for the worry you put her through." She shook her head and a mist of bright green drops gathered then faded. "I tried to tell her that it was my fault. I shouldn't have given you the idea to go and see Effra in the first place. I'll send word to Madam Blackwell to tell her you're safe, but I'm sure she won't believe it until she sees you for herself."

"I'm not alone." Marisee called back towards the cathedral, "It's fine, Robert. You can come out."

He appeared in the doorway. As soon as he saw Turnmill, his face lit up.

Turnmill gave him a big smile back. "So it's two of you to face Madam Blackwell's wrath!"

*

One thing was certain: Marisee was pleased to change out of the soggy dress. It had flapped around her feet, tripping her up as they trotted through the tunnels back to Clerkenwell. Luckily Turnmill had transformed into a stream and borne them some of the way. It was only when Marisee and Robert had risen up through Madam Blackwell's well that the dress had magically dried out. It was still tattered and stained with mud, though. Not even the strongest Chad magic could clean that.

"It's only good for patchwork," Grandma muttered, laying out clean clothes for her.

Grandma *was* furious. She even shushed Turnmill, who kept trying to explain that the trip to Vauxhall Pleasure Gardens had been her idea. Marisee was shocked. Were you allowed to shush a Chad?

"I trusted you to be careful, Marisee," Grandma insisted.

"I know," Marisee said. "I'm really sorry."

Grandma would not be appeased. She yanked a wrinkled linen dress from a trunk and threw it on the bed. "You were almost trampled by a river monster!"

"But I wasn't."

"Only because the Fumis saved you! And we both know why that isn't such a good thing, don't we?"

It was lucky that Robert was there. Grandma was

so pleased to see him that she kept her anger short. When Marisee was dressed, Grandma prepared them all mugs of rice milk. The scent of nutmeg and cinnamon warmed Marisee's insides before she'd even taken a sip. Grandma added currants at the bottom for Marisee to fish out with a spoon. That was a good sign that Grandma's fury had worn itself out.

They took candles and sat outside by the well because Turnmill complained about being inside Solid houses. She said it made her feel cut off from her source and she had to stop herself bursting out through the walls.

Robert sat hunched and nervous.

"Don't worry," Turnmill said. "Sadler's on watch."

Robert didn't look reassured.

"So this Domedary monster needs music," Grandma said.

"Yes," Marisee said.

"And London's music has…" Grandma looked confused. "Been disturbed?"

She started to hum a tune. Marisee recognized it; Grandma usually hummed it when she was poring over the ledgers. Though Marisee reckoned that "tune" was not exactly the right word. Grandma was not good at keeping in tune, but it was no worse than usual.

"Maybe whatever it is hasn't reached Clerkenwell," Grandma said.

"But it stopped the music at Sadler's Wells last night," Marisee said. "Perhaps … perhaps it's a certain type of music."

Grandma sighed. "I know, Marisee. Your mother was always polite about my bad singing too. What do the Fumis want?"

"They want us to find out what's happened to the music," Robert said.

"And fight a monster too, it seems. I will not let you fight monsters." Grandma glared at Marisee and Robert, defying them to answer. "Yes, if that's what they're demanding, I will do it myself."

"The Fumis won't accept that," Robert said quietly. "It's a favour for a favour."

"It was me who asked them to save Robert from the plague monster in the Serpentine," Marisee said. "*I* have to do it. *I* owe the favour."

Grandma shook her head so hard, her coil of dark hair tumbled on to her shoulders. "You *both* helped to save London. We all owe you *both* a favour."

"I agree," Turnmill said. "But Marisee is right. The Fumis are strict about this sort of thing. You…" She pointed to Marisee. "In their eyes, *you* owe them the favour. *You* have to repay it. They're worse than the Dragons for keeping to the absolute word of their deals."

"But you did it to save me," Robert said. "It's not just *your* deal, Marisee. It belongs to both of us. We might not like it, but we have to keep it. Remember how I tried to trick the tithe-master? He stole a tenth of my memories. Now all I can remember is that I had a brother but nothing about him, because those were the memories he took." Robert turned to Marisee. "But you don't have to come to the Poplar Gut if you don't want to. You could stay here and rest."

She crossed her arms. "I want to come."

Grandma crossed her arms too. "And that means I am most certainly coming as well. I'm not letting you both face goodness knows what by yourselves. And, anyway" – she gave them a quick smile – "I haven't been to Poplar Gut for a long while."

Marisee scowled at her. "What if something happens to you, Grandma?"

"And what if something happens to you two?" Grandma said.

Grandma and Marisee stared at each other. Turnmill stepped between them. "The clock's ticking," she said. "If Madam Blackwell knows the island, then I think she should go."

Marisee wasn't convinced, but she certainly wasn't going to argue with Turnmill.

"What island?" Marisee said instead. "And what does north south mean?"

"It's the Isle of Dogs," Grandma said. "Where the river loops around. The land on the north bank juts out so far it looks like it's on the south side of the river."

Marisee thought she knew London well, but there was always much more to explore.

"Who lives there?" she asked. What if the Fumi in the whispering gallery was just leading them to danger?

"Mostly cattle and sheep," Grandma said. "And there are windmills along the embankment. I went there a few years ago and the streams and springs told me in no uncertain terms that they want to be left alone."

"What *is* the Poplar Gut?" Robert wanted to know.

Marisee wasn't sure if *she* wanted to know. She imagined the land opened up like a fish, so she could see its insides.

"It's a lake," Turnmill said. "A very unhappy one. The story is that the Domedary punched through the embankment thousands of years ago and the river water poured in through the Breach. Now it's stuck in the Poplar Gut and can't return to Thames Rex."

Marisee shivered again. If the Domedary could

punch a hole in the embankment, she'd witnessed only a tiny part of its power.

"And 'the Squall'?" Robert asked.

"We-ell," Turnmill said. "There's a windmill next to the Gut. The sails turn even when no breeze reaches them. Many years ago, the Keeper of London's Mills lived there. When he disappeared, no one else came to replace him. There's a rumour that he's still there. Or at least his bones are." She laughed. "But that's never been proven. But the Squall… You know that expression, it's an ill wind that blows nobody good?"

Marisee nodded. Turnmill's laugh had not been a reassuring one. Marisee was suddenly pleased that Grandma was coming.

"The Squall is an ill wind," Turnmill said. "A bad-tempered, bitter puff of air as ever there was. But who can blame it after what the Dragons did to its friend?" She stopped, head cocked.

A sleek fox-like creature streaked towards them. Its fur shone as if it was wet.

"Sadler!" Turnmill said, jumping to her feet to meet it. "What's wrong?"

If Sadler was speaking, Marisee couldn't hear it, but Turnmill was listening intently, her head bowed towards the river spirit's snout. Sadler raced away again.

"We have to go!" she said. "They're coming!"

Marisee could hear them now, hooves pummelling the grass. They sounded like an army, ready for battle, and she, Robert and Grandma were in the wrong army.

She jumped up. "Robert! You have to hide!"

But it was too late.

"Madam Blackwell!" a voice boomed from the path between the fields. "Give up Robert Hibbert! He is my property!"

"It must be Lord Hibbert's cousin!" Robert's voice was full of panic. "He's found me!"

"Bring him to me!" The man's voice was closer. "He is mine."

The horses came from all directions – galloping from the village across the fields and along the bridle path that led to the main road to London. Lanterns bobbed on the riders' poles, throwing a sweeping light across the men's faces.

"That's Benjamin!" Robert said. "The Hibberts's groom!"

"Did you really think that you'd escaped for good, Robert?" Benjamin chuckled. "I'm glad I lost you the first time. The reward's six guineas now."

A solid man in a heavy riding coat dismounted his horse and stood in front of the riders. "It's taken a while, but our spies in the village didn't let us down," he said, tapping his sword hilt. "And you have cost me money, Robert Hibbert— No! You are mine! I am Lord Pritchard, so you are Robert Pritchard. *That* is your name."

He stepped forward. Robert edged back.

"Jump!" It was Turnmill's voice. Marisee glanced around, but Turnmill was nowhere to be seen.

"Marisee and Robert! Jump!"

It was coming from inside the well. Robert's pursuers looked around, confused.

"Be wary!" Pritchard shouted. "They may have planned an ambush."

There was the scrape of swords leaving scabbards.

"Let them try, Lord Pritchard!" the men shouted. "We are ready."

Grandma stepped in front of Robert. "You will not take him!"

Lord Pritchard grasped his own sword, raising it high. Lamplight flickered along the edge of the blade.

"Do you not understand, Madam Blackwell?" Lord Pritchard sounded amused. "I am the legal owner of Robert *Pritchard*. By the law, you cannot hinder me from taking back what is mine. A magistrate is among my party here to witness these proceedings. If you do not stand aside, you will be arrested and taken to Fleet Prison. You'll be placed in a basement cell riddled with so many lice that they'll crunch underfoot with every step that you take. The Fleet is so rife with fever that most prisoners rarely survive two weeks."

Grandma seemed to make herself taller. "I would rather be chained inside the deepest cell in the Fleet than step aside for you."

"Jump, Marisee! Jump!" There were two voices now. Turnmill's and – Robert's? Marisee glanced behind her. Robert was gone.

Just then, Lord Pritchard noticed that too.

"Trickery!" he yelled. "Seize the woman! Seize the girl! They have magicked away my boy!"

Two men grabbed Grandma's arms.

"No!" Marisee shouted. "Let her go!"

A snort, then a whinny wafted up from the well as if a horse was trapped down there too. Lord Pritchard's horse reared, almost knocking him over. The other riders were struggling to control the horses as they whinnied and stamped their hooves, the reins jerking free from their hands.

"If you let that woman escape, you will all be thrown into prison too!" Lord Pritchard shouted. "And you, Madam Blackwell! If you survive the Fleet cells, your next journey after that will be to the gallows!"

Lord Pritchard turned his attention to his horse. This could be Marisee's only chance to pull Grandma free! She ran forward but managed only two steps before a creature jumped from the shadows towards her. It was shaped like a fox, as dark as treacle and seemed to flow through her hands when she tried to push it away.

"Sadler?" she gasped.

Sadler hit her in the chest. She stumbled backwards and fell … and fell.

MR CECIL AND DAISY

Robert watched Marisee fall towards him, holding his breath even though he knew that she wouldn't be hurt. He breathed out deeply when Turnmill caught her with ease. But where was Madam Blackwell? Shouldn't she arrive next?

"I keep thinking my London Horse pronunciation is out of practice," Turnmill said. "But it seemed to work. It helps that the horses aren't too fussed about grammar. And they've little patience with most Solids and want any excuse to misbehave."

"We need to go back!" Marisee shouted. "They're taking Grandma!"

"I know," Turnmill said.

Why did Turnmill seem so calm about it? Robert had heard that those who helped people like him escape were punished harshly if caught.

"We have to rescue her!" Marisee was looking upwards as if hoping to climb the wall.

Robert's eyes followed her gaze, but he could see no footholds.

"We will rescue her," Turnmill said, still so calm. "They're taking her to the Fleet."

"I know!" Marisee said. "She can't stay there! She might catch the gaol fever. And there are some desperate people in the Fleet who might hurt her."

"Trust me, Marisee," Turnmill said. "Madam Blackwell will be safe in the Fleet."

"How can you be so sure?"

"Because it's the *Fleet* prison," Turnmill said. "By the *Fleet* River."

Now Robert understood! So did Marisee because a slow smile spread across her face.

"Sally Fleet will protect her!" she said.

"And the deeper the cell, the easier it will be to rescue her," Turnmill added. "As soon as I've taken you to the ferry, me, Ditch and Sally will make a visit to that prison. I'm really interested to know how that mean-spirited warder will explain a fountain bursting through the basement and a new prisoner disappeared!"

Robert felt safe walking through the old Roman water tunnels. Turnmill said that the tunnels were sinking further into the clay as new layers of London were built on top.

She patted an ancient plank of wood. "They were a clever lot, those Romans," she said. "And I did miss them when they left."

This time, Turnmill didn't change into a stream to carry them along. She said that she was saving her strength for Madam Blackwell's rescue. Robert was secretly pleased. The longer he remained underground, the longer he could avoid Lord Pritchard and the capture-creature.

But he also knew that he couldn't stay underground all his life. He'd been so bored stuck in the Red Guard Gang's boarded-up parlour. How could he ever live a free life?

Turnmill brought them back above ground through an abandoned well in a churchyard near to the docks.

"It's strange," Turnmill said. "This is usually a place of singing and music. It's the sailors – they can't help themselves. But tonight…"

Robert nodded. It felt that the world was being

pulled tight and it needed the music to loosen it again. Though perhaps the sailors sensed what lurked in the water beyond and were afraid. There was the tang of something else too. It sat on the air like thin ice on a river. It was sadness and fear and a wild animal fury.

Turnmill looked from Robert to the hulk of the Tower of London in the distance. "Do you feel it?"

"Yes." He could certainly feel it.

"That Tower is a prison for people, and animals too," Turnmill said. "Fear and cruelty are soaked into its walls. There are nasty things that happen there, even worse than the executions." She sighed. "Now take the Iron Gate steps down to the river. It's to the east of the quay. Mr Cecil is already waiting. He's a strange one, but he's the only one I know who I can trust to take you to the Isle of Dogs." She smiled. "And I must go and rescue Madam Blackwell." She rubbed her hands together. Shining green drops burst from between her palms. "I think I'm going to enjoy this! Good luck!"

Turnmill dissolved into a glow of green mist that hovered over the well mouth and disappeared.

"Let's find Mr Cecil," Marisee said, walking quickly towards the river.

They skirted the edges of the quay. It was stacked with barrels and boxes that had been unloaded from the mass of ships that bobbed hull-to-hull in the river beyond. Hundreds of masts criss-crossed the sky, sails drooping in the still night air. Voices called from the decks down to the dock and even at this hour, porters heaved cargo down the gangplanks. The biggest boats were anchored in the deeper water in the middle of the river. Robert wondered if any carried people like him.

"Oi!" a cracked voice called out.

Marisee and Robert stopped. A dark figure sat on a bulging bale by the gates. Robert's heart hammered harder. Could it be… No, the shape was all wrong. The capture-creature was wide and powerful and wore a woollen cap. It was full of strength and fury and would already have grasped Robert and borne him away. This man seemed softer and rounder and his hat was wide with the brim pinned back.

"Oi!" he called again. "That you, Saul?"

"Yes. I hear you, John."

"You don't believe them fairy tales, do you?" John said.

"Don't know for sure." Saul must be the porter that was weaving his way through the stacks of cargo. "There are monsters at sea," Saul said. "Everyone knows that."

"But this ain't the sea," John said. "This is the River Thames. If there's monsters in there, why haven't we seen them before?"

Saul shifted the load on his shoulder. "Maybe they got no reason to show themselves before."

John laughed. "The only folk who's *seen* this monster were at the Pleasure Gardens. I reckon Mr Tyers didn't build that orchestra stand properly. It all fell down and he made up some story to hide it." He laughed again.

"I heard that many people saw it," Saul said.

"It was a puppet, Saul! Or one of them new automaton machine things! You're going to hear about it soon. It was all a trick."

"I'm not so sure," Saul muttered. "There's definitely something wrong. My brother had his wherry out that night, between Lambeth Palace and Millbank. He said that he couldn't even whistle a song. It was like someone had stolen the tune away."

Saul continued on his way.

"That's just the dirty air!" John called after him. "That's all it is! It doesn't mean nothing! Fairy tales and dirty air!"

"It wasn't 'nothing'," Marisee said furiously. "If he'd been there and seen how that Domedary sliced the tree trunks…"

Robert rested his hand on her arm. "People choose to believe what they want. Even when in their hearts they know they're wrong."

They left the bales and barrels of cargo behind. Robert supposed that the merchants wanted their goods in sight of their ships as it was well known that much was stolen. Even the tithe-master's tunnels had been filled with goods smuggled out of the docks.

A tall iron gate blocked the way to a narrow path between two warehouses.

"This must be the way," Marisee said.

Robert pushed the gate; it swung open in silence. The tide was coming in, lapping halfway up the water steps. Robert was surprised how loud it was – a river that thought it was a sea. He wasn't looking forward to this. He didn't like boats at the best of times, but now he was going to be rowed across a river with a giant, murderous monster lurking below. But nothing could be worse than his journey from Barbados to England, sick and lonely, curled up in a hammock in a deck below the waterline, moving further and further away from his family.

"Well Keeper's granddaughter! We're waiting!" a voice called from the river.

Robert squinted down towards the water. A figure stepped from a boat moored just out of sight. They waited on the water steps holding a lamp high.

"Are you Mr Cecil?" Marisee asked.

The figure tugged the brim of a dirty green tricorn

hat that looked as if it had been fished out of the river more than once. "I am indeed."

Robert stared at him. *Mr* Cecil? Surely he couldn't be any older than Robert himself.

Mr Cecil stared back. "And you, sir?" he asked. "What name do you go by?"

"Robert," he said.

Mr Cecil's smile was older than his face. "Good," he said. "You are the correct passengers. Step into my vessel."

"And be quick!" a high voice called up from the river. "The tide's going to turn soon, Uncle Cecil. We want it high to get close to the Breach."

A child? Was Mr Cecil's oarsman a child?

"Coming, Daisy!" Mr Cecil smiled that old smile again. There was something not fully human about him, but Robert couldn't see him clearly enough to work out what. "Walk this way, Miss Blackwell."

Mr Cecil skipped down the steps. Robert looked from the firm, dry quay to the wet slabs, then followed him. The endless tides had worked hard at the stones. They were slippery and uneven, shaped by hundreds of years of different feet. It would not be so bad if the tide was low. A tumble on to the foreshore would be painful, but Robert would rather that than a fall into the dark high river.

The rowing boat bobbed in the water, waiting

for them. Mr Cecil stood on the prow, perfectly still in the rocking vessel. Daisy was much smaller. Robert was sure that the oar she held was longer than she was tall. He couldn't see her face; she seemed to be purposefully looking away.

Mr Cecil reached out a steady hand towards Robert. He grabbed the hand and stepped into the boat. It felt strangely still on the choppy tide. He settled on to the bench in the middle, grasping the edges tight.

Now it was Marisee's turn. The boat lurched away from the steps. Daisy pulled on a rope that was looped around a post and the prow jerked back towards Marisee.

"Tell her to hurry up," Daisy said. "Or we'll all end up out at sea."

Mr Cecil's fingers beckoned to Marisee. She took his hand and joined Robert. She looked as uncomfortable as Robert felt.

Daisy cackled. "You're the Well Keeper's granddaughter! You should like water!"

"Not this water," Marisee muttered.

Robert knew that the Thames was filled with nasty things that had been thrown from ships or carried through London in the many rivers that emptied into it. He felt the undercurrent tug at the boat, but alongside that, there was something more rhythmic, like breathing, as if the

Thames itself was alive. He stared at the water, almost expecting to see it dip and rise, but there were just small waves skimming across the darkness. Mr Cecil and Daisy were barely lifting their oars. Every little river breath was taking them closer to the far shore.

Marisee nudged him. "Is the boat moving by itself?"

He shrugged. His bad memories were returning and this time wouldn't be pushed away. His nails scraped the wooden bench as he gripped harder. Marisee touched his shoulder.

"What is it?" she asked.

"The last time I was on a boat like this, they were bringing me to the dock to take me to the Hibberts's mansion," he said.

"I'm sorry," she said, and they were both silent.

The moon was a smudge in the sky, but for a few moments the clouds parted and Robert saw the river start to bend. The embankment was buttressed by wooden pillions, with flights of steps leading to rows of boats bobbing on the tide.

"The Breach," Mr Cecil said.

The nearside bank had split apart. Robert could just make out the ragged edges of a wall that had crumbled and the river bulging through.

"Why don't they fix it?" Marisee asked.

126

"Because the Thames doesn't want it fixed," Daisy said. "Every time they build a wall or hammer in pillions, the river knocks them down. It's like it wants to remind us that it's still got some power."

It didn't feel powerful now; Robert was happy about that. The water was flat and still and the boat moved smoothly. The oars seemed to guide it rather than propel it along.

"The Gut lies just beyond the Breach," Mr Cecil said. "We'll leave you by the embankment. But we must go carefully. We mustn't alert the spies."

He pointed to three tall ships anchored in the centre of The Breach. They were without sails or flags to identify them. A solitary lamp burned dimly from the crow's nest of each of them.

"Whose spies are they?" Marisee asked.

"Whoever pays them the most," Daisy said.

Seven black shapes rose from the central crow's nest, silhouetted against the moon before flying away.

"The ravens," Mr Cecil said. "I think they've already seen us."

Robert's heart raced. "Who do you think is paying them now?"

Mr Cecil gave him a long look. Robert forced himself to hold it.

"Not the creature that pursues you," Mr Cecil said. "It won't pay for information. It enjoys sniffing out the clues itself."

"Stop it, Uncle," Daisy said. "You're frightening him."

"He already fears it, don't you, Robert?"

Robert nodded. "It had such strength. But it seemed old too. I thought it was taking me to Lord Hibbert, but it said that it had another place to deliver me."

"It could be—" Daisy began.

"Don't dwell on it now," Mr Cecil interrupted. "All of us are fearful of it." Mr Cecil held his hand to his brow, staring into the sky. "The ravens are heading north-west. It will be that Master Goldsmith. There are rumours that he's trained them to act on his command."

"The Goldsmith!" Robert and Marisee said together.

They looked at each other. They'd gone to the Lord Mayor for help when London had fallen under the enchanted sleep, but the Master of the Goldsmiths Guild had locked them in the Mansion House cellar to be fed to a Dragon.

"You know of him?" Mr Cecil said.

"We do," Marisee muttered.

"He wants to know about everything," Mr Cecil said. "He's probably trained the ravens to come to him whenever anyone stops at the Breach. But we've arrived. You'd better get your business done quickly."

The boat slipped into an inlet next to a wooden ladder slick with moss. Mr Cecil knotted the rope around the base of a mooring post and guided the prow closer to shore.

"We'll leave you here," Mr Cecil said.

"Will you wait for us?" Marisee asked.

Mr Cecil and Daisy glanced at each other.

"I help Miss Turnmill as I can," Mr Cecil said. "But I can't put my niece in danger."

"Since when?" Daisy said. "Remember when—"

"Quiet!" It was so sharp that Daisy stopped talking. "We'll wait for a while," Mr Cecil said, "but leave if we must."

Marisee stood up first, waited to find her balance, then took a wobbling step forward. She grasped the mooring post to steady herself then the ladder with her other hand. She paused, moved carefully on to the ladder and made her way up.

"It's not too bad." Marisee peered down at him. "There are only five rungs."

True, the bank was not far overhead, but the water was deep below the hull. A wave knocked the boat away from the ladder. It seemed to come from nowhere in this still water. Mr Cecil tugged on the rope, bringing the boat close to the ladder again.

"Uncle..." Daisy said.

Mr Cecil nodded. "I know, Daisy. The river shouldn't be fussing like this."

Robert reached for the ladder. The wood was damp and spongy. His foot crunched down on something – a barnacle or an oyster. He closed his eyes. That way he couldn't look down. But then the other memories filled his head, of climbing the ladder from the rowing boat in Barbados to the tall ship that would take him away from his mother and sisters to England.

"Hurry!" Daisy hissed from the boat.

He wanted to, but his legs wouldn't move.

"Robert?" Marisee's voice sounded so close to him. "Reach up. There's a rung above you. Just do that."

He braced himself and let one hand loosen on the rung that he was clinging to. Water splashed against the back of his legs as another wave broke against the embankment. He took a deep breath, let go of the rung and grabbed the one above.

"That's it," Marisee said. Her voice was clear and calm. "And now your foot."

He stepped higher, first with one foot and then the other.

"And again," Marisee said.

His hand reached up for another rung, his feet following.

"And one more time," Marisee said.

This time instead of a rung, Robert's hand was clasped by another hand.

"I have you," Marisee said.

As she pulled him up, Robert scrabbled his way up the last rungs and on to solid land.

"Thank you," he said. "I don't think I could have done that without you."

"You're welcome." She gave him a little smile.

He smiled back.

They were standing on a short wooden jetty. The moonlit land showed a narrow path leading to a long lake. Beyond that was a row of trees, and rising just above them, the broad sails of a windmill.

"I think we've found the Poplar Gut," Marisee said. "And somewhere over there must be the Squall."

THE SQUALL

The path led through marshland; it seemed to give the Gut a wide berth. The Gut was empty of boats and no reeds grew around the banks. There was a sheen across the water that reminded Robert of a fresh scar.

He and Marisee followed the path through the trees and stopped in an overgrown yard with a tumbledown barn. A squat windmill stood before them, its windows dark and glassless.

"It has five sails," Marisee said. "That's strange. I thought windmills only had four sails."

Close up, Robert saw that only the sails' criss-cross

frames were intact. The canvas that had once covered them dangled from the frames in strips.

"I don't think anyone's been here for a long time," Robert said.

"Not since the last Keeper of the Mills," Marisee said. "And no one knows what happened to them."

Robert would rather have not been reminded.

The windmill creaked. There was not even the smallest breeze. The sails shuddered then stilled. The strips of canvas swung to and fro. There was another long, loud creak and the whole of the roof turned, slowly grinding. A chain clanked inside as the sails disappeared from view then reappeared as the roof scraped to a stop.

Robert felt a ball of fear swelling in his throat and swallowed hard. He hoped again that the Fumi in the whispering gallery had not been setting a trap by sending them here. After all, they'd only been told to find the Squall. They'd been given no information about what it was and how it could help them. But, at the moment, it was the only clue they had.

"Who's there?" Robert shouted, more bravely than he felt. "Is that the Squall?"

"Fee-fi-fo-furl!" The sails spun slowly, as if pulling out words from inside the windmill. "I smell the blood of the Well Keeper girl!"

Marisee gave a little cry, a sound so small that she probably didn't hear it herself. But Robert knew that accent. It screeched like a weathervane in the wind.

"It's a Fumi," he said to Marisee. "Listen."

"Be you alive or be you dead…" The sails paused then spun the other way. "I'll grind your bones to make my bread!"

The dark windows turned white. The whiteness ballooned from the empty frames and squirmed like snakes. Marisee grabbed Robert's arm and backed away as the snakes twisted, dividing and stretching into – fingers. Five wide fingers like the windmill's sails. The air was heavy with a white powder that stung Robert's eyes and nose. Marisee was coughing hard, Robert too, as the powder coated his mouth. What was it? It wasn't flour. The cloud surrounded him, settling on his cheeks and filling his ears.

Then a gust of air lifted Robert off his feet. He tried to shout but he couldn't breathe.

"I'll grind your bones to make my bread!" the Fumi screeched.

"Put them down!" a voice ordered.

The cloud dissolved and Robert fell. It wasn't a long drop, but his knees gave and he slumped to the muddy ground. Marisee fell next to him. Everything around them was coated in white, apart from the old man who stood looking down at them. He was dressed like a beggar in a greatcoat that was much too great for him. Bare threads hung from the sleeve cuffs, matting together like fur. His boots were covered in fur too – just like the capture-creature.

Robert strained to see his face, but it was hidden beneath the brim of a top hat. It wasn't … it couldn't be the capture-creature. Surely it couldn't be here already! He scrabbled around, looking for something he could throw at it. If the thing was going to take him, Robert would not make it easy.

The old man removed his hat and beat the crown. White dust rose from it.

"That chalk gets everywhere." He held out his gloved hand. "But how can we talk properly with you down there in the mud?"

Marisee hesitantly took the offered hand. Robert scrambled up by himself. He stepped away from the old man, because it *was* there, however faint. Something wild and ancient. The old man's sandy-grey hair was thick and sleek. His eyes were round and bright. In the shadows, they seemed to be rimmed with black. His nose was wide and protruded out more than any human's, just like the capture-creature's.

He jammed his hat back on his head. "I have to apologize for the Squall. We don't get many visitors here and those that do come don't want no good."

The sails spun again. "Grind their bones… Grind their bones…"

"There's no bone grinding happening today, Squall," the old man said, "so behave yourself."

He walked towards the barn. Marisee was ready to follow him, but Robert held her back.

"Can we trust him?" he asked.

"We have to," she said. "We were told to look for the Squall and we've found it."

They stayed by the barn doorway, trying to look inside. It was pitch-black. They heard the sound of scraping metal, followed by the glow of smouldering tinder.

"I'm out of practice with the tinderbox," the old man said. "I don't need much light myself."

A candle was lit, then another one and another. They were stuck into a mound of melted wax on a millstone. There was nothing else in the barn apart from some bales of hay and a pile of blankets.

Robert and Marisee looked at each other and went inside.

"So you're the Well Keeper's granddaughter," the old man said to Marisee.

"Yes." She seemed to make herself taller. "I'm Marisee Blackwell. How do you know?"

"News gets to us eventually," he said. "Welcome, Marisee Blackwell." He smiled. Two long, sharp teeth protruded from his upper and lower jaw. "Well-keeping. That's a worthy profession. I'm Henry... I keep the Squall company. I suppose we keep each other company, as none of our own kind desire to be with us."

What is your kind? Robert longed to ask. There was something about him that still reminded Robert of the capture-creature. Marisee gave him a little shake of her head as if she'd known what he was thinking. He'd always been full of questions, but he had to remember to only ask the right ones at the right time.

Henry's gaze swept over Robert. "I know who *you* are, Mr Strong."

Robert flinched. He was right. Henry and the capture-creature *were* of a similar kind. He squinted into the barn. Was it waiting to pounce at him from behind a bale of hay?

"Don't worry, Robert. I won't cause you harm," Henry said. "I've been a fugitive like you. I know what it's like to be hunted. But tell me why you've travelled to our bend in the river."

"We have to find London's lost music," Marisee

said simply. "We were told… It was suggested that you or" – Marisee waved her hand towards the windmill – "the Squall might know something about it."

"Ah, the music's gone," Henry said. "So that's why the Domedary's raised its ugly head."

"You've seen it too?" Marisee asked.

"I have," Henry said. "Out by Blackwall Reach. I didn't believe my eyes. Then the Squall and I felt it pass beneath the tide last night, scuttling west along the riverbed."

"It destroyed the Vauxhall Pleasure Gardens," Marisee said, her voice quivering.

"This *is* a terrible business," Henry said. "But why must the Well Keeper solve it?"

"We owe the Fumis a favour," Robert said. Marisee might have been the one who made the deal, but it was Robert's life that they'd saved.

"Do you indeed?" Henry nodded slowly. "Those airheads – no offence to my good friend the Squall. Those Elders seem like they're full of smoke, but they're ruthless. *They* wouldn't send you here, though. The Squall is an embarrassment to them. In the Council's raggedy eyes, it doesn't exist."

"A Fumi we once helped, helped us," Marisee said. "*It* sent us to you without the Elders knowing."

"Well," Henry said, "Squall used to work in the Vauxhall Gardens. Well, not exactly work, but it certainly knows why them Elders are so eager not to be blamed for the missing music. And it can tell you a bit about blowing music around too. Let's find it."

Find it? Robert thought. It hadn't done much to hide itself when they arrived.

Henry leaned forward and blew out the candles. "Invisible is best," he said. "Especially when the spies have got eyes and very sharp beaks."

A WHIRL OF FIRE

Marisee took a step forward and bumped into Robert, who hadn't moved.

"Come on!" she urged.

Robert shook his head. "I don't know where he's taking me!"

"It seems safe here, Robert."

"I'm not safe anywhere," Robert said. "There's a reward on my head and anyone will betray me for six guineas."

Did Robert really believe that anyone would betray him?

"Even me?" she asked.

He didn't answer straight away. "No," he said. "I trust you."

Even after thinking about it, he didn't sound too sure. Perhaps it would take longer to build back the trust in each other than she had hoped.

"This way, please," Henry's voice called from the darkness. "And just to be clear, Mr Strong, I do not need or want money. And if I did, I would not obtain it through betrayal."

Robert nodded and they shuffled out of the barn, arms outstretched in the darkness. A flash of moonlight made the chalky ground shine as they picked their way across and entered the ruined mill.

The lower room was empty. Even the post that should hold the mill in place was gone. Marisee wondered if it was only Fumi magic that stopped it from falling down. They climbed a ladder into the room above.

"Squall!" Henry called. "They're safe'uns. They want our help."

"I'll grind their bones…"

"No, you won't," Henry said. "You'll come down from those rafters and tell 'em about Vauxhall."

"Vauxhall? Why do they need to know about that?" The Squall's voice, when it wasn't threatening to grind their bones, was surprisingly soft and sing-song.

"Because you know as well as I do that the Domedary's on the rampage again," Henry said. "And these poor souls got no choice but to stop it."

There was a soft gust of wind, almost like the one at the Pleasure Gardens. The Squall was definitely a Fumi, with the same shovel-shaped head and pole-thin body. Unlike the dark smoky Fumis of the Council, the Squall was a sandy white. The colour twisted around slowly; one moment Marisee could see through it, the next moment it was nearly solid. It didn't smell of the city like the others – she breathed in chalk dust with a hint of boiled ham and violin resin.

Robert was watching the Squall warily.

"I was telling 'em that you know those Pleasure Gardens up west well," Henry said.

"I know the tunnel," the Squall said. "I don't know much about the rest of it. And I haven't been back since I escaped."

Robert was suddenly interested. "Escaped?"

"I was stuck in a stinking tunnel full of stinking musicians," the Squall said. "It was hot down there and none of them used soap."

"The orchestra I saw was on a platform," Marisee said.

"The Pleasure Gardens are big," the Squall said.

"And the Tyers Solid who owns them wants to fill every corner with strange things. There was a tunnel to the east of the Grove where the musicians played secretly so the music wafted up through the bushes. It was my job to make it waft as far as possible."

"So Mr Tyers knows about the elementals?" Marisee asked. Was she one of the last people in the city to find out about Elemental London?

"It was that Handel Solid who told him about us," the Squall said. "I suppose the king told *him*. All the kings and queens know, but some of 'em don't have much to do with us. But that second George, he was always poking around elemental business – and he was no good at keeping secrets. When the Council of Elders saw fit to … um … punish me, I was confined to that wretched tunnel."

"Why did they punish you?" Robert asked.

"I didn't mind my own business," the Squall said. "I was accused of being 'too in harmony with the enemy'."

"Tell 'em what you mean by that," Henry said.

"I was never like the other Fumis," the Squall said. "I took no pleasure flitting around high above the rooftops. Yes, lower London was filthy, but it all seemed more … *vivace*. Full of life. I flew lower and lower … and soon I was talking to folk I wasn't supposed to."

"Like whom?" Marisee asked.

"There's a Dragon that keeps watch on Mary-le-Bow on Cheapside," the Squall said. "She speaks Weathervane and I'd pause to converse with her. She knows everything that's going on below. And some of the Magogs' statue-spies get bored stuck up there on their perches. They value a conversation now and again."

"Magog spies?" Robert said.

"Yes, Magog magic got the statues moving and talking," the Squall said. "While the giants sleep, the statues watch out for them. And Magog magic soaks through the earth. I heard that they made monsters from the glass shattered when Fleet Street shook."

Robert nodded. "They're called shard beasts," he said.

Marisee glanced at him. He'd met more magical monsters without her?

Henry sniffed the air. "Best tell your tale quickly, Squall. We won't be alone for long."

Robert jumped up. "Who … is it…?"

"It's not the one you truly fear, Mr Strong," Henry said. "But it isn't good news. Stay here." He climbed back down the ladder.

"I shall hurry," the Squall said. "*Accelerando.* One hot July evening, the musicians were tuning their instruments. The noise. The heat. Sweaty shirts and sweaty feet. I could stand it no longer. There were two of us Fumis by then. The other – my friend – was being punished for whispering a story of adventure into the ear of a goldsmith's sleeping daughter, just to see if she would remember it in the morning. It was silly, but not harmful."

Was that a shout from outside? Robert's head jerked towards the door.

"Someone's coming!" he said. "Please, Squall. Is there anything important we should know?"

A cloud of flour puffed around the Squall. "*Presto*! Yes, *presto*! I am trying! I rushed through that stinking tunnel and burst out of the end. I heard afterwards that the musicians were found in a dead faint. We had taken all the air with us. They were all revived, but their clothes and wigs were … were shredded like the old canvas that hangs from these sails. And their instruments were shattered into pieces."

Just like the orchestra earlier, Marisee thought. *Fumis definitely can make instruments explode.* No wonder the Fumi Elders were worried.

"My friend came with me," the Squall continued. "We flew east, following the river, not knowing where we would find ourselves. I had no time to stop and navigate.

I feared that the Council would send their warriors to catch me."

"The Fumis have warriors?" Marisee said.

"Indeed, they do," the Squall said. "But they are rarely called upon to fight. Though it was not them that we should have feared."

Now Marisee looked towards the door. There were definitely men's voices in the distance.

Please, she urged silently. *Please hurry up!*

"It was the Dragons who killed my friend," the Squall said.

Both Marisee and Robert snapped back towards it.

"Killed?" they said together.

"We strayed into their territory across the City of London. As you know, there is little love lost between Fumi and Dragon. The Goldsmiths Guild is rich and powerful. The Masters collude with the Dragons to hold on to wealth. After my friend's visit, that goldsmith's daughter insisted that she wanted to be a pirate. She turned down a wealthy husband and went to sea. Her father sought revenge."

"What happened to your friend?" Marisee asked quietly.

"The Dragons surrounded them." The Squall became almost completely invisible. "Not in their Dragon

146

shape, but in a whirl of fire. As the Dragons burned brighter, my friend faded. They called for me as they died, but I could not pass through that fire to save them."

Marisee wished that the Squall was more solid so that she could comfort it.

"Did they attack you too?" Robert asked.

"No," the Squall said. "The Fumi Council escorted me here, but in truth, the Dragons had no interest in me. The Council could do nothing to avenge my friend because we had escaped our confinement. We were fugitives. But they became fearful. They hadn't known until then that the Dragons could kill us." The Fumi turned pure white. "Beware! They're here!"

A raven shot through the glassless window in silence. It landed on the ground and stretched out its wings. They were as wide as a millstone. It tucked its wings into its body and cawed once. A second bird flew in and perched next to it. Both birds stared at Marisee.

The Squall transformed into a column of greyish dust, swelling to fill the small room.

"Run!" it squealed. "Run!"

The ravens made a low, gurgling sound like a well-pump before the water gushed out, fanning away the chalk dust with their wings. Marisee felt a hand on her arm. Robert pulled her towards the ladder. He scrambled down first, her following quickly, her feet catching in her skirt hem. She stumbled to the ground.

Henry was waiting at the bottom of the ladder, a trapped raven under each arm. The birds wriggled and cawed but couldn't free themselves. Henry snarled, his sharp teeth shining in the lamplight cast by the man standing in front of him. The flame flickered across Henry's hands; where there'd been fingernails, Marisee saw claws.

"Get out!" Henry roared at the man. "Or your filthy spies will die!"

"Release them, Henry," the man said calmly. "It's not you they want. Yet."

Marisee knew the man straight way. He was the Master of the Goldsmiths Guild, an ambitious, cruel man who'd once tried to feed her and Robert to a Dragon.

Henry roared again. The air shook. Marisee flinched. The Goldsmith stayed exactly as he was, a small smile playing across his lips. He lifted his arm to show a large bird balanced on his wrist. It was black, like a raven, but much bigger with curved talons and a wide, blunt beak like a mouth. Its feathers were as smooth and shiny as pewter. Its head jerked from side to side. Marisee thought she could hear a tick, tick, tick.

"Marisee!" Robert backed away. "It's not a raven! It's…"

148

There was a tick and click and the tang of gunpowder in the air.

"Perhaps you can conquer the ravens," the Goldsmith said, his voice still calm. "But what about a real challenge?"

The bird was edged with a fiery orange that glowed from inside it. As the Goldsmith hurled it towards Henry, its wings jerked. The tick, tick, tick became louder as the bird blazed. Flames shot from its eye sockets. A wave of heat hit Marisee's face. Henry swiped the bird away; it fell to the ground, still burning, then slowly started to rise again, clicking and ticking, its wings levering it upwards. A plume of fire rushed towards Henry. As he jumped out of the way, he lost his grip on the ravens and they careered away.

Tick, tick, tick went the burning bird.

"We left you in peace here, Henry," the Goldsmith said. "You and your rogue companion. That can change. It *will* change."

"Marisee!" a voice screeched. "Robert! Go!"

A chalky wind rushed past them, knocking the Goldsmith from his feet. Marisee and Robert stumbled outside, but there was no escape. A raven dived towards Marisee, cawing loudly, claws catching in her hair.

"Stop it!" she screamed, trying to bat it away.

It looped away then back, landing on her shoulder, its claws digging through her clothes to her skin. There was a flap of wings and a second bird landed on her other shoulder. They were circling Robert too, cawing and screeching as if they were laughing. Robert's arms flailed as he tried to fight them off. A raven clung on each of his wrists, forcing them together like handcuffs.

Shadows moved from the treeline. Soldiers carrying torches; archers with their bows raised. They stalked towards Marisee and Robert, surrounding them. The ravens shrieked one caw together then lifted into the air and flew away towards the Breach.

"Take them to the boat." The Goldsmith stood up, brushing down his jacket. He lifted the strange Dragon-bird; its fire dimmed. "But first…" He waved a hand towards the buildings. "I must tidy this away."

Tick, click, the smell of gunpowder.

The Goldsmith threw the bird towards the barn. A glow, then a fiery explosion drove it onwards. It landed in the barn in full blaze. The hay smouldered then burst into flames.

"No!" Marisee shrieked as the soldiers pulled her away.

"You deal with this." Now the Goldsmith waved towards the windmill. Two soldiers entered, torches burning. They returned a moment later as dark smoke billowed from the windmill's windows.

"You didn't have to do that!" Marisee cried.

"I didn't have to," the Goldsmith said. "But I wanted to."

SIR GEORGE NELSON, LORD MAYOR OF LONDON

As the soldiers pulled Robert towards the jetty, he strained to see any sign of Mr Cecil and Daisy. There was none. Robert hoped that they were safe, and even more, that they could find Turnmill to tell her what had happened. It might be more than one rescue she'd have to plan tonight.

He was placed in one boat, Marisee in a different

one. He sat rigid, almost crushed between two soldiers. The tide was strong, as if the Thames could smell the sea and was straining towards it. Mr Cecil's small boat had moved so smoothly, but the soldiers grunted as they rowed, fighting the undertow. Did *they* know what might lie beneath them? If the Domedary rose now, this boat would be as useless as wet tinder.

But their trip to the Isle of Dogs seemed useless too. They'd learned little of help from the Squall and were now the Goldsmith's prisoners. Perhaps Lord Pritchard was this very moment being summoned. His ship may still be waiting to carry Robert back to the West Indies. For a moment, Robert pictured Steeple swaggering through London spending the money he'd made from selling Robert's golden box. His betrayal had started all this. Robert breathed in and out deeply and gritted his teeth. He would do everything he could to ensure he never ever returned to a plantation.

As the boat passed the Tower of London, Robert felt it again, the fury and wildness that seemed to ooze from the bricks into everything around it.

The arches of London Bridge loomed ahead, but the boat moored just before it. Robert was ordered to stand up and was pushed up the water steps on to the jetty. The Goldsmith's barge moored next to it. The Goldsmith leaped nimbly on to the water step, his guards pulling Marisee behind them. She looked furious.

"You wait until my grandmother hears about this!" she shouted.

"Don't worry, my dear," the Goldsmith said. "You'll be able to tell her yourself when we throw you into the Fleet alongside her." He looked Robert up and down. "And you, runaway boy, will be much further away. I have sent word to Lord Pritchard of your capture."

Robert met the Goldsmith's eye. "No," he said. "I will not go back to the plantation."

"Do you really think that you have a choice?" the Goldsmith said.

The Goldsmith's carriage was waiting in a side street. Robert recognized the coat of arms on the side. Such comfort wasn't for him and Marisee, though. The Goldsmith watched carefully as their wrists and ankles were bound, before the soldiers lifted them and dropped them clumsily into the back of a cart.

"This is how they take the condemned to the gallows," Marisee said.

"Indeed," the Goldsmith replied.

He climbed into his coach and the driver urged the horses forward. Robert wished Turnmill was here to persuade the horses to behave badly, but the carriage clattered away into the night. The sturdy dray pulling the cart plodded north, away from the river.

Robert and Marisee didn't talk to each other on the journey, almost as if they'd agreed a pact to stay silent in case the soldiers eavesdropped and reported back. Marisee pressed them to tell her where they were going, but they ignored her. Robert glanced from side to side, listening out for the sound of hooves and Lord Pritchard's arrival. He thought, for a moment, that he saw a sleek, fox-like shape flitting alongside them in the shadows and tried to catch Marisee's eye, but she was lost in her own thoughts, sitting bolt upright, shoulders back, staring ahead.

The cart rattled to a stop outside the Lord Mayor's Mansion House. Marisee looked at Robert in alarm.

"He wouldn't dare!" she said.

Robert wasn't so sure. Would the Goldsmith try to feed them to a Dragon again? Perhaps even that would be better than returning to enslavement. This time if the Dragon asked a riddle, he'd refuse to answer.

They were untied and marched through the servants' entrance, but instead of being taken down to the cellar, they went up and kept going up to the attic rooms perched on the roof. Marisee was shoved through a door that was quickly locked behind her. Robert was pushed through another door. The key rattled in the lock outside.

There was no light at all. Robert felt his way across the room. His shin knocked painfully against the frame of something that might be a bed. He reached out and touched it. Yes, there was a frame, a thin mattress, a blanket. He climbed on to it and lay down. As early morning light trickled in through the small window, he fell asleep.

He dreamed that he was in the hold of a ship in total darkness. The boat creaked around him and somewhere high above, sailors called to each other. Something nudged his shoulder, but the darkness was so complete he couldn't see who or what it was.

"Keke!" It was his mother's voice. "Take this for your journey!"

He smelled the sharp-sweet scent of an orange.

He pushed the hand away. He didn't want food. He didn't want drink. He'd sleep and sleep and never wake up.

"Wake up!"

He kept his eyes closed.

"Wake up, Robert!"

He was shoved hard. He opened his eyes. Marisee was waving a chunk of bread above his face.

"They've brought us some breakfast," she said, pointing to a tray by the door. "Well, it's bread that must have been baked sometime last week. There's warm milk to dip it in. Well, it could have been warm when it left the kitchen. I persuaded the guard to let me come and eat with you."

Robert's stomach rumbled. His body was telling him that he needed food but he wasn't hungry. He pulled the blanket tight over himself.

"Lord Pritchard is coming for me," he said. "What's the point of eating breakfast? Going to the plantation is like going to the gallows."

Marisee ripped the blanket off. "You are not on that boat yet, Robert Strong! And even if you were, I would come and rescue you." She took a bite of bread and screwed up her face. "This bread could probably sink a boat. But anyway, we have to meet the Lord Mayor soon. Both of us. So no Lord Pritchard yet."

"The Lord Mayor?" Robert sat up.

"Yes," Marisee said. "The Goldsmith brought us here for a reason, and now we're going to find out why."

Robert swung his legs over the side of the bed, his hope returning. The Goldsmith could so easily have ordered the soldiers to take him to Lord Pritchard last night. But he was here instead.

"Is this Lord Mayor like the old one?" he asked.

"Grandma's not impressed." Marisee lifted the bread to her mouth again, then changed her mind. She threw it towards the tray. It thudded on to the wood. "But then Grandma's not impressed by any of them. She says that it's time to get a woman Lord Mayor for a change, but I can never see that happening."

"Who is he?" Robert asked.

"He's called George Nelson. Grandma says that he just wants an easy life. He lets the Guild Masters do what they want while he prances about in expensive clothes and jewels."

Robert laughed. It was good to be with Marisee again.

A guard soon came and ordered her out. Servants brought Robert a basin of water to wash himself and a set of clothes. They weren't new, but they were freshly laundered and darned. When he was clean and dressed, the guard let him out of the room. Marisee was waiting outside. She was wearing a ruffled pink silk dress and looking very unhappy about it.

"Apparently it upsets the Lord Mayor to see ill-dressed people," she said. "Though in this hideous thing I feel very ill-dressed."

Sir George Nelson, the Lord Mayor of London, stood at the end of the table in a large parlour. His arm was resting on the back of a chair, as if he was waiting for his portrait to be painted. He certainly wore more clothes than any man that Robert had ever seen – breeches, stockings and shoes, of course, then an open waistcoat over a white shirt which in turn was half-covered by a burgundy frock coat covered in embroidery and decorated with a row of small gold buttons. On top of this, a heavy dark gown was fastened around his neck and hung down to the floor. A gold chain nestled in its folds, a chain so thick that Robert imagined it lifting an anchor. The Lord Mayor's hair was covered by a short white wig. Robert wondered if the Lord Mayor's face was a cleverly embroidered mask hiding another mask underneath and another under that.

The guards pushed Robert and Marisee forward then stepped back. The Lord Mayor eyed them then let his glance slip away, as if they held nothing of interest to him.

"Passable," he said, waving his arm so the white shirt cuffs billowed from beneath the gown.

The door slammed open and the Goldsmith stormed in. He stomped over to the Lord Mayor and whispered in his ear.

"Oh!" The Lord Mayor looked confused. "A fountain, you say?"

"Yes, Lord Mayor. A fountain."

"Through the floor of the Fleet prison?"

"Through the floor of the Fleet prison."

The Lord Mayor shifted slightly to help the gown drape better. "And the Well Keeper is quite gone?" he said.

"Yes," the Goldsmith said, glaring at Robert and Marisee. "She has disappeared, Lord Mayor."

Robert was used to keeping his face free of expressions, but he felt a grin widening inside him. Madam Blackwell was safe! Marisee bowed her head to hide the smile twitching at the corner of her mouth.

The Lord Mayor waved his arm again. "Then we must send soldiers to find her!"

"Not yet, Lord Mayor." The Goldsmith spoke more calmly than Robert liked. "We can play this to our advantage." The Goldsmith walked towards Marisee. "I'm sure that this young lady knows that her grandmother could be severely punished for harbouring a runaway slave."

The Goldsmith poked Robert. Robert made his face stay blank.

"When we find her," the Goldsmith said, "and indeed we will find her, we will lock her in a cell that no ... Chad" – he spat the word – "can enter, and we will make sure it is well guarded."

"Well guarded?" the Lord Mayor said. "You mean by that smelly Dragon thing you showed me in the cellar?"

The Goldsmith didn't answer. He walked in a slow

circle around Marisee before returning to the Lord Mayor. "There are other Dragons. More fierce. More hungry."

The Lord Mayor picked a stray thread from his cuff. "I don't need to know about all that ugly magic stuff. I've told you to take care of that, Edward. Why are these children even here? I have to meet the king in a few hours because Queen Charlotte is most upset that harm may have come to the Mozart child. On English soil too! We don't want those Hapsburgs trying to start a war. They seem to like that sort of thing. Do you know how he is?"

"The boy's sister is outside waiting to see you," the Goldsmith said wearily. "Remember, you asked for her, Lord Mayor."

"Oh, did I?" The Lord Mayor looked annoyed. "Perhaps you can deal with her, Edward. My silversmith is due. The guild has a competition to design new buckles for my shoes and I wish to select the winner."

"Of course, Lord Mayor," the Goldsmith said.

"Oh, just one other thing." The Lord Mayor was inspecting his other cuff. "The servants are telling rather fanciful stories that it was actually a monster that destroyed the Pleasure Gardens."

"Trust me, Lord Mayor," the Goldsmith said smoothly, "there is no *monster*. It is most likely a clever mechanical puppet. As you know, Mr Dross, the automata maker, persists in hawking his machines across London. I believe it was one of his. The explosion was an unfortunate accident involving candles and fireworks."

"It is truly terrible," the Lord Mayor said, "that such a disaster should befall people of fashion. Mr Dross must be punished severely."

People of fashion? Robert thought. Were those the only people that mattered?

"The monster was not a clever mechanical puppet!" Marisee burst out. "It wasn't an accident! I was there! I saw it!"

The Goldsmith stepped in front of her. "With your permission, Lord Mayor, I will take steps to ensure that the Mozart child is safe, and we will be saved from a possible war. And" – he gave the Lord Mayor a reassuring smile – "I will deal with Mr Dross and his mechanical monster."

"Good," the Lord Mayor said. "But make sure that I have good news to pass to the queen."

He flicked his gown into the air so it swirled around him and strode out of the parlour.

"Let the girl enter!" the Goldsmith called.

She ran in as soon as the door opened. She was pale with blonde hair framing a tired face.

"I've seen her before," Marisee whispered to Robert.

"She was in the Pleasure Gardens and took Mozart as soon as the trouble started."

"Where is the Lord Mayor?" She spoke English with an accent Robert had not heard before. "He requested me. I want to see him. My brother is sick and needs help. He is … he is losing his music. It's in his head but the instruments just break. I don't understand!"

"It is indeed unfortunate," the Goldsmith said. "I have heard tales of such a strange affliction in London." He pointed at Robert and Marisee. "This boy and girl will find the cause and the cure."

Robert stared at the Goldsmith. Marisee was right; he wasn't to be handed over to Lord Pritchard! And Marisee wasn't being thrown into gaol. Not for the moment, anyway. The Goldsmith was not a man to be trusted.

The girl gave them a long look. "Who are they?"

The Goldsmith's mouth twitched into a thin smile. "Robert *Pritchard* and Marisee Blackwell. They helped cure our sleep predicament last year. They have a special understanding of London's problems. *I* believe that the air is to blame for our current difficulty. It can be very troublesome."

"The air?" The girl looked confused. "How can the air cause these music problems?"

The Fumi Council was right, Robert thought. *The Goldsmith is trying to blame the lost music on them.*

"Something, or some things, in the air affect the music," the Goldsmith said certainly. "Strange violent winds that blow it the wrong way. The boy and girl will prove it. By tomorrow sunset." He beckoned to the guards. "Show them out, please. They have work to do."

As the door opened, a man pushed his way in past the guards. He was wearing a strange red hat and a red frock coat crusted with mud.

Marisee started. "That's Dross!" she whispered to Robert. "He was at the Pleasure Gardens too."

"Mr Goldsmith! Mr Goldsmith!" he cried. "I still await payment for the firebird I constructed for you."

Dross? Robert knew that name and voice from somewhere.

"There is no payment owed," the Goldsmith said coldly. "You are a nothing in this city, Mr Dross. You should be honoured to receive such a commission from me."

"I cannot eat honour!" Mr Dross yelled. "My pantry is empty! My home is falling down! You and your rich friends are all the same. You commission my designs because they are the best in Europe then you refuse to pay me!"

Dross? How did Robert know – oh, yes! It was the man who'd shot at him from the window of the strange house in Soho. It had been the only other time that he'd left the Red Guard Gang's den and it had ended in disaster.

Mr Dross plucked at the Goldsmith's jacket. "I cannot survive, Master Goldsmith, unless I am paid."

The Goldsmith swiped Mr Dross's hand away.

"The Lord Mayor is outraged that your mechanical monster caused such destruction in the Pleasure Gardens yesterday evening," the Goldsmith said.

Mr Dross looked confused. "My what caused what?"

"Do not pretend innocence, Mr Dross," the Goldsmith said. "You call yourself the animateur extraordinaire. You have just claimed that you create the best designs in Europe. *You* built that monster to show off your skills, Mr Dross, then lost control of it. The Lord Mayor has demanded that you are punished severely."

"Are you accusing me of building that ... that river demon?" Mr Dross shouted. "You are blaming me for the deaths and injuries that it caused?"

"There is no other explanation," the Goldsmith said. "Not unless one believes in..." His face curled up in disgust. "Magic."

But you know about magic! Robert wanted to shout. *Why are you pretending that you don't?*

"As there is no such thing as magic," the Goldsmith continued, "I have no choice but to blame you for the disaster, Mr Dross. I can call a guard now who will hurl you straight into Newgate Prison, or I can be lenient. If you wish to avoid punishment, you will not ask me for payment for the firebird, or indeed for any other machine I order you to construct for me…"

"But, Master Goldsmith…" Mr Dross stuttered.

"Or for any machine I order you to construct for any member of my guild," the Goldsmith finished.

The shock on Mr Dross's face returned to anger. "You want me to create automata for any guild member who asks?" he cried. "Without payment? You will ruin me!"

"Your ruin is no concern of mine," the Goldsmith said and strode out of the room.

Mr Dross stared after him, eyes narrowed, lips twitching in a half smile. He seemed to have forgotten that he wasn't alone.

"I'm nothing in this city, am I?" he said quietly. "Well, it's time that I make my ruin your concern, Master Goldsmith. You'll soon find out what a *nobody* like me can do when my hand is forced."

SO MANY QUESTIONS

Marisee watched as the yeomen burst into the parlour and led Mr Dross out. He was smiling, a sly, secret grin that made Marisee shiver. The Goldsmith had certainly made himself another enemy. She, Robert and the girl were accompanied to the Mansion House entrance and the door was firmly closed behind them. They walked down the steps in silence. Marisee noticed a boy standing by the railings holding a whistle flute. He put it to his mouth and blew the first few notes.

As she watched him, a tiny breeze brushed against Marisee's face. She smelled ... was that frying chicken?

A loud squeal made her jump. The boy's face was screwed up with the effort of trying to force the rest of the song from the whistle flute. Then came a sound like a creature bellowing. It was faint and far away.

Marisee turned to Robert to see if he'd noticed, but he and the girl were already walking off. Nobody else seemed to have heard the sound. Perhaps it was distant thunder. Then she saw Mr Dross. He was leaning against the railings, a small frown on his face, his ear cocked upwards as if listening. His eyes flicked from the whistle-flute player to the girl at Robert's side. When he realized that Marisee was looking at him, he hurried away.

Marisee ran to catch up with Robert to tell him what she'd seen, but the girl was talking.

"If you are to help us, you must know more about us," she was saying. "Perhaps you can walk with me back to our lodgings. We only arrived two days ago and I am still easily lost."

Robert looked uneasy but said nothing.

"I'm Marisee," Marisee said. "What's your name?"

"Maria Anna Walburga Ignatia Mozart," the girl said. "But I am known as Nannerl."

"I saw you at the Pleasure Gardens," Marisee said. "You took your brother from the stage when the instruments started to explode."

"I thought it was a conjuror's trick at first," Nannerl said. "But then the harpsichord… That was a gift from Mr Shudi on Golden Square. We would never let it be broken."

"You said your brother was sick," Robert said. "How?"

"He has done nothing but sleep since we returned from the Pleasure Gardens," Nannerl said. "Music is his life. Now he says that he has no life. He feels the music moving around in his head, but it cannot come out. He can compose, but if he tries to play… The first notes are good and then it is terrible." Nannerl tapped her head. "The music is inside me too. But I cannot hum or sing. Even the music box I brought with me from Salzburg has broken." She stroked a pouch that she carried on long straps over her shoulder.

"You have a music box inside there?" Marisee said.

"I will show you."

Nannerl tipped the music box out of the pouch. It was a square wooden box with a hinged lid. The inside was lined with red velvet. The painted tin ballerina that must have spun slowly around when the music played was lying on its side.

Nannerl breathed in. "Even the smell of it reminds me of home," she said.

Could Marisee smell fried chicken again? She

looked around. There was a pie shop across the road. That must be it.

"Um…" Robert said, looking around nervously. "Can we carry on walking?"

"Yes, sorry," Marisee said, flipping the music box closed. "I think we should talk to your brother as soon as possible, Nannerl. He may have more to tell us about what happened to the orchestra at the Pleasure Gardens."

"Come back at midday," Nannerl said. "I will make sure that he is awake and ready to talk to you."

"Midday?"

Marisee wanted to talk to him now! They were supposed to find the music by sunset tomorrow. If they failed, both she and Robert had so much to lose.

On the other hand, she had to tell Grandma everything that had happened as soon as possible so they could plan a way to defeat the Domedary, and she definitely had to warn Grandma that the Goldsmith was hunting for her.

"We'll return at midday," Marisee agreed.

They left Nannerl on the corner of Frith Street in Soho and hurried towards the well near St Anne's church. Luckily, there was no one around to give Marisee a strange look as she called down the shaft. "Are you there, Turnmill?"

"Of course!" Turnmill called back. "Would I let you fall like a sack of coal?"

There was a snort too, that sounded like the Fleet Ditch boar laughing. Marisee was even happy to hear that.

"You go first," she said to Robert.

Robert climbed on to the wall. "Thank you," he said, stepping into the air.

"Your turn, Marisee," Turnmill called.

Marisee clambered up and let herself drop. The mist met her halfway down, curling around her and softening her fall. She used to love watching Grandma stepping into the Blackwell Well on Friday mornings, wishing she was allowed to follow her. Now, Marisee did it so often she'd almost become used to it.

Almost.

She would never become *fully* used to it because the world of the Chads was so strange. There were always new tunnels to explore, new springs to meet, new flotsam washing into the room of lost things. And at last, Marisee had Robert to share it with again. But, if they didn't find out what happened to London's music, Robert would be seized and shipped to the West Indies. And Grandma ... she would never be safe above ground again.

"You look so serious, my darling," Grandma said.

Marisee had been so lost in her thoughts, she hadn't noticed Grandma standing in front of her.

"Grandma!" Marisee rushed to her and kissed her. Grandma hugged Marisee, then Robert.

"I hope you didn't think that I was still stuck in that stinking prison!" Grandma smiled. "Though it stank much less after the boar smashed through the cell floor and let the water in."

"It *was* very impressive," Turnmill agreed.

They set off down the tunnels. Marisee grinned at Robert. It was so good to see that Grandma was safe. Robert didn't smile back.

"If they catch you, Madam Blackwell," he said, "they'll put you in a worse prison. Now you're a fugitive like me."

"Robert," Grandma said gently, "I've fought many battles against men like that Goldsmith. They're just bullies who like to strut around and make others do their dirty work. My biggest worry is you. I need to make sure *you* are safe." Grandma stopped talking as she crouched to pass beneath a low stone arch. "Those Romans must have been very short," she said.

The tunnel widened into a cavern. The vaulted ceiling was so low that Marisee could reach up and touch it. The floor was set with fragments of painted tiles.

Steps in the centre led down to a tiled square space that was filled with blankets and pillows. Marisee felt the exhaustion wash over her. Robert looked like he could hardly stay standing. She suddenly felt guilty because he'd probably only just gone to sleep when she'd woken him earlier.

"Rest now," Turnmill said. "We'll talk later."

"We can't!" Marisee said. "We haven't got much time!"

"You need to rest," Grandma said sternly.

"But we have to be in Soho for midday," Marisee protested. "To talk to Nannerl's brother."

"You still need to rest," Grandma said, nudging her down the steps. "Shoes off!"

Marisee kicked them off and was even happier to change out of the ugly pink dress. Grandma helped her slide beneath the blankets. She closed her eyes and it felt like she'd only blinked a couple of times before Grandma was waking her up.

"Feel better?" Grandma asked.

Marisee nodded, even though her eyes were sore and her stomach hurt. It was a twisting ache; it happened when she knew that she was expected to be brave. How could they ever find the music and defeat the Domedary by sunset tomorrow? She let Grandma guide her out of

173

the makeshift bed, threw back her shoulders and lifted her chin. She *would* be brave.

She smelled the hot rolls before she saw them. They were piled on a platter alongside a ramekin of butter and some chunks of cheese. Robert was already eating, chewing slowly, his thoughts elsewhere. Grandma poured tea into plain earthenware beakers for them all. Marisee took a sip. It was warm and sweet. It seemed to give her extra strength.

"You'll stay here now, won't you, Grandma?" Marisee said. "Where you're safe."

"No, honey. I'm too old to sleep in a draughty old cavern," Grandma said. "Turnmill has gone to plead my case to Lady Walbrook. It will be far more comfortable in the Mithraeum."

"Lady Walbrook?" Marisee had been reaching for more butter. Her hand stalled.

Lady Walbrook, the Chads' riverhead, did not like humans. She blamed them because her once mighty river, the Walbrook, was now an unknown underground trickle.

"We can't trust her, Grandma," Marisee said. "You know that. Please stay here."

Grandma placed her beaker down firmly. "Let me worry about me, Marisee. You and Robert keep your minds on the business in hand. What do we know so far?"

Marisee *would* worry, but Grandma was right. They had work to do.

"The Domedary has been asleep east of the Greenwich peninsula," Marisee began. "Effra said that London's music keeps it sleeping."

"Yes," Grandma said. "Turnmill told me that much."

"Do we know that for certain?" Robert interrupted. "Perhaps it's the Domedary waking up that's stopped the music."

Grandma raised her eyebrows. "That's a possibility. We can't make assumptions, though Turnmill seemed sure that the music must have been taken first."

"Effra said the same," Marisee added.

Robert nodded.

"Both the Fumis and the Goldsmith want the music found with great urgency," Grandma said. "Is that right?"

"Yes," Marisee said. "The Fumis are scared of getting the blame for the missing music and being punished by the Dragons."

"And the Goldsmith wants to blame it on the Fumis so they *are* punished," Robert said.

Or killed, Marisee said to herself. That was what the Fumis truly feared.

"The Goldsmiths have always wanted the Dragons to be the most powerful elementals," Madam Blackwell said. "The Whittington Articles just about keep them in check, but the Goldsmith will try every way he can to ignore the terms of the truce."

And it doesn't help that the Squall told us that Fumis really could blow music about, Marisee thought. What would happen if a Fumi really was responsible?

Grandma sighed. "The Goldsmith has the Lord Mayor's ear, so anything that Goldsmith says, happens. Whoever – or whatever – he wants punished, shall be punished."

That answered Marisee's question about what would happen. It also reminded her of something else.

"There's a strange man who makes machines," she said. "He's called Mr Dross. I saw him in the Pleasure Gardens and he was at the Mansion House earlier."

"The automata maker?" Grandma asked.

Marisee was surprised. "You know about him?"

"I've seen his business cards in shops in London," Grandma said. "What about him?"

Marisee described seeing him in the Pleasure Gardens and what had happened between the Goldsmith and Mr Dross in the Lord Mayor's parlour earlier.

"The Goldsmith was definitely blaming Mr Dross for what happened in Vauxhall," Marisee said. "He even pretended that magic didn't exist."

"That Goldsmith is nastier than the Fleet privies," Grandma said. "I swear that he wants to be Lord Mayor someday. Then we'll all be in trouble. And you heard Mr Dross threaten some kind of revenge?"

Marisee nodded. "And he was outside the Mansion House afterwards," she said. "He was watching a boy trying to play a whistle flute."

"I don't trust the Goldsmith," Grandma said. "But we do need to be completely sure that isn't what happened. You saw the Domedary close up, Marisee. Could it have been some form of automata or puppet?"

"No!" Marisee said. "It was real!" She hadn't meant to sound so angry.

"I believe you, darling," Grandma said softly.

Robert nodded. "So do I."

Marisee looked away for a moment, blinking back tears. She'd never been pleased that she couldn't dream before. She was now. If she could dream, that monster's scream and the old man's ear trumpet would return to her over and over in her sleep. It had definitely been real. Grandma drew Marisee to her. Her cloak smelled of hot rolls with a sniff of Fleet Prison.

"What did you learn at the Isle of Dogs?" Grandma said, still hugging her.

"There was a man … a creature called Henry."

Robert's voice faltered. "He… He tried to protect us when the Goldsmith came. I don't know if he… He may not have survived."

"I'm so sorry to hear that," Grandma said, hugging Marisee even tighter.

"The Squall told us how he was imprisoned in the Pleasure Gardens tunnel with the orchestra," Marisee said.

"And how the Dragons killed his friend," Robert finished.

Grandma looked furious. "It was a terrible business! A different Master Goldsmith, but just as cruel as the one we have now."

Grandma kissed Marisee on the forehead and let her go. She pulled apart a bread roll and laid a slab of butter inside it. They all watched it melt.

"I'm not sure if we learned anything useful," Marisee said. "It seems even more likely that a Fumi has made the music disappear, because the Squall told us they can actually do that."

"Do you think the music has been taken by any of the elementals, Madam Blackwell?" Robert asked. "Only something with magic can do that."

Grandma thought about it. "Well, we know it's not the Fumis. They're much too frightened of being punished. Just one word from the Goldsmith and – well, they know full well what the Dragons can do to them. It's definitely not a Chad. They have no reason to want a monster trampling London's wells."

"The Dragons could have done it just so they can blame the Fumis," Marisee said, though she wasn't sure *how* they could do it. It had really felt like the music had been blown away on a gust of wind.

Grandma looked doubtful too. "Dragons rarely leave the City," she said. "They draw their power from the gold and money. I honestly don't think that they notice music."

"What about the Magogs?" Robert asked.

"Yes," Marisee said. "Effra said that the Domedary first stirred when Gog and Magog fell from Brutus's ship."

"True," Grandma said. "But the giants are still slumbering. How could they wake the Domedary and, even more importantly, why? Unless... No." She shook her head. "The legend is that the Domedary guards the Magogs from any harm coming in from the sea. Perhaps they have woken it to stop a— No." She shook her head again. "If a war was coming, the elementals would know long before us humans." She gave Marisee and Robert a reassuring smile. "Turnmill would have told me. I don't believe that it's anything to do with the Magogs."

There was a silence.

Robert split his own bread roll in two. "May I ask another question?"

It was good to see that Robert hadn't changed too much, Marisee thought. He was still full of questions.

"Of course," Grandma said. "You ask such good questions."

Robert frowned, as if trying to sort out his thoughts. "Does *everyone* believe that music keeps the monster asleep? Whoever took the music might not. Maybe the music thief just wanted the music and waking the Domedary was an accident. Or it could have all been an accident."

"It takes powerful magic to steal a city's music," Grandma said. "I believe that whoever has the power to do that is fully aware of the consequences. But you are right again. We mustn't make assumptions. We need to gather more information. Marisee?"

Marisee knew what was coming next. Her stomach twisted harder. She made herself keep her shoulders square and clenched her fists to stop clutching her aching belly.

"Do you think you can go back to the Pleasure Gardens?" Grandma asked. "Turnmill and I think that it's best for you to go there first before talking to the Mozart boy. You saw the music leave and the Domedary attack. You know what to look for and what questions to ask."

"Of course," Marisee said brightly.

She stared at the warm buttered roll on her plate. She'd been so hungry. Now she was too worried to eat anything at all.

THE METAL SONGBIRD

Robert had heard of the Vauxhall Pleasure Gardens, but he'd never visited them. When he'd served tea to Lady Hibbert's friends, their conversation had been filled with it. Often, they were in competition to see who had witnessed the most breathtaking wonder. Lady Norbury had eaten the *most* delicate boiled ham, cut so thin that she could see through it, beneath the *most* sumptuous paintings by the *most* famous artists. Lady Hayward had been one of the select few invited to light the fuse that made thousands of coloured glass lanterns blaze among the trees. Lady Clapton had danced among automata that looked *so* like real nightingales but had been designed to tweet her name. Just *her* name.

Robert had thought that the automata were Lady Clapton's silly boasts, but now he wasn't so sure. When they returned, he'd tell Marisee and Madam Blackwell about his own encounter with Mr Dross and his automata.

They walked with Turnmill as far as they could through the tunnels and emerged close to Blackfriars water steps. The tide was out. Robert could see a little sand on the Thames foreshore between the broken bricks, piles of oil-stained canvas and frayed, dirty rope. It still made him think of his last glimpse of the Barbados shoreline when he'd been forced from the jetty on to the rowing boat ferrying him to the ship bound for London.

Marisee had become quieter as they'd walked, her shoulders slumping further and further down. She cast nervous looks towards the river.

"Perhaps I shouldn't come with you," Marisee said. "Nannerl *will* be waiting for us. Maybe it's better if I go and speak to her brother."

Robert touched her shoulder. "I think you should," he said. "I don't mind going to the Pleasure Gardens alone if it upsets you."

"I agree," Turnmill said. "You had a horrible fright last night. I don't blame you for not wanting to go back. I can take you the quick way underground to Soho. You'll be there by midday."

Marisee sighed. "No," she said with certainty. "I must go to Vauxhall. I can show you exactly where it all happened."

"Then I'll find a way for Nannerl to come to you," Turnmill said. "Effra will make sure you reach the Gardens safely, though at this time of day, you probably won't see her." She gave Robert a cheerful smile. "She looks like a giant spider. It upsets the horses." Turnmill waved towards the river. "Your wherry arrives."

A small rowing boat glided towards them from the opposite bank. A barge passed in front of it, its rowers heaving the vessel upriver towards Westminster. White pennants with red crosses flew from its masts.

"Navy men," Turnmill muttered. "I wonder if they've been asked to protect Westminster Hall while everyone else has to fend for themselves."

The rowing boat crossed the barge's wake with barely a shudder. Robert spotted a flash of dirty green tricorn hat.

"Mr Cecil?" Marisee laughed. "And Daisy."

"Indeed," Turnmill said.

The question burst out of Robert before he could damp it down. "Is he … is he like you?"

Turnmill cocked her head sideways. "There is no one like me, Robert Strong. And in answer to your question, I've known him for so long, it might be rude to ask him now."

"For so long?" Robert said. "He looks as if he's the same age as me!"

Turnmill placed an arm around Robert's and Marisee's shoulders. The air became fresh and it felt like a river thundered through Robert's head.

"Not all the secrets of Elemental London should be known to Solids," Turnmill said.

She let go of Robert. His head quietened and the Thames stink returned.

Daisy splashed her way through the shallow water on the edge of the shore. She was holding an oar. She tipped her felt hat towards Turnmill then jammed the blade into the sand. Mr Cecil handed her a rope; she looped it over the oar shaft and pulled the knot tight. Robert couldn't help staring at her face. It was as grey as Lady Hibbert's finest silk with eyes of shining green. She had no eyebrows or hair below her hat.

"Had a good look, have you?" Daisy said.

Turnmill chuckled. "As I said, Robert Strong. Not all secrets are for you to know."

*

Robert and Marisee tried to make themselves comfortable among the nets, buckets and rods heaped in the small boat.

"We're going oyster watching," Daisy said. "They're a bit amiss and we want to know why."

How can oysters be amiss? Robert wondered. Marisee nudged him as if she could feel the question working its way to his lips.

"Not now," she whispered.

"I'm glad to see you alive," Mr Cecil said. "That Goldsmith brought half his own army to the Dogs. He really wanted to catch you."

"He did catch us," Robert said. "Then he let us go."

"To do his dirty business, no doubt," Daisy said.

Yes, Robert thought bitterly, *it was*.

"I'm glad you're safe too," Marisee said.

Daisy laughed out loud. "Me and Uncle are good at being safe!"

"Shush," Mr Cecil said. "Let's get them to where they need to be."

The boat glided past the sailing ships anchored in the deepest water in the middle of the river. Robert held his breath until those ships were behind them. Would he ever be able to see a ship like that without remembering the pain of being taken away from his family and stowed like cargo?

"I don't like the river without the singing," Daisy said. "Sailors should always sing."

"It stops them fighting each other," Mr Cecil said. "A Spanish cook almost landed in my boat last night. The crew had thrown him off the bow for burning the mutton. Normal times they'd just chew it harder then sing along to the fiddle."

"If their jaws still had strength," Daisy snickered.

"What happened to the cook?" Robert asked.

"I threw him a rope," Daisy said. "And he held on until we were in the shallows. But we've heard it up and down the river, from Dowgate to Vauxhall. All them sailors bawling at each other. And shocking words too!" She snickered again.

Mr Cecil stood very still. "Listen," he said.

Robert strained, listening. Somewhere in the distance, bells clanged, then stopped.

"It's the church bells," Daisy said. "It's like they're all trying to ring but can't. I don't know about waking the dead, but that racket's going to make some ghosts really upset."

Mr Cecil shivered. "What can take the music from the church bells? That's powerful magic."

"Do *you* have any idea what it could be?" Robert asked.

How could he and Marisee, just two humans with no magical abilities at all, ever defeat power like that?

"None," Mr Cecil said. "But you have to find out what's doing it soon. That Domedary has no mercy."

Mr Cecil and Daisy kept close to the southern bank of the Thames, weaving between the wherries and lighter boats that crossed from one side to the other. Robert saw fewer houses on the south side; it was mostly timberyards and open fields.

Daisy lifted her oar from the water. "Is it safe to go beyond the bridge, Uncle Cecil?"

"We got dispensation," Mr Cecil said. "We can take them as far as the horse ferry. No further."

"I don't like it, Uncle Cecil."

"Then row quicker so we can get there quicker and leave 'em!"

"Why can't you go further?" Robert asked.

"Because folks like us can't go straying," Daisy said. "We stay where we're told."

"Why?"

"Read them Whittington Articles," Mr Cecil said. "If you can stay awake long enough to get to page one hundred, you'll see what that four-times Lord Mayor had to say about folks like us."

Us, Robert thought. *The Whittington Articles*

especially mention people like Mr Cecil and Daisy? What are they?

As if Marisee could read his mind, she nudged him hard. "Look, Robert! That's Lambeth Palace!"

"And the Horseferry stairs," Daisy said eagerly. "I can't see any horses, Uncle Cecil."

"The tide's too low," Mr Cecil said. "They'd sink the ferry."

"Can you wait for us this time?" Marisee asked as the boat eased towards the southern bank of the Thames.

Daisy shook her head so hard her hat almost tipped off. "I told you. Oysters."

She jumped out on to the sand, anchoring the boat with her oar once more. Robert disentangled himself from the nets and poles and carefully walked up the steps to the jetty. Marisee was right behind him. A few people and a donkey were waiting for the ferry which still bobbed on the other side of the river.

"This way," Marisee said, heading west.

If Effra was watching them, she was keeping to the shadows. A few riders galloped by, their horses rearing hard as they passed. Robert supposed that she must be there. He would have liked to have seen her. Some of the elders in Barbados had swapped stories about a trickster called Anansie, who was half-man and half-spider. Perhaps seeing Effra would have helped bring back the lost memories of his brother.

Because someone had told him Anansie stories at night-time when bad dreams had stopped him from sleeping. Someone had taken him outside of the cabin to catch a cool breeze, pouring a little water into the earth, then making Robert smear the mud across his face and neck to stop the mosquitoes biting him.

Robert squeezed his eyes shut. No matter how hard he tried, he couldn't remember what that person looked like, or how their voice sounded. His brother's face. His brother's voice, because surely it must have been him warding Robert's nightmares away.

"Robert?" Marisee looked puzzled. "Are you all right?"

Robert opened his eyes. "I was trying to remember Zeke."

"Still nothing?"

"I keep trying." Robert tapped his head. "But he's almost all gone."

"We'll find a way to bring him back," Marisee said.

She sounded so certain. Robert wished he could believe her.

*

Robert was surprised to see Nannerl Mozart at the gate to the Pleasure Gardens. She rushed forward to meet them.

"The strangest thing happened," Nannerl said. "I was waiting outside our lodgings for you, but instead a carriage arrived and stopped right by me. But ... but there was no driver. The horse stared at me and made – I don't know the name for horse noises in English." She made a neighing sound. "And it moved like this" – she nodded her head sideways – "as if I should climb inside. I looked through the window, but the carriage was empty, so I opened the door. There was a letter on the seat."

She produced a folded sheet of paper from beneath her cloak. Robert went to take it, but it was already in Marisee's fingers. Of course, she didn't know that he could read and write now. So much had happened in the last six months. Was it the same for her?

"It's Grandma's writing," Marisee said. "'But I don't understand the language."

"It's German," Nannerl said. "Does your grandmother speak German?"

She didn't, but Marisee knew a boar that probably did.

"It says that the horse is called Red Rum," Nannerl said. "He will take me to Vauxhall Pleasure Gardens to meet you. And here I am."

"Where *is* Red Rum?" Marisee asked. "Just in case we have to leave in a hurry."

"He trotted away as soon as I climbed out. It is so strange, though. A carriage with no driver." Nannerl laughed. "Perhaps one day, there will be a carriage with no horse! There are tales that London is full of strange things. Is it true that everyone fell into a deep sleep last year?"

"Yes, it is," Marisee said. "And Robert and I found out why and stopped it."

"Good," Nannerl said. "Then you are the perfect people to give my brother and me back our music."

The entrance gate to the Pleasure Gardens was wide open.

"There was a ticket booth here last night," Marisee said.

Today, nobody stopped them. One after another, they passed through a dark tunnel, their feet crunching on broken glass. And then they were in the Gardens. Except, they no longer looked like Gardens. The sailors on the ship that brought Robert to England, had told tales of mighty shipwrecks. They'd tried to frighten him with gruesome stories of wild mermaids and sea dragons with powerful tails that smashed through the masts and hull of the sturdiest boats. He *had* been frightened but had refused to show it.

The Pleasure Gardens really looked as if a sea monster had smashed through them, followed by a mighty wave that swept everything across the grounds. The stump of the orchestra stand was still there next to a ruined square building that looked like its roof had exploded outwards.

"That was the organ house," Nannerl said. "Herr Tyers gave us a tour." She turned away. "I don't think I can bear to look inside to see what has happened to the instrument."

Judging by the state of the building, Robert could make a good guess. He kept quiet. Strings of shattered lanterns trailed from the trees across paths slick with lamp oil. A row of elms along the avenue had been spliced in two. Leaves and twigs carpeted the grass mixed with chunks of plaster and painted canvas. The Domedary had caused all of this destruction; how could he and Marisee ever stop it?

Marisee gave a little gasp and turned away.

"I was in one of those trees," she said.

A group of men were gathered around a large plaster dome balancing on the debris. It had been lavishly painted but was cracked in many places.

"That was the roof over the orchestra stage," Nannerl said. "And those are the musicians."

"Did you see this happen?" Robert asked.

Nannerl shook her head. "Our papa is sick. I promised our mother that I would take the best care of Wolfgang. As soon as everything went wrong, I took him away. We had ordered a carriage to wait for us and the driver made his horse go so quickly. I didn't look back."

"How is Wolfgang now?" Robert asked.

"The music inside him still cannot come out." Nannerl gave a shy smile. "I am the same."

"You play too?" Robert said.

"I play and compose. But it is Wolfgang who is really suffering. Papa expects much from him."

"But not from you?" Marisee asked.

Nannerl shrugged. "I will be expected to be a good wife someday. Good wives do not tour concert halls." She nodded towards the dome. "We must talk to the musicians. They can tell us what happened to them last night."

She crunched her way over the broken glass towards the dome, Robert and Marisee following. Robert's foot kicked something metal from under the leaves. He bent down and scooped it up.

"What is it?" Marisee said.

It looked like a small bird. Curved pewter plates were bolted together to make its body. One wing was missing. The other stretched from the body as if in flight, though Robert could see no mechanism that would lift it into the sky or keep it there. Its head was cocked; its beak closed. Robert was surprised by how heavy it was. He shook it. Something rattled inside then its beak opened, and it began to sing like … like birdsong. Even better than birdsong. There was a click and it fell silent again. Robert and Marisee looked at each other.

"Music!" they said together.

Robert was about to slip it beneath his jacket when they heard a voice.

"You have found one of Mr Dross's creations?"

A man picked his way across the grass towards them. He was round-faced and wore no wig. His dark hair was cropped close to his skull. His clothes were those of a gentleman. Robert nodded and said nothing. He wished that he had not been noticed, but it was too late now.

"May I take it?" The man held out his hand. "I am Mr Staples, the manager. Mr Dross wishes to charge us a pretty penny for his mechanical songbirds. We have not paid him yet and now will never be able to do so."

The man slipped the bird in his pocket and walked on. Robert watched him go, imagining him rushing to despatch a rider to tell Lord Pritchard that his "property" was here in Vauxhall. But then the man stooped down to pluck something else out from the debris. He had barely noticed Robert at all.

Over by the ruined dome, Nannerl was having little luck with the musicians. Some were opening and closing their mouths, as if silently singing, their faces confused. One man wiggled his fingers as if playing a piano, another as if working the valves of a trumpet. Their expressions were of deep despair.

Nannerl carefully made her way back to Robert and Marisee.

"They are like my brother," she said. "They feel like they have lost part of themselves."

"And like you?" Robert asked.

Nannerl gave him a sad smile. "You understand how it feels to lose part of yourself?"

"Yes," Robert said. "I do."

Marisee looked from one to the other then away. "I'm not sure what else we can learn here," she said briskly. "Everything is crushed and torn. The paintings, the bandstand, even those little mechanical birds."

"Mechanical birds?" Nannerl's eyes sharpened.

"Made by Mr Dross," Robert said. "And it hadn't lost its music."

"We keep hearing Mr Dross's name, don't we?" Marisee sounded excited. "He *must* know more about what's happening. We should visit him, but how do we find out where he lives?"

This was the time for Robert to tell her about that night-time excursion to Soho. He opened his mouth, but Nannerl was already talking.

"I have his address," she was saying, taking a trade card from her pocket. "He gave me this when we met him outside our lodgings."

MR DROSS, ANIMATEUR
EXTRAORDINAIRE

Marisee was still reaching for the card, but Robert was quicker.

"Mr Jack Dross," he read. His words were slow but correct.

Robert could read and write now? In the last six months, she'd made big plans about how *she'd* teach him when they finally met again, but someone else had got there first. She bit back her frustration. So he could have written her a note to let her know that he was safe. If he'd tried hard enough, he might have found someone to deliver it for him.

She watched him study a word for a few seconds. Nannerl gave him a patient smile as if he was a young child. Marisee wondered if she looked at her little brother like that.

"Animateur?" Robert asked.

Nannerl nodded.

"Mr Jack Dross, animateur. Removed from the Anchor near Blackfriars to the Rose, Dean Street," Robert continued. "Genius ... genius extraordinaire. Creator of ex..."

He showed the card to Nannerl. Oh, how Marisee wanted to crane her neck to see the word he was stuck on so *she* could help him.

"Exquisite," Nannerl said.

"Creator of exquisite automata as close to life as God will allow. Will also repair music boxes."

"I showed him this." Nannerl tapped the pouch with the broken music box. "He was interested, but then the carriage arrived. I said I would call on him later."

"Then that's exactly what we should do," Marisee said.

As they walked back towards the entrance, they passed two men sawing through the trunk of a toppled tree; another man swept the mess from the path. He had only cleared a small patch and as the others worked, more leaves and branches fell and covered it again. Marisee sighed. Nothing would ever clear away her memories of what had happened here.

She was cheered when she saw the coach waiting outside, pulled by a familiar brown horse. "Red Rum!" She gasped and ran towards him. The horse neighed in reply. She grinned at Robert. "Aren't you pleased to see him too?"

"Yes," Robert said, though he looked more pleased to be safely hidden inside a carriage.

"Will it take us to Mr Dross?" Nannerl asked.

It? "I'm sure *he* will if we ask him nicely," Marisee said.

Red Rum nodded his head.

"Dean Street, please," Marisee said, and climbed into the coach.

As they sat back, Robert said, "I have been to Mr Dross's before."

"When?" Marisee said. "You didn't mention it earlier."

"I wasn't sure if it was important," Robert said. "We went at night-time." He looked a little embarrassed and lowered his voice. "Through the back way."

Marisee could only think of one reason why Robert

might be creeping around someone's house at night-time. She glanced at Nannerl, who was looking at them with curiosity. Whatever Robert had done, Marisee didn't want to air it in front of this girl they'd just met.

"Is there anything you think we should know?" Marisee asked.

"It's daytime," Robert said. "And we'll be knocking on his front door, won't we?"

"Yes," Marisee said.

"Then no," Robert said. "Not for the moment."

Marisee nodded, but she knew that she was definitely making Robert tell her the full story when they were alone.

Nannerl pressed her nose against the window as the carriage crossed Westminster Bridge and joined the traffic heading north. Last year, Red Rum had carried Marisee and Robert along Piccadilly, when darkness came early as the sky had filled with the sickly yellow mist of the enchanted sleep. The gates to Burlington House had been locked then and the roads empty. Now, carriages and traders' carts pulled in and out of the grand houses – coal men, milk carts, a gardener balancing a small tree in his wheelbarrow. Marisee even spotted a young eel-seller slip through the gates hoping to sell her wares at the kitchen door.

Marisee turned to Nannerl. "London is wonderful, isn't it? If we don't find out what's happened to the music, the monster will destroy it all."

"This city is so big and noisy!" Nannerl glanced away from the window. "I prefer Salzburg."

London should be noisy and full of life! Marisee could not even see the paving stones because there were so many people! Men and women strode in and out of shops, liveried messengers weaving between them to place and collect orders. A stagecoach waited outside the Hatchett's Hotel, the horses fretting as the coachmen loaded a pile of luggage on to its roof. More people were waiting to travel than could possibly fit. Marisee wondered if they had heard rumours of what had been awoken in the Thames. She'd heard that when the earthquakes shook Fleet Street a few years before she was born, many Londoners had fled to the countryside.

"Over there," Nannerl said, pointing.

A child sat on a draper's doorstep idly tapping a drum with their heels. Their younger sibling bashed the ground with a fiddler's bow. Musical instruments were now nothing but toys.

"I cannot imagine this world without music," Nannerl said. "My father taught me to play the clavier when I was seven years old. He said I was gifted. But

Wolfgang … he started to play when he was four. I realized quickly that my path would be different from his."

They all sat back, lost in their thoughts. Nannerl looked a little sombre. Robert twitched the curtain aside and took quick peeps at the world outside. Marisee tried to forget last night's events, but her head filled with the giant white shell, the ear-splitting roar and the orange legs that stamped Vauxhall Pleasure Gardens into the earth. She felt heavy with sadness.

The coach jolted to a stop outside a tall brown-brick house, with red bricks edging the windows as if the builder had felt a moment of cheer. Some of the bricks were missing, so now it looked neglected. Green paint flaked from the cracked wooden door.

"The house is so different from the front," Robert said.

A trade card was stuck inside a window. It was the same as the one Nannerl had shown them.

Nannerl had made a plan. It was very simple. She would knock on Mr Dross's door asking if he could fix her music box. She would introduce Robert and Marisee and say how excited they were to see the exquisite creations he talked of on his trade card. Hopefully, they would all be invited in.

"Yes," Marisee had said. "It is simple. What if he recognizes us from the Mansion House?"

Nannerl had given her a little smile. "I imagine that he will. You are easy to remember."

Marisee scowled at her. "What do you mean?"

Nannerl looked slightly embarrassed. "I have not seen people like you in Salzburg."

"Well, there are many people like us in London," Marisee said.

"And it's a good thing if he recognizes us," Robert said quickly. "We actually heard him say that he made the best machines in Europe. It should be easier to convince him that we'd love the honour of seeing them."

"Yes," Nannerl said. "Of course."

The silence had lasted until the coach arrived at Mr Dross's.

Nannerl strode up to the door and banged the knocker hard. The door was flung open straight away. Mr Dross glared down at them. He was wearing a faded red banyan coat buttoned from his neck to his bare feet. Silver songbirds were embroidered along the hem, with delicate musical notes scattered around their heads. Perched on Mr Dross's head, was a red nightcap with a tiny silver bird stuck to the crown. It opened and closed its beak, chirruping.

Since Marisee had discovered Elemental London, she'd seen many strange things. Mr Dross was certainly not the strangest, but she *was* impressed by how Nannerl ignored his odd appearance.

"Good day again, Mr Dross," she said. "I hope you don't mind us calling upon you."

Mr Dross squinted at Nannerl. "Ah!" he said. "Miss Mozart!" He stepped on to the doorstep, pulling the door to behind him. "I am very pleased to see you."

"You are?" Nannerl looked surprised.

"Indeed." He glanced towards her pouch.

"May we come in?" Nannerl waved a hand towards Marisee and Robert. "My friends and I are very excited to see your creations."

"No!" he said. "That is totally out of the question." He squeezed his lips into a thin smile. "I have no servants and my home is cold and unwelcoming."

A girl's voice came from behind the door, so muffled that Marisee could not hear words. But she was singing – in tune. Then another voice joined it and an instrument, a harpsichord or a clavicle. Marisee felt a breeze, like a small child's sigh, the same as outside the Mansion House. The breeze brought a sour smell, like malt mashing in a brewery, and a moment later the instrument stopped, but the voices carried on.

Could Mr Dross make that happen? Could he protect music?

Mr Dross's face cracked into a smile. "So it is as I thought," he muttered.

"What is, sir?" Marisee asked, keeping her expression innocent. If he became suspicious, he would never let them in.

Mr Dross's smile dropped away. "It is none of your business. But perhaps there is something I can help *you* with, Miss Mozart," he said, glancing towards the pouch again. "Something you may perchance have on your person."

"I do," Nannerl said. "My music box is broken. Perhaps we can go inside and—"

Mr Dross shook his head. "I am too ashamed to show you my home. I have fallen on hard times. It is barely fit for me, let alone esteemed guests such as you and your friends." His hand twitched towards the pouch and stopped. "But I am happy to help you for a much-reduced fee. It is the least I can do."

Nannerl seemed uncertain of what to do next. Her plan had been too simple after all. She stroked the pouch then looked back at Mr Dross. Robert was looking around and fidgeting. Marisee knew that he just wanted to be out of sight. They couldn't stand around waiting.

Marisee stepped forward. "Perhaps we can help *you*,

Mr Dross. It's very unfair of the Goldsmith to blame you for what happened at Vauxhall Gardens. We can help you prove your innocence."

Mr Dross's smile returned. "That is so kind of you, but I do not require any help. No help at all! Perhaps, Miss Mozart, if you show me your music box, I can at least let you know if I can repair it. I believe that it may have an extraordinary mechanism."

"If we can come inside," Marisee said.

Mr Dross gave her a little nod. "Show me the music box, I will show *you* the workshop where I will repair it."

"Thank you," Nannerl said.

She tipped the music box out of the pouch. In one quick movement, Mr Dross grabbed it from her hand, stepped back and slammed the door shut behind him. They stared at the flaking dark green panels.

"My music box," she whispered. She hammered on the door. "Mr Dross! Mr Dross!"

Passers-by were staring at them.

"I can't stay here," Robert said. "Word spreads quick. If anyone has read the notices in the coffee shops…"

"Nannerl?" Marisee took the girl by the shoulders. "We have to go!"

Nannerl shook her off. "I am not leaving without my music box!"

"Nannerl!" Marisee pulled the girl away. "We'll come back here, but we have to speak to your brother. Remember?"

Nannerl's eyes flashed with anger, but she let herself be drawn away. "We will certainly return! But yes, let us go and speak with Wolfgang."

The Mozart family was lodging in Frith Street, not far away. Robert's eyes darted back and forth along the street. He didn't relax until they were ushered into the hallway of the house.

"My father is sick," Nannerl said. "It will be easier if I bring Wolfgang down here."

She raced up the wooden steps. A moment later, she thundered back down again.

"He is gone!" she cried. "Wolfgang is gone! Mama was sitting with Papa. She thought that Wolfgang was asleep, but he is nowhere."

"You are certain?" Robert asked. "Perhaps he woke up confused. Is there … is there a window in his room that perhaps he…?"

Marisee could see that Robert didn't know how to finish the question. No one wanted to think that the boy may have fallen out of the window in a sleepy confusion.

"There is a window," Nannerl said. "But Mrs Lyle,

who owns the lodgings, said that the men were supposed to come and clean the privies last night. The stench could be truly terrible, so we locked and shuttered our windows against it. They are still shuttered now. My brother is not there, but I found this on the floor by his bed."

This time Marisee took the trade card.

"Mr Jack Dross, animateur," she said. She turned it over. Three words were written on the back.

I have music.

CLICK, TICK, HUM

Robert understood why Nannerl wanted to run straight back to Mr Dross's house to find her brother. On the Hibberts's plantation in Barbados, he was always watchful of his younger sisters and would have done anything he could to protect them. Perhaps his brother had been the same with him – he wished he could remember.

"You can't go back yet," Marisee said. "He knows we suspect something. He won't let us in. We need a plan."

"Did you not hear the harpsichord?" Nannerl cried. "That must have been Wolfgang! Mr Dross told him he had music and he was right!"

"You don't know for certain that your brother's there," Robert said. "Perhaps Mr Dross has machines that make music – maybe like a giant music box. He could have taken your music box to make his machines better."

Nannerl looked at him as if he'd suddenly sprouted scales. "It is just a simple music box. And it certainly does not sing. I know in my heart that my brother is in there."

But Marisee was right. They needed a proper plan. Mr Dross wouldn't open the door again, no matter who was banging on it. And a dropped trade card and a few notes of music were not proof to Robert that Wolfgang was inside that house. He could be anywhere in London.

Robert, himself, wanted to be away from the streets. He studied every man he saw. Were those grey fur-trimmed boots over those white stockings? No, the light just made it look that way. And that tattered frock coat? It was being worn by a small, thin gentleman holding a basket of leeks, not a ruthless capture-creature. Still, Soho was close to the St Giles rookery and the alley where the capture-creature had first stalked Robert and seized him. It was close to the Red Guard Gang and Steeple who'd betrayed him. He wondered what the others were doing now. Did they care that he was gone?

And Soho was much too close to Bloomsbury and the Hibberts's mansion and Benjamin and the other grooms who'd hunt him down to collect their six guineas. It would take just one wrong step, one moment of not looking where he was going, and he would find himself lashed to a mast on a ship sailing past Gravesend and out to open sea.

Marisee gave him a worried look. "We'll find somewhere less busy so we can plan what to do next. And we'll be quick."

He followed Marisee and Nannerl along the crowded Soho streets to Golden Square. They sat down beneath a hornbeam tree. Robert pressed himself into the trunk, hoping that he was in the shadows.

"Yesterday morning, we came to Mr Shudi's workshop here for Wolfgang to choose his harpsichord," Nannerl said. She jumped to her feet again. "What if Wolfgang has gone there? What if he hopes that their instruments will inspire him again? I will go to them!"

She ran off. Robert hoped that she would return trailing a small boy behind her. Somehow, he knew that hope was wasted. He inched a little way from the tree so that he could catch the sun's warmth on his face.

"Where have you been since *that* morning? And who taught you to read?" Marisee asked. Every question she'd been holding back had burst free.

He told her about the chase and his life with the

Red Guard Gang, stuck in their secret parlour, having to decide if he'd rather be safe than lonely, knowing that the capture-creature prowled the alleys looking for him. And then, the big betrayal. He still wondered if Steeple had been planning it from the beginning. Were the others part of his plan? No, how could they be? Garnet was too young and Turpin and Duval – Robert was sure that they would only betray someone if it was to save each other. And Emma – would she have spent all those hours teaching him to read and write if she was planning for him to be sent to the West Indies? He'd heard her voice shouting his name through Mr Gripe's door. He was sure that she hadn't known.

He was still filled with great sadness. He might never see them again.

"Emma taught me to read," he said. "There wasn't much else to do. She was one of the Red Guard Gang."

"Were they your friends?"

"I thought so."

Marisee patted his back. "I'm sorry."

Silence fell. Robert gripped a handful of grass and scrunched it in his hand. He breathed in the fresh spring smell. The sun cut through the hornbeam branches. A tiny beetle balanced on a blade of grass near Marisee's feet. Robert knew that he should hide himself away, but even when he'd been the Hibberts's servant, he'd never had a chance to sit and enjoy the sun like this.

"What have you been doing?" Robert asked.

Marisee gave him a big smile. "Grandma lets me help her more and" – her smile widened – "you didn't see it in the dark, but my name's on the sign now! It's Madam *and* the Misses Blackwells' medicinal well."

"Misses?"

"Misses," Marisee said certainly. "Me and Mama."

"Of course! Sorry! I'm so pleased for you, Marisee," he said. He really was! He knew how badly Marisee had wanted Madam Blackwell to let her help more.

"But…" Marisee said. She looked a little embarrassed. "It *is* good, but it's just … well … a bit boring. It's the same rude customers who don't want to pay for their water. And I love being with Sally Fleet…" She shrugged. "I sometimes wonder if that's it. Listening to Chads complain or rich people grumble about paying their debt."

"At least you can walk about freely," he said. It came out more bitterly than Robert had meant it to. She looked at him, shocked, then even more embarrassed.

"I know," she said quietly. "I'm sorry. If … *when* … we've found what's happened to the music and the monster has gone, I'll make sure you never have to hide again."

"Will you?" he said. "How?"

Marisee threw back her shoulders and looked him straight in the eye. "We'll find a way," she said.

And as he sat there, with the sun warming his face, he decided that for this moment at least, he'd let himself believe her.

"He is not there!" Nannerl flopped back down next to them. "Mr Shudi has closed his workshop and I had to bang on the door. He opened it like this." She mimed someone peering around a door. "He said that he dare not play his instruments. He was tuning a clavichord early this morning when he felt a strange breeze and the keys…" She wiggled her fingers wildly. "They jumped into the air and fell to the floor. He gathered them together and put them in a basket." Suddenly she was sobbing. "I am so tired! Everything is wrong. Papa's illness. Wolfgang gone! Our music gone. I don't know what to do!"

"We'll find your brother," Marisee said. She sounded so sure that Robert wanted to believe her in this too. "And the music."

"How?" Nannerl wailed. A lady and her maid turned to look at them. Robert inched back into the shadows. "If Mr Dross won't let us in his house, what are we supposed to do?"

"We can't be certain that your brother is there,"

Marisee said. "He might be somewhere else, so we'll keep looking. We know … um … people who have a good view of what's happening in London. They might know if your brother's been seen on the streets."

"They will?" Nannerl wiped her eyes. "That's good. But what if he hasn't been seen? We must still search Mr Dross's house."

"I have an idea for getting into Mr Dross's house," Robert said. "From when I was there before."

"Were you … were you with the gang that time?" Marisee asked. She glanced at Nannerl as if she was worried about what Nannerl might think of him. But now Robert had been asked to tell the story, he realized that *he* was worried – not about Nannerl, but about Marisee. What would she think of him when she found out that he'd been sent to check which houses might be easier to steal from?

He sighed. "Yes, but we didn't do anything … well, much … wrong."

Marisee gave him a suspicious look. She must know about the child gangs in London and what they had to do to survive.

"What happened?" Nannerl asked impatiently.

Robert told them about how bored he'd become stuck in the den. When the others went out, he was always left behind with Garnet. Facing the capture-creature had been starting to look better than being in the same room day and night, week after week. Even the reading and writing lessons hadn't become less of a distraction.

"The trip was organized by Steeple," Robert told Marisee and Nannerl.

"The one who betrayed you," Marisee grumbled.

"Why are you making that face, Robert?" Nannerl asked.

Part of it was because he was thinking about Steeple. But there was another reason.

"We were pretending to be night men," he said.

"Oh," Marisee said and made a face too.

"The ones who clean the privies?" Nannerl asked.

The night men came after dark to clean the waste from the toilet cesspits. Robert had often been ordered to stay awake to let them in and out of the Hibberts's mansion. If there was a word stronger than "stink" that he could have used, he would have. He'd had to hold his breath when they came in and even more so as they'd carried out the barrels of waste.

Even though Robert had known exactly what night men were, he'd been excited about finally leaving the den.

"We'll be going with my cousin," Steeple had said cheerfully. "No one wants to go near him, so he gets a good look around the big houses. He knows when some of those rich folk go off to the countryside and leave their places empty. And he knows when there's new folk in town." He rubbed his hands. "The ones who don't know their way about London yet and might stop in a dark alley to help a sick boy." He winked at Turpin. "And leave the alley without their watch fob or rings."

Turpin grinned at Duval. "Last time Steeple stole a Frenchman's periwig!"

Spindrift nodded towards the trunk. "And it's still in there! Where did you think we were going to sell it?"

Steeple gave a crafty smile. "Back to the Frenchman, of course! He was as bald as a bullet under that false hair. He would have paid good money to cover that shiny pate back up again!"

"No tricks tonight, Steeple," Spindrift said sternly. "Looking only. We want easy pickings. No one hurt, no one sent to the gallows."

"Of course not!" Steeple agreed. "Looking only."

Robert, Emma and Steeple had left the den after midnight. St Giles folk were too poor to leave candles burning in the windows to light people's way – few even had windows. The narrow alleys were pitch-black. They walked in single file, Emma leading, as she knew the paths better than anyone. Robert held on to the back hem of her jacket, and Steeple walked behind him. Occasionally, they were passed by other shadows or a broken shutter threw a splash of weak light on to the street. A link boy ran past them, holding a flaming torch, followed by two well-dressed gentlemen, striding to keep up. They climbed over the rubble from a collapsed roof and found themselves on a wider street.

"There's my cousin," Steeple said. "Over there!"

As they walked over to the cart, the stink made Robert's eyes water.

"How long can you hold your breath?" Emma whispered.

Robert had known that it would not be long enough.

Steeple's cousin was a large man, with a crooked face like a boxer. He gave them a wide, friendly smile.

"You!" He nodded towards Steeple. "Up next to me. The other two of you, in the back."

The cart was loaded with the night men's scraping poles and the familiar long barrels. The smell was so bad that Robert had reckoned most of those barrels were full.

"I can go in the back instead," Steeple offered.

"No!" His cousin sounded cross. "You're the only one who looks like he could be working with me. And anyhows, you all might turn up your noses, but someone's got to empty those privies. Just thank God it's not you."

Emma nodded. As she'd climbed into the back of

the cart, she'd pulled her Red Guard kerchief over her nose. Robert had done the same and, like Emma, had found a space where he didn't have to touch the barrels.

Steeple's cousin's voice rumbled in the front of the cart, but Robert made out few words between the clop of the horse's hooves and the clang of the barrels as they rocked against each other. He hoped so hard that they wouldn't topple over.

The horse stopped for a moment. "Soho Square," Steeple's cousin announced. "William Beckford lives there. Got rich from his business in the West Indies."

Robert knew exactly what business that was. He shivered.

"He's got a laundry maid," Steeple's cousin said, "and a footman, who are happy to pass on items that their master won't miss."

That had made Robert feel a tiny bit better.

The cart wobbled on and stopped in the lane between two houses. The tailgate of the cart was lowered.

"I want you to see this," Steeple's cousin said.

He'd opened a back gate into a small yard. The house was tall and narrow and had reminded Robert of the Hibberts's townhouse in Bloomsbury Square. It was in darkness.

"The man who moved in is from out of town,"

Steeple's cousin said. "He's called Mr Dross and he makes strange machines."

"Strange machines?" Emma wondered. "What do you mean?"

Steeple's cousin shrugged. "I've told you what I know. Find out more if you're interested. But if he's living in a place like this, he must have money." He pulled Steeple towards him. "The cellar's just down some steps. Sometimes folk forget to lock it. I think we should have a look around. If anyone stops us, we've come to check the pit."

"Are you sure?" Robert said. "Spindrift said—"

Steeple winked. "Looking only. That's what he said and that's what we're going to do. Just look." He and his cousin headed away.

"Strange machines," Emma said again. "I wish I knew what that meant."

Robert wondered if the house was full of a new type of weaving machine or machines that built stronger, bigger ships.

"Can you hear singing?" Emma asked, suddenly.

Robert heard the church bells across London ringing the hour. Then, when they stopped, there was another sound, a hum that reminded Robert of his mother when she was sitting sewing in the evenings, trying to catch the last rays of the sunshine. Robert could never quite catch the tune; it was like the song was for herself and no one else.

"There's more than one voice," Emma said. "Like a choir. Perhaps he makes singing machines."

The humming stopped suddenly and was replaced by clicking and ticking, that became louder and louder.

The shutters in the two highest windows flew open, smacking against the wall. Candles blazed behind the glass. A large, perfectly round face appeared in each window, shining as white as the moon, with curls of silver hair that seemed to explode from the skulls.

Emma gasped. "What in the name of—"

Steeple ran up the steps from the cellar. "It bit me!" he squealed. "It bit me!" He pelted across the yard and through the gate, followed at great speed by his cousin.

Tick, tick, tickety tick.

Something crawled across Robert's foot. He bit back a scream of pain as two sharp points that felt like fangs pierced the skin above his ankle. He'd looked down. The creatures swarmed across the yard. Some rolled and unrolled like giant woodlice, ticking as they moved. Others hooked their fangs into the ground and heaved themselves along.

"Robert!" Emma pulled at him. "Come on!"

A shutter in a lower window was flung open. A man's voice called out. "Thieves! Show yourselves!"

"That was Mr Dross," Robert told Nannerl and Marisee now.

"What happened next?" Marisee asked.

Robert had barely heard that first shout because he'd been swiping at the fanged creature fastened to his leg. Its shell was cold and hard. For a second, he'd felt the tick, tick, tick of its body as he'd grasped it and thrown it into the air. He kicked at the other creatures in his path. They landed on the ground with a clang.

A bang echoed through the garden and something smashed against the wall.

"I have a blunderbuss!" the man shouted. "You will not steal my creations!"

Robert had run. Steeple and his cousin had already taken off in the cart. He and Emma chased it to the end of the lane, where it waited long enough for them to throw themselves into the back before clattering into the night.

They'd all agreed not to tell Spindrift too much about what happened that night, and as far as Robert knew, no one had. But Robert had not been allowed out on any adventure again until the trip to Mr Gripe's.

When he'd finished talking, there was silence.

"If that is the only way in, then we must take it," Nannerl said.

"But we have to wait until nightfall," Marisee said.

Robert nodded. He wasn't looking forward to returning there at all.

THE BROTHERS IN
COVENT GARDEN

Nannerl returned to her lodgings to wait in case her brother came home. Marisee and Robert left the square quickly, Robert walking with his head down.

"Now to Cheapside," Marisee said.

"Cheapside? Can we go to Covent Garden first?" he asked.

"Why?"

"Perhaps we can find some more help for tonight."

Marisee gave him a curious look. "You mean the Red Guard Gang?"

"Perhaps."

"I thought they'd betrayed you," Marisee said.

"I think… No, I'm *sure* it was only one of them," he said. "It was Steeple. He stole the gold and told Mr Gripe who I was. It was only him that the capture-creature mentioned when they talked about the reward."

"If you're sure you can trust them," Marisee said.

How could he tell her that he was never fully sure if he could trust anyone at all? But he gave her a little smile and nodded. It would be good to see Emma again too, to let her know that he was, well, as all right as he could be under the circumstances.

Robert heard the market stall-holders shouting enticements to buy long before he set foot in Covent Garden. Panic rose in him. Just there, off Drury Lane, Mr Gripe had locked him in the shop and the capture-creature had… Robert's heart slammed against his ribs.

Robert knew he had to calm down. He breathed in deeply. The usual London smells hung in the air. The capture-creature's scent did not. Mr Gripe's shop was too far away to see into the market. And the market itself was teeming with carts and carriages, and people crowding the stalls and shops. That's why thieves loved this place.

It was easy to pick a pocket and escape into the mass of people.

Robert looked around. He hoped that his instincts were right. They should be here.

"Who are we looking for?" Marisee shouted above the noise.

"Two boys," Robert said.

They weaved their way between the fruit and vegetable stalls. Robert kept his eyes towards the ground. He'd seen the boys in action; they were quick, a bend and scoop, then away.

There! Robert was sure of it! The flash of a hand grabbing a fallen potato then away again. But that's all there'd been – a hand. He couldn't see who it belonged to. And there! Again. Another potato, scooped from by the wheel of a handcart. This time Robert glimpsed the owner – it was Duval, crouching by a row of carts. Turpin must be close by.

"This way," Robert said to Marisee. They pushed their way towards the edge of the market. "It's best if I let them see me. Then it's up to them if they want to talk to me."

"What if they don't?" Marisee asked.

"I'll have to change my plan," he said.

Robert walked slowly, Marisee at his side. He kept

227

looking straight ahead until he stooped by the cart and bent down, as if adjusting his shoe.

"It's Robert," an excited whisper came. It sounded like Duval. "It's him!"

"I thought he was taken away!" Turpin's higher voice.

"He's come back! He's safe."

"And I need your help," Robert said.

"He needs our help!" Turpin said. "Can we help him?"

"It depends what he wants," Duval said. "Spindrift said that we mustn't get into any big trouble."

"I want you to pass a message to Emma," Robert whispered quickly. "Ask her to meet me at the house with the machines at midnight tonight. We need a distraction. Tell the shard beasts they'll have the fight of their lives."

Robert stood up slowly. When he glanced down again, the boys had gone. Marisee was looking around, confused.

"So who is it that you want to talk to?" she said.

He laughed. "It's done. So why do we have to go to Cheapside?"

"To talk to a Dragon."

"Oh." His laughter died away.

*

The church of Mary-le-Bow was on Cheapside. He and Marisee stood by the door to the bell tower. High above them, an immense gold dragon-shaped weathervane pointed south. It looked so heavy Robert reckoned that only magic could move it.

"I always remember the churches called Mary," Marisee said. "It's not just because of me. It's my mama's name too."

Robert knew that. Madam Blackwell, Marisee's grandma was Mary-Ay. Marisee was Mary C. In between them, Marisee's mama was Mary-Bee. Marisee didn't talk about her mother much. She'd disappeared when Marisee was young.

Marisee nudged him. "I think we're being watched."

She pointed to two statues of cherubs on a stone ledge above the door surrounded by one, two, three – seven carved cherub faces. Robert stared at them to see if they would move. After the statues on the steeple of St George's church in Bloomsbury had come alive in the enchanted mist, he'd always wondered – with a slight tremble of fear – if it would happen again. The cherubs didn't move, not even a blink. But he still felt like he was being watched.

"Let's go inside," he said.

A round window set between the cherubs let a

little light in the vestibule. Robert imagined the cherubs' necks creaking around and the statues pressing their noses against the glass, still watching as he and Marisee entered the church.

"I suppose we go this way," Marisee said, starting up the narrow stone stairs ahead of them. "The Dragon's on the steeple. We can't climb all the way, but let's see how far we can go."

Steeple. Robert thought of the climbing boy and the betrayal. He trudged grim-faced behind her.

"I hope the Squall was right and the Dragon does see everything that's going on below," Marisee continued. "Not just Nannerl's brother, but maybe she's seen the Domedary too. I'd certainly like to know where it is now."

Up, up, up. Being trapped in the Red Guard's den had taken its toll on Robert. He used to run around the mansion for Lady Hibbert and her cruel housekeeper, Mrs Wandle, from dawn until night-time. He had hardly walked anywhere in the last six months, let alone run – except out of Mr Dross's garden. Now his legs hurt and he was out of breath.

The stairs went up until they stopped in a room with ropes dangling between the rafters. A ladder led to a large trapdoor in the ceiling.

"This must be the bellringers' room," Marisee said. "Hello!" she called. "Is anyone here?"

There were certainly no Dragons that Robert could see – nor smell. But suddenly, he could smell something else, something far worse. His aching legs felt like they were going to give way.

"I think... I think..." He needed to tell Marisee. He needed to move quickly. His legs, his mouth – neither would work.

Surely, Marisee could smell it too – spoiled meat and ancient dust.

Surely. *Surely!*

"Robert?" Marisee was looking at him, confused. "What's wrong?"

He breathed in, tried to hold the air in his chest, then breathed out hard. Now! He had to move now! Because the capture-creature wasn't coming for him. It had found him. It was already here.

Its voice was low but clear. "There's nowhere to run, little boy. Nowhere you can hide."

Marisee glanced down the stairs. "Who ... who is that?"

Robert couldn't talk. He mustn't even think about talking. He must use all his strength to escape. He scrambled up the ladder and tried to shove the trapdoor in the ceiling open. It wobbled but didn't move. He just didn't have the strength.

"Little boy?" the voice from the stairwell called. "Come quickly. Come easily. I don't want to hurt you."

Robert tried to grip the ladder with one hand and shove the trapdoor open with the other. It still wouldn't budge.

He felt an arm around his waist pulling him down.

THE DRAGON'S RIDDLE

It was Marisee who was pulling Robert back. "Let me try it," she said.

Robert half-slid back down to the floor. The capture-creature's smell filled the room. He could feel its wildness. He'd escaped before. This time it would show no mercy.

"Robert!" Marisee had opened the trapdoor and climbed through. "Come on!"

He tried to stand up. The creature turned the corner of the stairwell, bringing with it a wave of pure anger that seemed to pin Robert against the wall.

"Robert!" Marisee shouted. "I'm coming for you."

The capture-creature stepped into the room. Robert wriggled backwards. He felt Marisee tugging his arm. His fingers brushed the ladder and he tried to hold it. Marisee climbed up ahead of him and stretched down.

"Take my hand, Robert!"

The capture-creature shook its head slowly. The pale curls beneath the knitted cap seemed almost transparent. Its eyes were as bright as fire. It rubbed its hands together; the backs were covered in dense fur. "And now I am here, little boy," it growled.

The wide paw of a hand grasped Robert's ankle. Claws dug into his leg. Robert made a grab for the ladder, fingers gripping the rung. The capture-creature's hand clamped around Robert's other ankle and pulled.

"No!" Robert tried to shake his legs free. "I am not letting you take me."

"'Let me'?" The capture-creature pulled harder. "I need no permission."

Robert felt as if he was being wrenched in two. His fingers were loosening. One by one, they uncurled.

There was a shriek from above him. He looked up to see Marisee disappear as if hurled away from the trapdoor. A wind rushed past Robert, tossing him on to his side. The capture-creature fell too, thumping to the ground and releasing Robert's ankles. A whirling cloud of chalk dust swept around the bellringers' chamber then lifted Robert from the floor.

The capture-creature roared and tried to seize him. A louder roar answered. An old beggar in a ragged greatcoat strode out of the cloud of chalk dust. He pushed back the brim of his top hat. His eyes were narrowed and his lips bared into a snarl, curved teeth protruding from his top and bottom jaws. He pounced.

"Henry?" Robert whispered.

Yes, it was him! And that cloud of chalk dust – the Squall!

The capture-creature clenched its fists and claws sprung from the knuckles. Henry landed just short of it as it jumped to its feet. They were like two mongooses that Robert had seen in Barbados, reared up, facing each other, ready to fight. Neither moved.

"You took the oath too, Henry," the capture-creature growled. "But it won't hold forever."

He turned and walked back down the stairs.

The Squall wrapped around Robert and swept him up through the trapdoor and into the belfry itself. It lay him on to a wooden frame by an enormous bell then curled upwards through a gap in the wooden ceiling. Robert coughed. He'd breathed in too much chalk dust. But he was happy with that, happy to be alive.

Marisee looked from Robert to the trapdoor in shock. "Is that ... the capture-creature?" she said.

"Yes." Robert's voice sounded tiny.

Marisee held her hand to her heart. "It's ... full of hate, isn't it?"

Robert nodded.

A hairy hand appeared on the edge of the trapdoor hatch, then the crown of a battered top hat. Henry pulled himself through and slammed the trapdoor shut.

"Thank you," Robert said. "You've saved us twice now."

"Which is why I was such a bad assassin," Henry said.

"Assassin?" Marisee said. "What's an assassin?"

Henry shook his head. "It's a long story. But what brings you here?"

"What brings *you* here, Henry?" Marisee said. "Though I'm glad that you *are* here. The last thing we saw was the windmill on fire and..."

"We didn't know if you'd survived," Robert finished for her.

"Me and Squall are good at surviving," Henry said. "We don't have many friends in the City of London, especially with the Goldsmith and his allies, but we're safe here." He looked towards the closed trapdoor. "Or we thought we were."

His worried eyes met Robert's. *Henry knows exactly what's after me,* he thought. He knows what the capture-creature is, something even worse than Lord Pritchard or Lord Hibbert.

"We came to see the Dragon," Marisee said, her voice wobbling a little. "A small boy's lost in London and we wondered if she'd seen anything. Is she..." Marisee pointed upwards. "Is that really the Dragon up there? For everyone to see?"

Henry smiled. When his mouth was closed, he seemed more human – if you didn't look too closely.

"One lesson me and the old Squall learned was that sometimes it's easier to hide in plain sight," he said. "Squall's just up there telling her you're here. I thought she'd have noticed with all that roaring, but most of the time, her eyes and ears are in the far corners of London. That's why her and the Squall used to love gossiping so much. But then he got punished by those airhead Fumi Elders for consorting with Dragon enemies."

Henry sat down, stretching out his legs. "I never thought that I'd meet Haakon again."

"So you do know him," Robert said. "What is he? And why is he hunting me?"

"It's what he was made for," Henry said. "It's what we were all made for." He lifted the hem of his loose breeches. He wore no stockings. His legs were covered in pale brown hair. "I don't know your modern-day name for folk like us, though some of our folk call themselves Variegates. I think they're partial to the Latin."

"Variegates?" Robert said. "What does that mean?"

"Look at me," Henry said. "And you've seen Haakon close up. You know what it means. Just let yourself believe it."

Robert's eyes moved from Henry's legs to the wide snout-like nose and the mane of light brown hair. "You're like..." He shook his head. "I don't understand. You look like a lion. But a man too."

"And there you have it," Henry said.

"Lion men?" Marisee shook her head. Robert could see that she was struggling to believe it too.

"Lion *man*," Henry chuckled. "There's only one lion man that I know of. I'm supposed to be the king of all beasts. How I disappointed them all."

"But how did you... Were you always..." Robert couldn't find the right words. He thought of the many times that strangers had rubbed his skin, sometimes even scraping their nails across it to see if he was white underneath the brown. Should he even have asked Henry what he was?

"How did I become like this?" Henry asked.

Robert nodded. Marisee too.

"I don't remember it myself," Henry said. "Which is a good thing. I wouldn't have enjoyed the process. You know what an alchemist is, don't you?"

"They try and turn common metal into gold," Marisee said.

"There are others like them," Henry said. "Part alchemists, part necromancers. Necromancers are the ones that try and seek knowledge from the dead. There is a room below the deepest cellar in the Tower of London set aside for their experiments."

"What type of experiments?" Robert asked.

"Experiments like me," Henry said. "Experiments on the helpless by ruthless people. If you pass the Tower, you feel it." He leaned forward. Robert could see a sprinkle of freckles below his nose, and stiff strands of whisker-like hair. "The anger. The sadness. The desperation."

"I know," Robert said.

"The Tower is a prison for man, woman and child," Henry said. "Many have died there. But it has long been a prison for beasts too. For hundreds of years, they brought us from around this world, from the hot places and the cold and tied us up in the menagerie for visitors to poke at and mock." He gave a little snort. "We were cold and lonely. Food was thrown to us. I missed the power of

239

running across the plains hunting my own meat. Many of us died long before our time. I suppose that I died too."

"But you can't remember," Marisee said softly.

"No," Henry said. "But I know now that they started by taking fish from the moat and swans from the rivers. They took human prisoners who were sick and would not survive long enough to meet their executioner. I don't know fully what happened in that room, but I believe that there was earth magic. Even from their sleep at the bottom of the river, the Magogs can breathe life into stone and clay. Perhaps they know other ancient secrets too."

"You think that the Magogs helped make you?" Marisee asked.

"The necromancers roused the spirits of the newly dead," Henry said. "Those who were executed in secret rooms with no witnesses. They persuaded them to stay in their bodies, promising them a new life, a new power. The alchemists and corrupt apothecaries infused the cooling blood with metals to keep the bodies supple and potions made from the hearts and other parts from the captive beasts in the menagerie."

Robert shivered. He'd heard how the dead were taken from the gallows at Tyburn and delivered to the surgeons for experiments. In the secret rooms in the Tower of London, it must have been so much easier.

"Some of the prisoners welcomed it," Henry said quietly. "They wanted that new life. They wanted that power. Anything was better than the life they'd lived before."

"And Haakon?" Robert asked. Suddenly, he wanted to know everything about the creature that hunted him.

"He was the first of us," Henry said. "The oldest. Hundreds of years ago, the King of Norway sent a polar bear called Haakon as a present to the king here. That Norwegian king must have hated the bear to do that. One day, Haakon was free, roaming the snow and ice. Then, after what must have been a terrible journey, he was imprisoned on the end of a chain fishing for food in the filthy Thames. He died still furious, pining for his homeland."

Robert didn't want to imagine Haakon's pain. He didn't want to feel sorry for the creature that was so eager to hurt *him*.

"When Haakon was dying," Henry said, "they took his still-beating heart and buried it in the place where they carry out the executions." Henry sighed. His whiskery beard shuddered. "Imagine, that mighty heart, thudding away in its casket in the ground below where so many lost their lives. Then, when they were ready, they placed it inside a dying murderer."

"Who was he?" Marisee asked.

"His name was never recorded," Henry said. "Many Variegates were made before Haakon, but none survived. I believe that when the hearts were buried in the ground they were infused with Magog magic. Along with Haakon and a few others, I was given to Jonathan Wilde, the Thief Taker General. Do you know of him?"

Robert didn't, but Marisee was nodding. "Didn't he steal things?" she asked. "Then if there was a finder's reward, he'd pretend that he'd found the goods and take the reward."

"He kept a gang of thieves," Henry said. "He was ruthless. He claimed he was a hero protecting the law while sending thieves to the gallows that he, himself, had instructed to steal. He told us to hunt men like prey. We were assassins, but we all secretly swore an oath to never hurt each other."

"A Guild of Assassins," Marisee said.

"A Guild of Variegate Assassins," Henry said. "I hated it. Catching humans who themselves had so little didn't make me happy. And we, ourselves, weren't safe. Some of us were caught by collectors who wanted to display our stuffed hides in their mansions. I am sure to this day that Jonathan Wilde took money to tell them how to find us. I ran away. They sent Haakon to find me,

242

but he honoured our oath. I promised to stay on the Isle of Dogs, out of sight and out of mind." He sighed. "Now, neither the Squall nor me can return there. And Haakon? The murderous rage inside him will never let him rest."

A wind whirled through the room, carrying white powder speckled with black and gold. It uncurled into the Squall's thin long body and shovel-shaped head. The black and gold speckles drew out from the smoky white like they were being pulled by threads. They clustered together, bulging like a bag of water peppered with sparks of orange. The cluster exploded. Hundreds of tiny black, gold and orange dots dropped to the floor and scuttled towards Robert and Marisee.

"Dragon!" Marisee gasped.

The dots clustered again and started to take a shape. Robert recognized the long head broadening out into a wide brow, the black, gold and orange dots overlapping like scales. There was the smell too, though much lighter than he had smelt before. It was the bitterness of a lime kiln and the stink of an abattoir.

"Yes," Robert said. "Dragon." And he hoped that he could trust the Squall and this one didn't want to eat them.

And so far, it was just the Dragon's head. There was nothing beyond the neck. When she opened her mouth, a flame appeared, as tiny as a rushlight. Robert was grateful. There was too much wood in this high up room for Dragon flames. Two bright sparks looked like eyes.

"Forgive my incompleteness," the Dragon said. "I must not fully leave my post. I hear you are seeking my advice?"

"We are," Marisee said. Her voice quavered. She cleared her throat and tried again. "You must see so much up there. When you were watching the streets today, did you see a small lost boy? He'd be well-dressed, though not in our style. And perhaps wearing a powdered grey wig."

"I see many lost people," the Dragon said. "But I am a Dragon. I am not permitted to pass on knowledge without a price."

Robert and Marisee looked at each other. They knew what Dragons demanded.

"Do we have to solve a riddle?" Robert asked.

The head bobbed as if nodding.

"And ... and if we don't know the answer?" he said. A nub of fear lodged itself in his stomach.

"If you don't know the answer?" The Dragon's long jaw split in two. Spike-like gold teeth poked out from her mouth. "Perhaps I should eat you." She sighed, and every scale turned black. "But I lost the taste for Solid human flesh a long time ago. If you do not know the answer, you will leave here with nothing. You will not find the boy. You will not stop the Domedary." The Dragon glowed then darkened again. "And that would be such a pity. I know so much that can help you."

The Dragon's orange eyes sparked out as if her eyelids had closed. Her head bulged and tiny black dots fell to the floor and started streaming back towards the Squall. All that was left was the Dragon's mouth.

"Don't go!" Robert shouted. "Tell me your riddle!"

If playing the Dragon's game meant they'd get the help they needed, then of course they'd do it.

"As you wish." Her gold teeth shone as she spoke.

"I am a Wren on a Fish.

I am a baker's mishap.

I am an eye in the sky

With a flaming gold cap.

And I am there in my glory,

At the start of a story.

What am I?"

Robert looked at Marisee. He knew that a wren was a bird but why would it be on a fish near a baker's shop. He had an idea. "Isn't there a song? The one with blackbirds in a pie? Maybe…" Now his idea didn't sound quite as good as he said it out loud. "Maybe the mishap was the pie. Maybe the baker should have used wrens and ... er ... fish."

Marisee was gazing out of the narrow windows of the belfry. "I know exactly what it is," she said. "I can see it from here."

Robert joined her by the window. The pale column of the monument to the Great Fire of London stuck out from between the many church spires. The sun glinted off the golden urn that topped it.

"It's on Fish Street Hill," Marisee said. "And wasn't it Mr Wren who designed it?"

The Dragon nodded. "This church too."

"The start of the story is because it's where the fire began," Marisee continued. "They said it started at a baker's."

"And you are there in your glory?" Robert said.

"I am," the Dragon said. "Carved into one of the panels."

"I solved the riddle?" Marisee said, pleased.
"Indeed."

The black and gold sparks streamed back and shaped themselves into a face around the mouth. "I will tell you what I know about the boy. The Solids chatter about him, so I have been watching him. He went to

Vauxhall Gardens last night but escaped before the Domedary came. Is that true?"

"Yes," Marisee said. "What happened this morning?"

"The boy entered the house of the clockwork man," the Dragon said. "He went willingly. I have not seen him leave."

"So he *is* there," Robert said. He hoped so hard that Emma had received his message and that she would be willing to help him tonight.

"You know about the Domedary too," Marisee said. "How do we stop it?"

"I know little of its history," the Dragon said. "We were mere sparks of fire in ancient times. We didn't form our Dragon shapes until London became rich. But I can tell you what I see now. The Thames is swollen. The Domedary is still weak, lurking below the waves, feeding and gathering its strength. It will attack again soon. East of the peninsula, the wind blows more trouble this way. There is a ship and it moves far quicker than any I have seen before. But enough now. I must return."

The Dragon's face fell apart and the creatures scuttled away. The Squall lifted them up, back to the weathervane.

"So Nannerl's brother is definitely in Mr Dross's house," Robert said.

At least they knew that for sure now and it gave them even more of a reason to find a way into the automata-maker's house.

"But the monster is getting stronger." Marisee sounded almost defeated. "And we're no closer to finding the music."

"We are!" Robert said. "It all leads back to Mr Dross! We'll find out much more tonight."

"I hope so." Marisee said. "Because it seems like there's even more trouble coming our way."

"A ship driven by magical winds." Henry was leaning against a bell frame watching them. "I've never known that before and we get all sorts sailing past the Dogs."

"Have elementals from other places ever come to London?" Robert asked.

"The London elementals are part of the city itself," Henry said. "I haven't heard of them travelling, but it doesn't mean they don't. You'll need a wisdom more ancient than mine to answer that one."

"You mean … Haakon?" Robert asked. The nub of fear had returned, and it was growing.

"He might know," Henry said. "But he's not going to answer none of your questions, is he? I meant the Panyer Boy. His business is knowledge."

There was a creak. A wooden wheel turned and a bell clanged.

"Even Bow bells have lost their music," Henry said sadly.

A white smoky shape spun between the bells. "The Dragon has seen Lord Pritchard!" the Squall said. "An apprentice spotted you in Golden Square and found the lord in his coffee shop on Poultry. He will be here within minutes."

Henry opened the trapdoor and peered down. "The way's clear," he said. "Go! I'll be behind you, just in case."

Robert scrambled down the wooden steps, Marisee close behind him. They raced down the staircase and stopped by the door to the vestibule. Henry opened it and breathed in.

"Haakon's scent has gone," he said.

But Lord Pritchard was on his way – that was bad too. Robert dodged Henry and ran out into the churchyard.

"Where's the nearest well?" he shouted at Marisee.

"Across the street by the Guildhall!" she shouted back. "Quick!"

THE NIGHT MEN

Sally Fleet caught Marisee as she fell through the well. Marisee was very relieved about that. It was a mixture of mists and silver threads and was definitely one of Sally's better catches. Even Robert didn't look too sick when he landed.

"Do you think anyone saw us jump?" Robert said.

"Maybe," Marisee said. "Though the merchants are usually too busy thinking about making money to notice much else. And other folk will probably decide that their eyes were playing tricks on them."

Grandma was waiting for them in the place where

they'd rested and eaten earlier. The blankets were neatly folded on the benches, the beakers lined up as if waiting to be refilled with tea.

"I was starting to worry," Grandma said. "I thought that the monster might have made another appearance in the Pleasure Gardens."

Marisee shook her head. "There isn't really much of the Pleasure Gardens left."

Grandma sighed. "And that's what the Domedary can do when it's still quite weak. Imagine it at full strength. So what else happened?"

"Well, Robert…" *was tracked down by the capture-creature and nearly caught again.* She wanted to tell Grandma that, but when she looked at Robert, he gave a little shake of his head.

"We know that Mr Dross is definitely involved," Marisee said.

"And I have a plan for finding out more," Robert added.

The rest of the day was spent preparing for that night's adventure. Marisee was pleased that everything they needed could be found in the room of lost things. They would certainly raise a few eyebrows if they tried to buy them in a shop. Robert walked around with her, choosing what to take. The last time they'd been here together, they'd found Sally Fleet's Foundling Hospital uniform and name tag. They had feared it had been left there because she had come to harm in the river. They could never have imagined what she had become now.

But neither Marisee nor Robert could have imagined what *they* had become now. Marisee was officially a Well Keeper and Robert, well, he was far from the lonely, starving boy he'd once been. He'd made friends. Someone called Emma had even taught him to read and write. That was good. Somehow, Marisee hadn't managed to make any more human friends herself. Her only close friend from before the enchanted sleep was Camille. She'd tended the cows at the nearby Bagnigge pumprooms, but she had moved to Chelmsford with her mother.

Marisee wasn't sure why she felt a bit cross. Was it because Robert had been out having adventures without her? Or maybe because she'd spent six months worrying about him when he'd been safe all along. At least she'd managed to persuade Grandma not to come to Mr Dross's with them. If a watchman looked at her too closely, he would easily see through the disguise. And, as much as Marisee loved Grandma, she knew that her grandmother would not be able to run fast enough if they had to escape in a hurry.

When everything was prepared and their disguises

were in place, Grandma handed around a plate of ratafia biscuits.

"A present from a grateful Venetian merchant," Grandma said. "He'd visited every apothecary in Westminster to try and cure his red eye. Just a few drops of *our* water" – Grandma smiled at Marisee – "brought back his natural sparkle."

Marisee made herself smile back. She nibbled at the biscuit, trying to enjoy its crumbly sweetness, but this waiting was making her even more nervous. Robert was taking little nibbles of his biscuit, his face serious. Marisee was sure that he was worried too. And behind Grandma's smile, Marisee could sense the tension.

"I really should come," Grandma said suddenly. "I could never forgive myself if something happened to you."

"Sadler will watch out for us," Marisee said. "And Turnmill and the Fleet Ditch Boar will be close by."

Grandma sighed. "I know. But I want to be there to protect you as well."

Grandma made them go over the plan again and again. It was so simple. They'd go in the back way and creep in through the cellar. If Mr Dross was alerted, he'd come to the first-storey window at the back. Hopefully, Robert's Red Guard Gang would be there to help fight the machines and to keep Mr Dross distracted. She, Robert and Nannerl would search the ground floor quickly, then one by one check the other rooms, being very careful to listen out for the owner. It was a big house. There were three of them and only one Dross.

Each time they talked about it, it seemed too simple. What if Dross expected them and set his own trap? What if the cellar was locked? What if they couldn't fight off his strange machines? What if the Red Guard Gang didn't turn up? Marisee still didn't understand why Robert was ready to trust them so easily after Steeple's betrayal.

By the time Turnmill came to lead them to Fleet Bridge, Marisee's stomach was churning with worry. Grandma helped them carry the equipment to the tunnel exit. Marisee kissed her goodbye and tried to give her a reassuring smile.

"Don't worry, Grandma," she said. "We'll be back soon."

Grandma hugged her tighter as if she could see behind the smile, then finally let go.

Marisee and Robert climbed up the bank under the bridge and on to the street. A cart was waiting for them, harnessed to a familiar horse.

"It's Red Rum!" Marisee said.

"Of course!" Turnmill said. "Who else could I trust?"

Marisee and Robert loaded the equipment into the back of the cart as quickly and quietly as they could. At one point, a watchman walked past. He raised his lamp, glanced into the cart, nodded and walked briskly away.

Marisee straightened her breeches and greatcoat and tucked her hair firmly into her hat.

She whispered into Red Rum's ear. "Are you ready?"

The horse neighed quietly. Marisee stroked his nose and climbed up on to the seat of the cart next to Robert. She was glad that Red Rum was ready. *She* wasn't. Who knew what they were walking into?

"I'm ... I'm frightened," she said to Robert.

"Me too," Robert said. "But that's not going to stop us, is it?"

"No," Marisee said, certainly. "It isn't."

Robert held the horse's reins as they set off. They had to look the part – the part of night men cleaning out the muck from the cesspits below London's privies, only allowed to work after dark because of the stink. The poles and barrels in the back of the cart rattled and rumbled.

They clattered through the dark streets until Red Rum stopped in the narrow alley at the back of Mr Dross's house. As agreed, Nannerl was waiting for them, shading her lantern with her hand.

"It's so difficult telling lies to Mama," she said. "I

255

didn't want her to worry so I said that Wolfgang has been at Lady Montague's house today and that she has sent a coach for me to go and collect him."

Marisee nodded. "Good idea," she said. But what if Nannerl and her brother didn't return safely? She had to push that thought away. No one would be safe if they didn't stop the Domedary.

Robert looked around. "Have you seen anyone else here?"

"No one," Nannerl said.

"I hope your friends come," Marisee said.

The night was too silent for her. It reminded her of London under the enchanted sleep. A silent London meant something bad was going to happen.

"Of course we were going to come," a girl's voice said from the end of the alley.

The girl stepped into the weak halo of Nannerl's lantern. Two young boys were behind her. Marisee was pleased it was dark so no one could see the disappointment on her face. She had expected – well – more from the Red Guard Gang. There were only three of them and they were all so small and thin. They didn't carry as much as a cudgel between them! And where were the rest of them? A gang was more than three people!

"I thought I would never see you again!" The

faint light showed the girl grinning at Robert. "I was hammering on the door as soon as Mr Gripe locked it! I knew something was wrong because I smelled that thing. The capture-creature. It was the same stink from the alley when it first tried to take you."

"Spindrift had to pull Emma away, didn't he?" the taller boy said.

"Before the watchmen came," the other said. "Or the constables."

"Then he and Steeple shouted at each other."

"And he made Steeple leave the den."

"Steeple left?" Robert said.

"Yes," Emma said. "He didn't want to, but Spindrift made him. We all did. Steeple knew the rules. We never betray each other, not even for a trunk full of guineas. And then we had to find somewhere else to live in case Steeple took a finder's fee to show the constables the den. There's a reward for Spindrift too." She looked over at Marisee. "Is this the friend you told me so much about?"

Marisee couldn't help smiling. Robert *had* mentioned her! She'd started to wonder if his new life with the Red Guard Gang had meant he'd left his memories of her behind. "I'm Marisee."

"I'm Emma. And this is Turpin and Duval."

The boys stared back, unsmiling.

"Did you bring anyone else?" Robert asked.

"Spindrift stayed with Garnet," Emma said. "But don't worry. We have the shard beasts. They couldn't resist a fight."

Shard beasts? Marisee wondered. *What are they? And even more importantly,* where *are they?*

But Robert seemed satisfied. She squeezed back her doubt. She'd have to trust him; true friendship meant trusting each other fully – again.

"Don't put yourselves in danger," Robert said. "Just make a distraction and give us time to get into the house."

"Good luck," Emma called.

Robert nodded and opened the gate.

Marisee heard the ticking straight away, but Nannerl was shading her lantern and it was so dark ahead that Marisee could not even see her feet, let alone what made the noise. Was it the machine with fangs that had dug itself into Robert's ankle? Or was it something even more ferocious? Marisee shuffled slowly, tensing herself.

Suddenly, the shutters in the two highest windows flew open. Robert had warned her about this too, but she still jumped. The lamps blazing inside showed that the house was falling apart. The shutters sagged on their hinges. Panes of glass were missing from the windows.

"Ignore it," Robert whispered. "The cellar steps are just ahead. Hopefully, the door's unlocked."

Marisee couldn't stop herself from looking. A shining moon-like face appeared in the upstairs windows. Curly silver hair sprung from its head. Behind her, Nannerl gasped and said something in a different language. Marisee made herself look away, but the bright face seemed to hover behind her eyelids. Would the house be filled with creatures like that? She hoped that there weren't any in the rooms she was searching.

"They're Mr Dross's machines," Robert said. "I think they are set off when the back gate opens. Last time, this was when Mr Dross threatened us with his blunderbuss."

Marisee wasn't sure if the blunderbuss or the shocking shiny-faced machines were worse.

The ticking and clicking was louder now. The ground seemed to ripple.

Nannerl squealed. "Something has bitten me!"

But there was no Mr Dross. No blunderbuss. Where was he? Was he in the house at all?

"Robert!" Nannerl's voice sounded desperate. "I do not like these things at all."

"Emma!" Robert called. "Now!"

In Nannerl's dimming lamp, Marisee saw Duval dive forward, scoop up something that looked like a giant woodlouse and hurl it over the gate into the lane. Turpin did the same, grabbing the thing that had dug itself into Nannerl's foot. It was almost round, the size of a rat, with two points jutting out from what should be a jaw.

Tick, click. Tick, click.

The darkness moved around them. Mr Dross's creatures were swarming through the garden, a sea of slithering, ticking, clicking, rolling, unrolling. Marisee's fear stopped everything – her feet, her thoughts, almost her heart. These things were not truly alive. They would keep coming and coming, a wave of metal and clicking, knocking her over and burying her beneath them. Nothing would stop them.

"Robert!" she hissed. "Throwing a few of them over the fence isn't helping! There are too many of them."

"Wait," Robert said, too calmly for Marisee's liking. This was not a time to be calm!

How could she wait when the machines were digging their fangs into the earth, dragging themselves towards her?

Tick, click. Tick, click.

Then another sound, like the soft tinkle of broken glass in a stream. Was this a new horror from Mr Dross's workshop?

"The shard beasts have arrived," Robert said.

The light from the upstairs windows fell on living, moving creatures covered in spikes of glass. They raced into the yard. Did they have three...? Yes, they had three legs! Marisee had seen Chads of all shapes and sizes, but nothing like these! One shard beast jumped into the air, spinning, legs splayed out like a broken stool, sending the machines flying in a whir of ticking metal. Marisee ducked as a metal twisted thing flew towards her and more smashed against the wall. Another shard beast threw itself to the ground, twisting and turning so its quills jammed the mechanisms. A third crouched low then released a volley of quills that pierced between the machines' casings, making them judder and stop. Then, with each leg in turn, it stomped on them. These shard beasts were terrifying but wonderful!

"Careful," Emma warned, as she stepped out of the quills' flight. She produced a wooden staff that must have been hidden in the alley. She slammed it down on the crawling contraptions before batting them over the wall.

"Thank you!" Robert called.

"After what Steeple did, we owed *you*!" Emma called back.

Nannerl was staring open-mouthed at the shard beasts. "Are they real or machines?"

Marisee glanced up at the windows. Still no Mr

Dross. They couldn't wait any longer in case a watchman had heard the noise and came to investigate.

Marisee tugged Nannerl's jacket. "Let's go and find your brother," she said.

"But those things…"

"Later," Marisee said. This wasn't the time to explain about magical London.

They ran down the steps to the cellar. Wide ramps ran along either side of the steps. A few creatures ticked and clicked up them towards the garden. Nannerl paused, uncertain.

"I don't think they can see us," Robert said. "They just go forward and forward until they stop." He pointed to the cellar door, which was wide open. "Instead of dogs, Mr Dross guards his home with his machines."

"But where is he?" Marisee asked.

He couldn't have missed all that noise. Was he too busy planning something terrible to care about what was happening outside?

"I don't know," Robert said. "We need to be extra quiet and extra careful."

Nannerl held up her lamp so they could see into the cellar. It was a small brick room. A sack of metal screws spilled out across the floor. A few of the machines lay on their sides, twitching. Nannerl stepped carefully over them. A box overflowed with old-fashioned periwigs. Marisee picked one up. It was cheap, made from horsehair.

A door from the cellar led into the room beyond. Marisee reached forward to try it.

"Wait," Robert said. "Mr Dross may guard this room too."

Nannerl pressed her ear against the door. "It is silent. Those creatures go tick, tick."

Marisee listened too. "I can't hear anything," she agreed.

If Mr Dross was waiting for them in there, he was very quiet indeed. She gripped the doorknob and gently twisted it, pulled the door open less than an inch and waited. There was no sound, no movement. She peered through. Nannerl's lantern revealed more crates and a wall of barrels.

"Is it safe to go in?" Robert asked.

Nannerl gave the door a little push. "If we don't go in, we will never find my brother," she said, and walked through.

Nothing happened. Marisee breathed out in relief and followed her.

"It's just a storeroom," Marisee said.

A lid flipped off a barrel. A pale bald head sprung

from its depths, then wobbled from side to side. Marisee jumped back in shock, clapping her hand across her mouth to stop herself from screaming.

Nannerl raised the lamp. Her hand was shaking. Marisee forced herself to take a step closer to the barrel and touched the head. It was shiny and smooth, resting on an old-fashioned lace ruff.

"It's made of porcelain," she said.

The head's wide blue eyes had been painted on, but the lashes and eyebrows looked like horsehair. Silently, the head's jaw fell open. Marisee just stopped herself from jumping back again. Instead, she went closer. Now she could see where the jaws were hinged together. She held the head in both hands; it felt cold and delicate. She gave it a gentle pull.

"It's attached to a spring," she said. "And there's a lever on the side of the barrel to crank it back inside."

"It is a..." Nannerl scratched her head. "Eine Schachtelmännchen. I don't know the English word."

"A jack-in-the-box," Robert said. "The overseer had one sent to Barbados for his child."

"As big as this?" Marisee asked, letting the head go so it wobbled again.

"I suppose not," Robert said. "Though we were never allowed close enough to look at it."

"Let us not be distracted," Nannerl said. "We must find my brother."

"And clues about the lost music," Marisee said.

They crept through the storeroom and up the servants' steps at the side of the kitchen. They stopped in the hallway. There were closed doors either side of them. Was Mr Dross behind any of them? Was Nannerl's brother?

The plan was to search this floor first. Marisee stepped carefully towards a door, listening. She opened it. Nannerl lifted the lantern – there was nothing but more boxes inside.

"I can hear music!" Nannerl's voice sounded much too loud. "Singing! It's coming from upstairs."

"But Daisy said that the sailors can't sing any more," Robert said. "No one can."

"Except for here," Nannerl said. "We heard singing when Mr Dross opened the door this morning. He did not lie. He does have music!"

The three huddled together at the bottom of the stairs. Marisee knew that in a moment's time she'd have to face whatever was up there.

The singing stopped. A horse neighed outside and a carriage rattled past. Inside, the house was silent except for the tick, tick, tick in a distant room. The step creaked as Nannerl started up the next flight of stairs.

"Robert!" Nannerl whispered – but still, too loudly. "Marisee! It's a clavichord!"

Marisee strained and could just hear the soft plonk of notes. Nannerl crept towards it. They were supposed to avoid Mr Dross, not try and find him! But the Goldsmith wanted this solved by tomorrow. Mr Dross definitely still had music. The answer to the mystery must be up those stairs. Marisee straightened her shoulders and followed Nannerl.

Nannerl was standing by a door; the music was coming from the room on the other side.

"Oh, Wolfgang," she sighed. "The music has truly returned to you." Her hand was on the doorknob.

"What if it's a trap?" Robert said. "What if it's an automaton and it's luring us in?"

"An automaton is not real," Nannerl said. "It cannot lure."

"But Mr Dross is real," Robert said. "He can make machines to trap us."

"And he could be in there," Marisee said. "What do we do if—"

"My brother is in that room." Nannerl's voice was full of determination. "No matter what or who else is in there, I must go to him."

She twisted the knob and the door opened.

There was a gasp and then a scream. Marisee and Robert looked at each other and ran in after her.

A solitary candle burned inside a glass case. Light flickered across the small figure sitting behind the clavichord, fingers tapping the keys. He wore a red velvet jacket with sleeves so long that they brushed the keyboard. His head twitched from side to side.

Nannerl shook her head. "I thought… I thought it was Wolfgang." She sniffed. "I'd hoped that it was him."

She walked slowly towards the musician. He continued to play, ignoring her as she circled him. She reached out carefully and tapped the musician's shoulder. He still didn't turn.

"It's one of Mr Dross's automata," Robert said.

"He is like a work of magic," Nannerl said. "Bad magic that tricks us into thinking it's real."

Marisee stepped closer to examine it; the automaton was playing the clavichord like a human musician. Inside, were wheels and levers, but its eyes moved, following the movement of its fingers that were actually striking the keys.

"It even holds its body like a musician," Nannerl said.

"Remember Mr Dross's trade card?" Robert said. "He makes automata as close to life as God will allow. I

267

wonder how he does it." He moved closer too. "Perhaps it's like the Variegates. Perhaps he takes parts of musicians and…"

Nannerl spun round. "Takes parts of musicians? What do you mean, Robert?" she demanded. "Do you think he has stolen my brother" – she pointed to the automaton – "and turned him into that? No! I will not believe that!" She raced out of the room. "Wolfgang!" she shouted. "Where are you?" A door was flung open along the hallway. "Wolfga—"

"I'm sorry." Robert looked upset. "I didn't mean to frighten her."

"I was thinking the same thing," Marisee said, although she'd kept the thought to herself.

There was another scream. Robert and Marisee ran towards it. Wherever Mr Dross was, Marisee thought, he must surely have heard them by now. Nannerl was staring into a room filled with barrels; a porcelain head wobbled above each one. These ones wore wigs; eyes in the painted faces opened and closed with a soft clack.

There was one face that Marisee recognized. It was the child, Mozart.

"That's … that's my brother," Nannerl said.

Porcelain Wolfgang's mouth dropped open and he sighed.

THE PORCELAIN CHOIR

Robert stared into the room, then walked towards the head and flicked it. There was the "ting" of porcelain.

"Wolfgang!" Nannerl was crying so hard, her words were sobs. "You have been turned into a machine!"

"No, Nannerl," Robert said. "It's just another jack-in-the-box. I'm sorry for frightening you just now. I didn't mean to. The clavichord-player was just a machine – a clever one, but just a machine. And this is just another porcelain head on a spring."

Although it was even stranger than the musical automaton – a jack-in-the-box with a painted porcelain head and a jaw that moved.

Marisee put her arm around Nannerl's shoulders. "Robert's right. It's been painted to look like your brother. It's not him."

Nannerl delicately touched the cold, smooth face. "It is true. This is not my brother. But when I see such things in this house, how can I still hope that Wolfgang is safe?"

"I can assure you that Master Mozart is perfectly safe." Mr Dross stood in the doorway, holding a lantern. All three turned to look at him. Robert felt the ball of fear swelling beneath his rib cage.

The brighter light made the porcelain heads look ghostly. Mr Dross placed the lantern on the floor and picked up a large pair of bellows from the hallway outside. A leather tube ran from a nozzle, snaking around the edge of the room behind the boxes. He pulled the bellows handles apart then clapped them together. The porcelain jaw flapped open and sighed again.

Even though Robert knew how it worked, the clack and gasp still made him jump. The fear inside him grew more solid.

"A childish invention," Mr Dross said, walking past them towards the barrels. "In that I constructed my first one when I was a child."

He lifted the porcelain Wolfgang's head tenderly,

holding it so close to his own that his nose brushed the painted one. Marisee saw the leather air tube enclosed in the spring.

"But I *have* created a good likeness, haven't I?" Mr Dross continued. "Until today, I had only seen the boy genius's image from engravings." He gently lowered the head back into the barrel. "But pray, may I ask why you have stolen into my house at this hour?"

"Stolen?" Nannerl shouted. "*You* have stolen my brother!"

"You accuse me in error," Mr Dross said. "I have not *stolen* your brother. I have borrowed him, and he came to me willingly."

"I do not believe you!" Nannerl took a step forward. "I will look for myself!"

Mr Dross stepped aside from the doorway. "Will you indeed?"

The hallway filled with the clicking and ticking of automata. The metal creatures rolled and spun and tottered into the room. There were metal birds like the one Robert had found in the Pleasure Gardens, but with wheels instead of feet, their beaks quivering as they sang like true birds. A snake squirmed across the floor, its leather-like scales puckering around the cogs and spindles underneath. A clockface with a giant key on its back glided towards them, the clock's case covered in pins. Palm-sized iron spiders skimmed across the floor, each of their eight legs ending in a bright red marble. There were tiny creatures too – hundreds of juddering beetle-like beasts that scuttled across the smooth stone until Robert could no longer see the floor.

They were soon surrounded by the machine creatures. Robert lifted his leg to move, but they immediately filled the space where his foot had been. He didn't have the shard beasts' clay legs. The boots he wore had thin, uneven soles. The creatures' metal cases would cut right through them. He balanced on his toe. The creatures scuttled over his other foot, and pushed at it as if it was an obstacle in their way.

Robert imagined every door in the house opening to release more and more of these horrors. They would surround him, push at him until he fell, crawl over him. Or – even worse – Mr Dross would know Robert's value to Lord Pritchard. He would be locked in the storeroom until Lord Pritchard arrived.

Mr Dross smiled slowly. "Do you like my little guards?" he said. "I have fine-tuned the mechanisms so they can run for hours. They are not like humans. They are better than humans because they don't lie. They are not greedy. They need nothing but the tightening of a spring and a drip of oil."

"That is very interesting," Nannerl said. Her voice sounded stronger and calmer than Robert imagined his would. "But *where* is my brother?"

Mr Dross's eyes widened like those painted on the porcelain heads.

"Do you not understand the seriousness of your circumstances?" he said. "Housebreaking is punishable by death. Destroying my property ... the jury will be even less inclined to spare your lives. I have a mind to call for a watchman to take you straight to a magistrate."

Who would send for Lord Pritchard, Robert thought. If he ran now, could he escape? Mr Dross couldn't chase them all.

"We've done nothing wrong," Marisee declared.

Mr Dross held up his lamp so he could study them closely. "You broke into my house. You destroyed my creations outside and in. You have done much wrong. And you, young sir." He swung his lamp closer to Robert. Robert flinched away. "I'm sure I saw a notice in the Jerusalem coffee shop describing a young man such as yourself. He has fled his owner. There is a reward for his return."

Robert felt a prickle of fury as he looked Mr Dross in the eye. "I do not belong to anyone!"

"But the law says that you do." Mr Dross turned his lamp towards Marisee. "And *you* could hang for trying to

273

rob me tonight." He rubbed his hands. "Or at least, be transported to the Americas."

"We were not trying to rob you!" Marisee shouted. "We want to find Nannerl's brother. Give him back to us or *you'll* be punished for kidnapping a child!"

"Please, Mr Dross," Nannerl said, her voice still calm. Though this time Robert heard the tremble beneath it. "Bring Wolfgang to me and we will go. You do not even have to return my music box."

Music box? Robert had forgotten about that. Mr Dross had deliberately asked to see it and then stole it. Why would he do that?

Mr Dross plucked a silent mechanical bird from the ground, took a nail from his banyan pocket and inserted it into a hole in the creature's underbelly. As he twisted the nail, the tiny mechanical legs wriggled, the beak opened and it began to sing again. He replaced it on the floor where it rolled forward.

"Your brother came here of his own choice," Mr Dross said. "I promised him music and music he has. He is indeed a genius."

"So now let him leave of his own free will," Nannerl pleaded. "Take me to him."

"With pleasure," Mr Dross said. "While there is still time."

Marisee looked at Robert. "Time for what?" she mouthed.

Robert let questions unfurl in his head. He wished the answers were unfurling at the same time. Whatever time there was, was going to be much too little.

What did Mr Dross want time for?

What did he need the boy musician for?

Why did he take Nannerl's music box?

Why didn't the automata music get stolen?

And what were those last words that Mr Dross had muttered to the Goldsmith this morning...?

"Time for what?" Mr Dross said out loud, looking at Marisee. "Young lady, it is time to test the fruits of my labour." He made a hand flourish towards Nannerl. "And those of your prodigy brother."

He swept out of the room, Nannerl running after him. The automata twitched, shuffled and crawled, but slower now. Some of the birds still chirruped and sang.

"They're like clocks," Robert said, "and need to be wound up."

"I think he's letting us go." Marisee gave Robert a relieved smile and glanced towards the door.

"And leave Nannerl?" Robert asked.

"Well..." Marisee sighed. "No, I suppose we can't leave Nannerl."

"And don't you think it's strange?" Robert said. "That after he threatened to call the watchman and send me back to the plantation and you to the Americas, that he'd just let us escape so easily?"

"Perhaps he realizes that he's been found out?" Marisee looked hopeful.

"I don't think he was ever going to call the watchman," Robert said. "Think about it, Marisee. If the Domedary is calmed by music, who is the only person in London with music?"

"Mr Dross," Marisee said, a little impatiently. "I know. But it won't be for long, will it? Surely other craftsmen can learn to make music machines. I mean, a music box is nothing but a music machine, isn't it? Perhaps the Goldsmith has already ordered the craftsmen to build bigger ones."

"Perhaps," Robert said. "But by the time they're ready, the Domedary may have gained its full strength and destroyed half of the city. So for now, Mr Dross does have the only music. He's the only one who can calm the monster."

"Maybe so," Marisee said. "He can make the monster sleep, Robert, but it doesn't mean that he can control it. It's awake and angry because London's music is being" – she shrugged – "blown away. He can make it sleep, but he can't make it wake up."

"What if he starts his automata playing then stops them again?" Robert said. "He'd send the monster to sleep then wake it up again. Wouldn't that make the monster angry?"

"Ye-es," Marisee said. "I suppose so. But I don't know, Robert. It's like the monster needs more than that. Maybe little bits of music can soothe it for a while, but not forever. It's almost like the city sings to it. And we still don't know what's stopped the music. It's definitely magical, but what?"

"I'm sure Mr Dross isn't magical," Robert said. "He'd stand up to the Goldsmith much more if he was."

Marisee flicked a metal snake away with her toe and shuddered. "No, Dross isn't magical, but he definitely knows something about the disappearing music. It can't be a coincidence, can it, Robert? He was in the Pleasure Gardens when the orchestra exploded. Then outside the Mansion House when you and Nannerl were walking on, he was looking at the whistle-flute player on the steps. When he saw me watching him, he hurried off. Maybe he'd realized something."

You and Nannerl… Those words hooked themselves into Robert's thoughts. *You and Nannerl… Nannerl.*

Why hadn't he thought about Nannerl earlier? At last, some of the answers to his questions were unfurling too.

"Marisee, when you, me and Nannerl knocked on his door this morning," he said, "what did Mr Dross do?"

"Slam the door in our face," Marisee said, crossly.

"Only after he'd snatched Nannerl's music box!" Yes, this was definitely starting to make sense to Robert now. "Why would he want that?"

"I don't know," Marisee said. "It didn't even work. Maybe he wanted the mechanism for one of his creatures."

"But that's it!" Robert swept a path with his boot through the automata. "Didn't he say something about its 'extraordinary mechanism'? Wasn't he the one who asked her to show it to him?"

Marisee frowned. "Yes, he did seem eager to see it." Her frown deepened. "You think that the music box has something to do with the missing music? It didn't feel magical when I touched it."

"Mr Dross wasn't the only one at the Pleasure Gardens when the orchestra exploded," Robert said. "Nannerl was there too, wasn't she? And near the Mansion House when the whistle-flute player stopped playing."

"But music's disappeared from across London," Marisee said. "Not just where Nannerl's been."

"True." Robert kicked a metal spider extra-hard. Marisee winced but said nothing. "But there has to be a reason why Mr Dross wanted the music box so badly. There's a secret to it, and he knows what it is."

"Maybe he thinks it can control the monster?" Marisee didn't sound certain.

"It must do somehow," Robert said. "And he's just told us that he's going to test the fruits of his labour. So whatever he needs the music box for, it's happening now."

"And we need to see what it is!" Marisee grabbed Mr Dross's lantern from the floor and ran out of the room. "And we must get that music box back!"

They darted up the wooden stairs. The door to a large parlour was thrown open, lit by spluttering tallow candles. The room was bare of furniture, the threadbare curtains too narrow to cover the wide windows. Barrels of all sizes were stacked on a wide wooden box. Mr Dross was going from one to the other, releasing a catch on their lids.

"You didn't run when you had the chance?" Mr Dross said, without looking around. "The bigger the audience, the better. Behold the superlative Jack Dross choir!"

Click. Another lid loosened.

"I've spent years perfecting every singer," Mr Dross said. "I have created the most delicate of mechanisms, chimes and whistles that pass through intricate valves until they sound like the human voice. I have tuned those voices to vocal excellence, both in solo and in harmony."

Click.

"I had even asked Mr Tyers's permission to perform our debut piece at the Vauxhall Pleasure Gardens," Mr Dross continued. "But he is like all the other wealthy villains in London. He wanted my creations as long as I was happy to receive no payment. But then I heard that the prodigy Mozart was visiting London and hoped against hope that he'd compose a piece for us." Mr Dross released the last catch and stepped back. "Now he is here in my parlour performing the most important music of his life. Dreams can come true."

A harpsichord stood in the middle of the floor. Nannerl and a small boy, who must be her brother, sat together on a stool in front of it. At least he seemed well. The boy turned to look at them. He was smiling. Nannerl was staring at the keyboard, touching each key gently as if soothing the instrument's pain.

"Our audience has arrived," Mr Dross said. "Let them witness the most important musical performance that London will know." He grinned at Marisee and Robert. "Please enjoy the Jack Dross choir performing a new piece composed by child prodigy Wolfgang Mozart, who along with his sister will briefly accompany them. Performance length – unknown."

He crouched by the wooden box. There was a *snap*

280

and the front panel dropped to the floor. Screwing up his face with the effort, he pumped the bellows inside it. There was a click and whoosh. The barrel lids flipped back on their hinges and the porcelain heads sprung up. Their jaws flopped open and they began to sing.

"It's like the voices we heard this morning," Marisee said.

"It was his choir," Robert said, staring at the strange choir of ghost-like heads with trembling jaws. It was frightening, but Robert couldn't help admiring Mr Dross's skill.

The sound was human, but not. There were no words, just "ahhs" when the jaws seemed to open wider, and "ooos" and "mmmms". But it was still beautiful. For a moment, Robert closed his eyes and let it wash over him.

"Now your turn!" Mr Dross instructed.

The Mozarts played together, their hands jumping over and around each other's. Their tune was a counter-melody that weaved between the unhuman voices. It made Robert think of his youngest sister when she was a small child, running between the cabins singing to herself, before she knew of the pain around her.

Mr Dross's hand rested on the pocket of his banyan. Robert could see the thin fabric stretching around a square shape – Nannerl's music box. Was it his imagination or did it give a little shudder? Something was definitely happening, but the choir was still singing and the Mozarts were still playing.

"It is like we are ourselves again!" Nannerl said, her fingers flitting across the keyboard.

Robert didn't understand it. Surely the music should have been taken by now. He glanced back at Mr Dross's pocket. It was still. Why? Was it because it was Nannerl's music box and it didn't want to take her music? It seemed to accompany her everywhere. If London's music soothed the Domedary, perhaps the Mozarts' music soothed what was inside the box. Robert shuddered. He hoped it wasn't another monster.

Even Mr Dross was looking uncertain. "Why? Why? Why?" he muttered. "The music should stop! The monster should come to destroy the thing that has awoken it! I cannot be wrong."

Marisee's head whipped round. *Monster should come?* Robert had heard too.

Marisee hurled herself towards Nannerl and tried to pull her away from the stool.

"The Domedary's coming, Nannerl! We must get out of here!"

"Leave me alone!" Nannerl shoved Marisee away.

"You were supposed to help me, but you were no help at all. Mr Dross has helped us! He has brought us back the music!"

Mr Dross's banyan pocket bulged as if the music box was trying to force its way out. There was that faint smell of fried chicken again.

"He isn't helping you, Nannerl!" Robert shouted above the music. "He just wanted the most famous musician in London to compose music for his choir."

"That Goldsmith said I was a nobody!" Mr Dross stroked a tall, curly wig on a porcelain head. "But here I have the child prodigy himself in *my* drawing room composing work just for me! How can I be a nobody?"

"But that's not all you're doing," Marisee yelled. "You've found out how to summon the monster?"

Except that the monster hasn't come yet, Robert thought. They had time to escape. He grabbed Wolfgang around his waist, but the boy made himself heavy and floppy, even while he still played on. Had Robert and Marisee risked their lives to save him just for them all to be crushed by the Domedary because the boy wouldn't leave?

"It's dangerous here!" Robert panted. "We have to go!"

"Our music has returned!" Nannerl said. "You go and let us be happy!"

Robert was very tempted to obey.

"You won't be happy for lo—" Marisee started.

Robert felt a breeze. It rippled across Mr Dross's banyan. The smell of fried chicken grew stronger. It was mixed with a sweet, earthier smell like near a brewer's yard. The porcelain heads swayed on their springs. Suddenly, a wild gust blew through the room towards the harpsichord. It landed in a small explosion of air that made Robert's ears hurt. Wolfgang was hurled backwards into Robert. Nannerl flew off the stool on to the floor. The harpsichord toppled over, the keys tossed into the air like a handful of coins.

"It is happening!" Mr Dross cried. "It is happening!"

The choir still hummed and cooed.

"But hush, my darlings," Mr Dross said, pulling a lever in the box beneath the choir. The porcelain jaws clicked shut. There was a moment's silence.

"Let me see if my theory is correct," he said, prancing towards the window. He threw open the shutters. "The music came. The music went. And in here..." He tapped his pocket. "I have the culprit. Come and find it, monster! And bring your fury and chaos with you!"

"Nannerl!" Wolfgang wailed. "The music is gone again."

Robert wasn't going to wait and see if Mr Dross's theory was correct. If the monster was coming, they had to get back to the safety of the tunnels now. He hoped that Emma and the boys had already escaped.

"Come on!" he shouted, trying to pull Wolfgang away again. "Now!"

Marisee helped Nannerl up. "Let's go!"

Nannerl touched the harpsichord's cracked frame. "It's ruined."

"Ruined? No." Mr Dross backed away from the window towards them. "A harpsichord can be repaired, even replaced. But a city ruined takes centuries to rebuild. I gave the Goldsmith and the others every chance to pay me for my work. They laughed at me and called me a nobody. Now it won't just be me who's ruined. It will be this whole city."

Nannerl stood up slowly and took a shaky step towards Mr Dross. "Give us back our music!"

"Nannerl!" Marisee shrieked with frustration. "The Domedary can split trees in two! Leave him! Come with us!"

Mr Dross swept a hand towards the silent heads. "Did you not enjoy your brother's composition? I call it … I call it the 'Monster's Lullaby'."

"I do not care what you call it!" Nannerl said, taking another step towards Mr Dross. "You have stolen our music! Give it back!"

"Me, stolen the music?" Mr Dross laughed. "Oh, Miss Mozart! You really don't know, do you? It was you who was stealing the music all along!"

He drew the music box out of his pocket. Robert glanced at Marisee. Her eyes were fixed on it. They'd thought Mr Dross wanted it because of a special mechanism, but now they knew it was worth much more than that. Somehow it held the magic that stopped the music and summoned the monster.

He and Marisee had to steal it back. But how?

"I don't understand its workings," Mr Dross said, stroking the music box's lid. "I dare not take it apart until its services are no longer required." He lifted his head, as if listening. "But I do know that it works very well indeed. If I hum, the notes are taken from me. If my choir plays, they are allowed to sing. It does not like the music of machines. I hurried past Mr Shudi's workshop this morning after I had taken the box from you. I heard Mr Shudi demonstrating a fine new harpsichord to a buyer. The harmonious notes shrieked and stopped as I passed. And then..." He grinned. His teeth were as bright as the singing heads. "I am sure that I heard the sound, the very faint sound, of a creature's fury."

Marisee jolted. "So I did hear the monster," she said.

Robert wanted to ask her when, but there were

286

more important matters to deal with – like saving their lives.

"My music box takes music?" Nannerl was laughing. "That's impossible, Mr Dross!"

"Is it, Miss Mozart?" He held the music box level with his eyes. "Were *you* not by the stage when the orchestra lost control at the Pleasure Gardens? Were *you* not by the Mansion House when the whistle-flute player could no longer play? Have you not heard the church bells clanging and the theatre owners complaining that their singers and musicians cannot work?"

"No," Nannerl said. "We have not been here long. I've been busy with Wolfgang or caring for my father. I have not been to theatres or visited churches. You cannot blame me for that."

"Well, Miss Mozart," Mr Dross said, "these strange events have only happened since your arrival. But there was one last thing I wondered. I saw the monster rise for the first time on the Greenwich peninsula. Mr Potter, the ferryman, told me that it was angered because London's music had been taken. They said that it would destroy the whole of London to find what had awoken it. Now, not only do I possess what awakened it, I possess the only music in London that cannot be stolen. I am the only one that can soothe it."

"Are you sure about that?" Marisee said. "I've heard that it needs the music of the city to make it sleep."

Mr Dross flicked one of the heads. His nail made the porcelain ring.

"Right now, the Jack Dross choir *is* the music of the city because it is the only music of the city. But let us see what happens."

Mr Dross stood still, as if listening. The bellow was distant, a sound that was low and sharp at the same time.

"The Domedary," Marisee whispered.

"And what a fine beast it is," Mr Dross said.

The Domedary bellowed again. If the monster had been biding its time, resting on the riverbed since the attack on Vauxhall Pleasure Gardens, it certainly sounded like it had recovered its full strength now. The bellow was followed by shouts and screams from the street. Mr Dross glanced towards the window, smiling. This was it! Robert's chance to grab the music box! He dived towards it, but the animateur must have seen the movement reflected in the window glass and swiped Robert away. The music box clattered to the floor, sliding towards Nannerl. Robert stumbled and fell against the barrels. The choir's jaws fell open and they seemed to gasp.

"Then I will take this!" Nannerl yelled. "I will have my music box back!"

Mr Dross charged towards her. Nannerl hurled the music box to Marisee, who just about caught it. Mr Dross raced towards the door, blocking their way. He held out his hand.

"Give it back to me!" he said. "And I'll give you time to run and hide before the chaos monster arrives."

Marisee shook her head.

"Very well." Mr Dross dropped his arm and leaned against the frame. "Stay here and watch the monster lay waste to London."

The Domedary's cry cut through the air. Robert could hear the clatter of horse hooves and people yelling. There was a faint orange glow of fire.

"I've seen the monster," Mr Dross said. "It's a destroyer that cannot be destroyed. Everyone you know will die. Everything you care about will be trampled. Only I have music." He nodded towards his choir again. "Only I can stop it. I'll do so if you give the music box back to me."

"If I don't," Marisee said, "you will die too."

Mr Dross shrugged. "I have nothing to lose. I will die happy knowing that I ruined the city that tried to ruin me."

Nannerl pointed to the window and shouted something in German. For the first time, Robert saw the monster himself. It was taller than the houses, bringing its own light, a shimmering silver that crackled furiously across its shell-like body. Its legs were bent in many places as they gathered strength to plunge through brick and tiles. Just one step and houses would crumble; one swing of those legs and trees would split apart. While the capture-creature's rage was like the point of a deadly sword aimed at Robert, the Domedary was like a cudgel flattening everything around it.

"Give him the music box, Marisee," Nannerl pleaded. "Just let Wolfgang leave here with his life."

"That is an excellent plan," Mr Dross said. "It is Miss Mozart's music box. You must do as she says."

The monster's cries were louder. It was closer. The only chance of escaping it was by giving Mr Dross the music box.

But just by the hem of Mr Dross's banyan, wasn't that...? Was it a hand?

Marisee was nodding slowly. "I'll give you back the music box, Mr Dross. But you'll have to catch it!"

She threw the music box low. As Mr Dross bent down for it, the hand that scooped it out of the air wasn't his.

"Duval?" Robert said. "Turpin?"

The brothers dived through the doorway either side of Mr Dross.

"You caught it, Turpin!" Duval said.

"Now you catch it!" Turpin threw the box to Duval, who took it with ease.

"Give it to me!" Mr Dross shouted, lurching towards Duval.

The doorway was free! It was time to run. As Mr Dross reached for Duval, Duval hurled the box over Mr Dross's head towards Marisee who was running towards the door. Mr Dross's arm shot towards it, but it bounced sideways off his fingers.

"I think this is mine," Nannerl said, snatching it.

"No, it isn't!" Mr Dross yelled, grabbing her jacket and throwing her to the floor.

Nannerl screamed. The music box dropped from her hand – into Turpin's.

"To me!" a voice called.

It was Emma, in the hallway by the door. Turpin threw; Emma caught it smartly and handed it to Marisee.

Nannerl stood up, seized her brother's hand and ran from the room.

"Go," Emma said to Robert. "We can keep Dross busy."

"Won't the river monster keep you busy enough?" Mr Dross said nastily. "Don't forget, I'm the only one with music and I'm certainly not going to calm it now."

"Perhaps so," Emma said, "but here are some smaller monsters to keep *you* busy." She stepped aside to show the shard beasts behind her.

Mr Dross's mouth fell open. "Is this city full of the devil's creatures?"

"You, Duval and Turpin have to take shelter," Robert said. "The Domedary's coming and we can't stop it."

"I know it's coming," Emma said. "But I believe you'll defeat it. Stay safe, Robert."

"Let's go, Robert!" Marisee brushed past him. "Hopefully, Red Rum's still waiting in the back." She nodded towards Emma. "And thank you."

They raced back down through the storeroom to the cellar, stumbling in the darkness. Robert could hear the Mozarts ahead of them.

"Be quick, Wolfie!" Nannerl urged. "But be careful! You cannot play if you fall and hurt your hands."

"My hands have no use!" he whimpered. "They cannot play the music in my head."

Robert heard a neigh from outside. It sounded as sweet as music! The cart was still there! He threw himself up the steps into the courtyard. His feet crunched and slid across cogs and panels; the shard beasts had certainly enjoyed their fight.

The others must have sped ahead of him and were

already waiting on the cart. A cannon boomed and the monster bellowed. Breathless, he flung himself through the gate. The cart *was* there. No, this one was bigger. And that horse certainly wasn't Red Rum.

"Marisee?" he called. "Nannerl?"

Two dark figures stepped out of the shadows. One was wide-shouldered with the battered face of a boxer. He carried a length of rope in his hand. The other wore the clothes of a climbing boy.

"Steeple?" Robert said.

And the other man – Steeple's cousin. This was a proper night men's cart, just as before. The barrels were stacked high and smelled like most had already been filled.

"Pleased to make your acquaintance again," Steeple said. "Six guineas would be a true pleasure. Though handing you over to Lord Pritchard will give me even more pleasure." He rummaged in his pocket and pulled out the golden Freedom box. "Six guineas as well as whatever we get for this!"

"You betrayed me," Robert said. "I thought you were my friend."

Steeple laughed. "Friendship or money?" He lifted his hands up and down, like a grocer's scales. "Friendship or money? It will be money every time."

A cannon boomed again. Steeple's cousin pulled the rope taut between his huge hands.

"Listen!" Robert said. "Can't you hear that? Something terrible is coming! It doesn't matter if you have money or—"

Steeple shoved Robert towards his cousin. Robert's arms were gripped hard and the rope coiled, then tightened around his wrists. Then tighter still. Robert gulped back pain. Steeple's cousin picked Robert up like he was a small child and dropped him into the back of the cart.

Marisee was lying between the barrels, her ankles and wrists bound, a rag tied across her mouth. Her eyes blazed with fury.

"Where are Nannerl and Wolfgang?" Robert asked.

"We had no need for them," Steeple's cousin said. "We weren't getting no coin for those two."

"Yes," Steeple said. "We kindly let them take their chance with the monster."

"But aren't you afra—"

Robert didn't finish, because Steeple's cousin thrust his face close to him. "I'm not going to gag you, because if you call out, your friend here" – he prodded Marisee – "is going to end up on the same ship as you."

Steeple snickered. "Maybe we should do that anyway! We'd get good money for her."

There was a flash of white. It glinted above the distant rooftops over Steeple's shoulder.

"Don't you understand?" Robert yelled. "There's a monster coming!"

Steeple shrugged. "Can't *you* hear? The army's already there dealing with whatever it is. It'll be dead soon."

He disappeared, leaving Robert and Marisee in the darkness and stench. Robert tried to bury his nose in his chest, but even still, the stench made his eyes water. The cart bowed and Robert heard a grunt. Steeple and his cousin had climbed into the driver's seat.

Marisee's eyes widened with terror. She was staring at Mr Dross's house. The Domedary's pale body appeared above the rooftops like a giant moon, crackling with magic. It lifted its legs high, bands of thin darkness. Then came the sound of shattering tiles and splintering wood, people screaming, horses whinnying, dogs barking. Another boom from a cannon.

A whip cracked.

"Move!" Steeple's cousin screamed. "MOVE!"

The horse reared, and the cart tipped, throwing Robert against a barrel. The Domedary's leg smashed through a roof. Candles flashed in the back rooms of the neighbouring terraces, doors slammed and people shrieked as they ran for their lives. The cart bounced. Steeple's cousin must have jumped out and made a run for it. Steeple ran past the cart then stopped.

"Untie us," Robert pleaded. "Please, Steeple."

Steeple ignored him; he was looking up at the Domedary. He gave a little whimper. The beast's underbelly was splitting open, broken oyster shells scattering across the street. One of its legs swung across the top of the cart. Steeple dived out of the way, dropping his lamp. Robert felt the whoosh as the leg sliced through the air. The cart jolted again and Robert heard the sound of hooves galloping away. The Domedary must have cut through the shaft and harness.

At least the horse was free. But he and Marisee – there was nothing they could do as the claw-tipped foot swung towards them. Robert was thrown sideways. There was a crash, then nothing but total darkness.

THE CHASE

Marisee's heart was beating so hard it was making her head hurt. The cart tipped, teetered then crashed, upturned, to the ground. The darkness was complete. She was trapped beneath it, wedged between the barrels; if any were crushed, or even split, she would be covered in… She took a tiny breath through her nose. She'd heard of night men who'd climbed into cesspits to clean them, then fainted or even died from the fumes. She mustn't think about that.

She wriggled her hands. They were tied tightly, her ankles too. The cart's driver had made sure of that. She tried to move her shoulders, but she was stuck. She could hear nothing of the world outside. Was the monster waiting for them or had it moved on? She wanted to call for Robert but the filthy rag tied around her mouth wouldn't shift no matter how much she wriggled her face.

"Marisee?" It was Robert!

If he could talk, he couldn't be too badly hurt, could he?

Suddenly, the cart flew off her and the barrels rolled away. Marisee looked up and was staring into the Domedary's underbelly. It was as deep as a pit. Its fangs curved out from its jaw, but smaller teeth spiralled deep into its body. There were no eyes. Air rushed over her as the monster's leg swung across her, the sharp tip of its foot just missing her face.

She couldn't stay here! Next time, it might not miss!

Marisee sat up, then struggled to standing. She almost fell over when she tried to walk. She had to find something to cut the rope.

Robert, where are you?

The Domedary's leg swept past her again. It missed her but the barbs caught the side of a barrel. The stinking muck oozed out. Marisee tried to cry out, but her mouth was filled with rag. Suddenly, Nannerl appeared, brandishing one of the night man's poles. She ducked beneath the Domedary's flailing leg.

"Get away!" Nannerl cried.

Hooves sounded behind her. A troop of soldiers charged at the beast. Nannerl dropped the pole and untied Marisee's gag.

"Our cart is at the end of the lane!" she said.

More soldiers arrived on horseback, their swords raised, shouting and whooping. One sliced at the Domedary's leg with his weapon. "Devil! Return to hell!" he cried.

Nothing happened.

"I said, 'Devil, return to hell'," he cried again.

They all charged, swords clashing against the monster's legs. But there were so many legs. Perhaps they hadn't realized how many. A leg flicked out, knocking two soldiers from their horses. Another shouted in anger before he too was swept from his saddle. A clawed foot stamped through the night men's cart, the barbs shredding the wood as it freed itself. Stinking slop exploded out of the barrels. Shrieks of disgust filled the air.

Nannerl looped her arm through Marisee's, but Marisee could only take tiny, tiny steps, the rope rubbing the skin from her ankles. She nearly fell again, trying to squirm around the stinking puddles spilling out of the barrels.

"Where's Robert?" she said.

"I made him go ahead," Nannerl said. "Do you have the music box?"

Marisee nodded. Thankfully, Steeple hadn't checked her jacket pockets.

More men arrived: some on foot, others on horses. They were armed with flaming torches and makeshift weapons – broom handles, curtain poles, even a butter paddle.

"Satan's beast! Return to the pit!" they yelled.

"This way!" Nannerl said, pulling Marisee along.

Marisee hobbled and hopped. It seemed hopeless. She couldn't even walk, meanwhile the Domedary crushed houses with every step. But at last! There was their cart. They *might* have a chance of reaching a tunnel before they were crushed by the Domedary's fury. Wolfgang was perched on the driver's seat, peering up the lane through his fingers. Marisee's heart bounced. Robert was safe and unhurt, leaning against the back of the cart trying to wriggle free from the ropes around his wrists.

"They're too tight!" he said.

"We brought tools, remember?" Marisee said. "There should be something back there to help."

Nannerl climbed into the back of the cart.

"This?" she said, holding up an iron chisel.

"Yes!" Marisee couldn't keep the panic out of her voice.

Nannerl jammed the chisel into the knot binding Robert's wrist until it was loose, then did the same for Marisee. Next came the ankle ropes.

"We thought you were gone," Marisee said.

"We want our music back," Nannerl said, throwing the chisel back into the cart. "I should have believed that you were the ones who really wanted to help us." Nannerl looked guilty. "And if Mr Dross is right, it's my fault that the music has gone. I brought the music box to London. I must help to mend the chaos it is causing."

Red Rum neighed. Marisee didn't need to speak London Horse to know that they were being urged to hurry. They squeezed into the driver's seat and Red Rum sped into action. Behind them, the Domedary loomed over the men who dodged between the swinging legs, beating at it with their weapons. The houses looked like *they* had been hit by cannon balls. Roofs were smashed; chimneys were leaning, crooked and jagged. A wall had crumbled and a bed hung out of the gaping hole.

And somewhere, Mr Dross would certainly be planning his revenge. The Domedary was strong and furious. It would destroy London in days.

"I hope your friends are safe," Marisee said to Robert.

"I think they will be," he said. "They are used to looking after themselves."

"And they have shard beasts to help them," she said.

Robert smiled. "Yes. That too."

Marisee breathed in the night air. For a few moments, they were safe too, but it wouldn't be for long. Behind them, the Domedary bellowed. It didn't sound as far away as Marisee had hoped. They had to get back underground as soon as possible.

A troop of soldiers galloped past them and disappeared down the road. Marisee looked back. The Domedary's pale body rose above the houses, shrieks and screams trailing behind it.

"Red Rum!" she said. "Can you go quicker?"

The cart swayed as Red Rum spun sideways into a narrow street then out into a wider one.

"Covent Garden," Robert said.

It was past midnight, but lights burned in windows around the square. Link boys bearing flaming torches huddled together, casting worried looks towards Soho. Marisee wanted to shout out to them – *run for your lives!*

"Mr Gripe lives down there," Robert said, pointing to a street. "I wouldn't mind if the Domedary crushed *his* shop."

Red Rum didn't pause. The cart swung from side

to side, throwing them against each other. The poles and empty barrels rattled in the back. A cannon boomed behind them, followed by two more. Marisee knew that it wouldn't stop the monster. Only music could do that. They'd discovered that the music box had stolen the music from London, but not how or why. And certainly not how to get the music back. As far as she knew, Mr Dross was still the only person whose creations could sing and play without being stopped. What if he really was the only person who could calm the Domedary?

Wolfgang spoke to his sister in German. Marisee could hear the fear in his voice.

"Where are we going?" Nannerl asked. "Is it safe?"

We're on Drury Lane, Marisee thought. *Where is the nearest well? Can we reach the Fleet Ditch?* The Domedary bellowed once more. Wolfgang whimpered as the curve of its shell rose behind the houses. There were more cries as people spilled out on to the street, more gun blasts as soldiers took aim.

The Domedary kept coming, its legs cutting through buildings as if they were cheese curds.

"We must hurry!" Nannerl screamed. "Hurry!"

Red Rum careered into another narrow street. Marisee was sure that she could hear waves washing against the wharves and smell the dank water. They must be near the Strand, the road that ran close to the north bank of the Thames. Fleet Ditch was still some way beyond that.

Where else could they go? Where else?

There was a crash. The Domedary seemed to drop from the night sky. It landed behind the cart, its shell knocking tiles from the roofs. A gable fell away and smashed into the street. The monster lowered itself, squatting among the bricks and broken tiles, its many jointed legs pressing down like Mr Dross's jack-in-the-box heads and—

It sprang into the air, this time landing in front of them, its flailing legs shattering windows and spearing the roofs of the huddled houses. Nannerl shrieked as Red Rum reared back, then stopped still.

"Nannerl, help your brother down," Robert said. "Red Rum is giving us time to escape!"

Nannerl wrapped her arms around Wolfgang and ushered him from the cart. "Where are we escaping to?"

Where to? Marisee thought. *Where to?* And then she knew.

"There's a well in Clement Danes churchyard," Marisee said, forcing herself to look away from the Domedary. She pointed to the dark shape of a church. "That's St Mary's. Clement Danes is behind that."

"A well?" Nannerl said.

"Yes," Marisee said. "Please just trust me."

Nannerl stared up at the Domedary. Tears poured down her face as she held her brother close. His face was blank, as if refusing to see the horror ahead of him.

"Nowhere is safe for us," she said.

Robert and Marisee looked at each other. Then they looked up at the Domedary. Robert could see the line across its underbelly as it started to split open.

"Nannerl, we'll try and keep its attention," Marisee said. "You and Wolfgang run to Clement Danes."

The line in the Domedary's underbelly grew wider. Nannerl gave her a little nod and started running, pulling Wolfgang behind her.

"How long do we leave it?" Robert asked.

The underbelly split into a mouth.

"That's enough time," Marisee said. "Run!"

They dashed sideways, but the Domedary's foot flicked out and caught Robert. He tumbled over. Marisee fell over him, her knee slamming against the muddy cobbles. Clawed feet clacked down around them, trapping them. Marisee could see the fangs clearly, as long as tree branches, and the teeth spiralling deep down inside.

"A favour for a favour! A favour for a favour!"

The air swelled around them, filled with the smell of coal smoke and burning tallow fat. It was a Fumi!

"I can help you," it said in its screechy Weathervane accent. "I can call on the others. We can tie the winds together and blast it back into the river. We could do it right away!"

That's when Marisee saw the Domedary's eyes. There were four of them, yellow balls mounted on stalks that were uncurling from inside its body.

"We can help you," the Fumi squealed. "But there must be a favour for a favour."

A favour for a favour! A favour for a favour! Why did Fumis always have to demand something in return for help? That's how Marisee and Robert had ended up here!

But there was no help coming from anywhere else! Those teeth. Those eyes. They needed help now or they would die.

"I agr—"

"Shame on you, airheads!" Turnmill Brook strolled out of the darkness towards them.

"Turnmill!" Marisee wheezed. "Thank goodness!"

Was it bad manners to hug a Chad with relief? Even if it wasn't, there was no time. The Fleet Ditch Boar was on one side of Turnmeill Brook, Sally Fleet on the other.

Loops of silver threads crackled around them. "How can you demand a favour when a Solid life is at stake?"

"What do we care about Solid lives?" the Fumi said. "They care nothing for us. A favour must always be paid back with a favour."

There was a rush of dark greasy air and the Fumi disappeared.

A silver thread shot from Turnmill's fingers and looped around one of the Domedary's legs, catching one of the barbs. She pulled it back towards her and the leg started to buckle. Sally Fleet lifted her hands, weaving thin bands of silver into a spiky ball that she hurled into the monster's mouth.

"Such an impresario!" Turnmill muttered.

The Domedary's eyes shot back down into its body and the belly-mouth clapped shut. The Ditch boar charged into another leg, which tried to flip the boar away, but the clawed foot passed straight through the water spirit. Turnmill shot another silver coil towards a rear leg, pulling it tight. The Domedary stumbled. Then it dropped into a crouch and sprang, silver threads trailing behind it.

"We'll distract it!" Turnmill yelled at Marisee. "You all get into the tunnels!"

The Domedary crashed back down again, its legs juddering as it regained its balance.

Marisee's fear turned into power. It was like a storm driving a windmill's sails. She ran so quickly her feet barely touched the cobbles. Soon, she had caught up with Nannerl and Wolfgang. The little boy was stumbling and Marisee could hear him crying. Robert's boots smacked down next to Marisee, a quicker beat that made her run faster, keeping time. Her sides hurt and her chest felt like it was filled with pins.

There it was! The church of St Clement Danes! It looked like a sleeping creature blocking the road, but she could just make out the well, shining with a faint silver-green glow. Marisee darted towards it, struggling to find enough breath to speak.

"Jump in!" Robert shouted. "I don't think they can hold the monster much longer!"

"You want me to jump into a well and die?" Tears were pouring down Nannerl's face again. "These are bad dreams. Please tell me that I will wake soon."

"You must!" Robert said. "The monster's getting ready to leap!"

Turnmill and Sally Fleet were winding silver thread back and forth between its legs in a shimmering web, trying to trap it. The Ditch boar charged again. The Domedary wobbled but didn't fall. Its jointed legs squeezed together like a lady's fan.

Any moment now it would—

"Jump into the well!" Marisee shouted.

"No!" Nannerl shouted back. "I will not send my brother to his death!"

"He won't die," Robert said, climbing on to the well's wall. "I promise you both."

He stepped off the edge.

Nannerl screamed. "He has killed himself!"

"No," Marisee said. "Please, please trust me. I'll explain when you're safe."

The Domedary leaped. Marisee realized with horror that it was going to land bang on top of the well.

"But you won't be safe if you don't jump now!" Marisee shrieked, pointing at the moving beast. Its legs spread, then drew in close to its body.

"Jump or not jump…" Nannerl's voice quivered. "Either way, we may die." She gave Marisee a desperate look. "I don't want to die."

"You won't," Marisee said.

Nannerl gathered her brother in her arms, climbed on to the well wall, closed her eyes and stepped into the empty space.

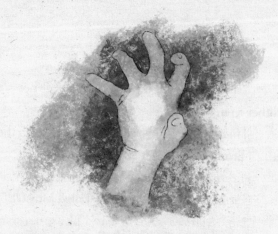

THE NO-MUSIC BOX

Robert's body broke through the green glow and plummeted into the darkness. Should he have stayed to make sure Nannerl and Wolfgang would follow? Had he saved himself and left everyone else to be killed?

And was there even anyone at the bottom of the well to catch him? Turnmill and Sally Fleet were overhead fighting the Domedary.

Madam Blackwell's there. Madam Blackwell will make sure we're safe.

But Madam Blackwell wasn't a Chad water spirit. Even she couldn't jump into the wells if there wasn't a Chad to catch *her*. What if there was no one and he—

Robert landed in a pool of water. He let his tense body relax. He hadn't slammed into hard ground. The surface of the pool was stretched so tight that he gave a little bounce. As the watery skin lowered him, he realized that it wasn't just a pool; it was Chads joined together, their linked hands raised. They weren't quite solid, weren't quite water.

There was a shriek. Nannerl and her little brother tumbled on to the bouncy water and were tipped on to the well floor.

And Marisee? Where was she?

Here she was! She plunged down the shaft, surrounded in a watery mist that sparked with silver. As she landed, the Chads lowered their arms and blended together into a stream that spun around the walls of the well, keeping the ground dry. Nannerl and Wolfgang huddled together, wide-eyed, mouths open. Robert felt sorry for them. The first time he'd jumped into a well it had felt like his body had been turned inside out.

The mist around Marisee stretched and split away from her, shaping itself into Turnmill Brook and Sally Fleet. Wolfgang gave a little cry and buried his face in his sister's shoulder.

"So we *are* dead," Nannerl said, shaking her head.

"That's what he thought the first time," Turnmill

said, nodding towards Robert, "but as you can see, he's still very much alive."

Robert stood up and brushed himself down. There was a crack overhead and a section of the well wall landed by Robert's feet, the bricks flying apart around him.

"If you want to stay alive, you'd better move further into the tunnels," Turnmill Brook said. "Little ones!" she called. "Thank you for your help! You can go home now."

For a moment, the only sound was the Chads still circling the well wall, then a *whoosh* as they rose into a wave that slammed against Robert, washing him and the others further into the tunnel. He gasped as his nose and mouth filled with water. Then the stream flowed past him and away. He was certain that he saw the flap of a lawyer's black coat and the pale curls of a judge's wig in the shimmer of the stream before it disappeared out of sight.

"They're the Lincoln's Inn Chads," Turnmill said. "Keep the wells flowing for the law students."

The Domedary's cry echoed from above, followed by the thud of more tumbling bricks. An orange leg and claw-tipped foot scraped its way down the inside of the well wall.

"Oh, no, no, no!" Turnmill cried.

Marisee looked towards the well mouth. "Effra

said it had no mercy. It could do this to every well in London."

The Domedary's foot swung from side to side, digging between the mortar, loosening bricks. They spilled into the well in a cloud of dust.

"To the whole of London," Robert said.

If they returned to the surface, there might be nothing left. They had to find a way to fight this thing!

Nannerl was already on her feet, her arms around Wolfgang's shoulders, hurrying him along. Marisee stared up at the destruction. Robert didn't move.

Madam Blackwell appeared from the further down the tunnel. "We won't let this beast win," she said. "We will stop it."

The Domedary bashed the wall so hard the whole well shook.

"But how, Grandma?" Marisee cried. "How?"

More chunks of bricks and sand fell around them.

"We are the Keepers of London's Wells," Madam Blackwell said, firmly. "We will find a way."

Robert followed Marisee as she guided Nannerl and Wolfgang around the jutting foundations of old buildings and through the dip of ancient channels that criss-crossed the tunnel. Robert knew that Nannerl would be full of questions. He remembered his own confusion when he found out about London's elemental world. Every answer just led to more questions.

"Are we in heaven?" Wolfgang whispered.

"It certainly is not heaven," Nannerl said. "There would not be monsters like that in heaven." She jerked her thumb upwards. "And in heaven, I think we would be made of music, not searching for it."

"Then we are ... we are..." Wolfgang's voice caught. "In the other place?"

"No." Nannerl squeezed Wolfgang's shoulders. "We are certainly not there either."

Wolfgang touched a broken wooden strut sticking out from the tunnel wall. "So where are we?"

Marisee pointed to Madam Blackwell, who was striding ahead. "That's my grandmother," she said. "Her full name is Madam Mary-Ay Blackwell and she's the Keeper of London's Wells. We have our own well in Clerkenwell that cures eye sickness." Marisee sounded very proud. "But Grandma has to make sure that all of London's wells are full of good water."

"How?" Nannerl asked. "Is she a scientist?"

"By taking care of the Chads, London's water spirits," Marisee said simply.

Nannerl glanced back at Turnmill and Sally Fleet, then at Marisee. "Is that what they are?"

"Yes," Marisee said. "They care for the rivers and streams."

Nannerl seemed to be taking this more calmly than Robert expected. Though, she *had* been chased by a river monster, owned a magical music box and jumped in a well and lived. Perhaps it made it easier to believe in water spirits.

"And if there are water spirits?" Nannerl said. "Are there other spirits too?"

"There are four Elemental London spirits," Marisee said. "The fire spirits are Dragons."

"Dragons!" Nannerl and Wolfgang said together.

"But not like you'd imagine," Marisee said. "They're very, very small."

Though sometimes they can be very big and threaten to eat you, Robert thought. But he kept that to himself.

"That is water and fire," Nannerl said. "What are the other two?"

"The earth elementals are called Magogs," Marisee said. "They keep themselves to themselves, except when…"

Except when the statues talk to me, Robert finished in his head. "We think the Domedary – that

315

monster – guards the Magogs," he said out loud. "They're two giants sleeping at the bottom of the Thames."

"Giants sleeping at the bottom of the Thames," Wolfgang said. "Are there giants in the Salzach?"

"I hope not," Nannerl said.

"Oh." Wolfgang sounded a little disappointed.

"The Fumis are the airheads." Turnmill had caught up with them. She made her voice screechy. "A favour for a favour! A favour for a favour! They're more ruthless dealmakers than the Dragons."

"I wonder if we have spirits like this in Salzburg," Nannerl said.

Wolfgang smiled. "I hope that we do."

They surfaced in the crypt of St Bartholomew's church. Nannerl jumped when she saw the pile of bones.

"Old monks," Turnmill said. "All bones, no ghost."

"Stay away," Nannerl said, but Wolfgang ran over to them, picked up a thigh bone and held it to his eyes.

Nannerl sighed.

Robert hung back in the tunnel, sickness churning his stomach. This was where he'd betrayed his friends, where he'd nearly died. He felt an arm around his shoulders. It was Madam Blackwell.

"Forget the past," she said. "Use your wonderful brain to help us find a way to save London again."

Robert gave her a little smile and nodded.

"You should be safe here for the moment," Turnmill said. "I'm going to find the boar. Sally will keep guard here."

Sally Fleet smiled and settled herself against the wall.

"Tell me everything that happened," Madam Blackwell said.

"Mr Dross took Wolfgang," Marisee said. "To compose music for his choir of automata heads to sing to the Domedary."

"My brother was bored," Nannerl said testily. "Mama was tending Papa. I was gone. Mr Dross left his card with our landlady. How could Wolfgang resist a chance to have his music back?"

Over in the corner, Wolfgang had laid out bones of different lengths and was tapping them and listening. He picked up a thin, very old-looking bone and blew through it. Dust sprayed out of the end. Nannerl went over to him and snatched it from his hand. She spoke to him crossly in German.

"The Dross man knows that music soothes the monster?" Madam Blackwell asked.

Robert nodded. "But he also knows what wakes it up."

"Does he now?" Madam Blackwell said. "What is it?"

Wolfgang picked up the bone again.

Marisee held out the music box.

"It's something to do with that," Marisee said. "But I don't understand what."

An odd tooting sound came from Wolfgang. He was blowing into the hollow bone, his finger half-covering the end of it. He grinned back at Nannerl. "It is like a flute," he said. "I wish it was magic and could soothe the monster too."

Nannerl took the music box. "We go from city to city, lodging house to lodging house," she said, "and I wanted to bring something with me that reminded me of home. I wrapped it up so carefully, and I didn't take it out until we arrived in London. Then Wolfgang opened it and—"

"I did not!" Wolfgang said. "I didn't touch your music box."

"You must have!" Nannerl said. "I found it open."

"It was not me," Wolfgang said. "And that is not a *music* box. You and I make music. That box made sounds." He blew another note through the bone.

"Well," Nannerl said, glaring at her brother, "the *music* box was broken and it wasn't me!"

"So you found it open," Robert cut in. "And neither of you had opened it."

"Perhaps Mama did," Nannerl said. "I don't know. I suppose I didn't wrap it carefully enough because it would no longer play."

"And that's when you started shouting," Wolfgang said.

"Because it is precious to me," Nannerl said quietly.

Wolfgang adjusted his finger on the hollow end of the bone and played a different note.

"D Major?" A smile crept across Nannerl's face. "Wolfgang! Is the music coming back?"

"Yes!" Wolfgang shouted.

Nannerl hummed a couple of notes. "It is!"

The music box jolted open. There was a rush of air and a smell of river water, brewery malt and fried chicken. The tiny ballerina that was lying inside flew out like a firework, red velvet lining swirling around her like a cloak. Wolfgang shrieked as an invisible hand seemed to knock the bone from his fingers. It shattered as it fell.

The music box lid dropped shut again. They all stared at it. Then Nannerl tipped it from her hand. Madam Blackwell caught it just before it hit the floor. It made Robert think of Turpin and Duval. He hoped they were safe.

"What..." Nannerl's jaw worked. The words struggled to come out. "My music box really is magic?"

"I don't think the music box is," Robert said. "I think there's something magic inside it, something we can't see. Did you feel that breeze? And the smell…"

"I smelled home," Wolfgang said. "Our real home in Salzburg."

"It must be some type of air spirit," Madam Blackwell said. "But not a London one. A local Fumi wouldn't hide in a music box. They hate being trapped and they certainly don't smell of chicken and beer."

"I don't think it's trapped," Robert said. "It can come in and out when it wants."

"True," Madam Blackwell said. "It leaves to take the music, but goodness knows what it does with it when it finds some. Or why it's even doing it. Though I think you were right all along, Robert." She gave an embarrassed smile. "It had no idea of the consequences. Waking the Domedary was an accident."

Robert bit back his smile. He *had* thought that Madam Blackwell had waved away his earlier suggestion too quickly.

"I still don't understand," Nannerl said. "The music has been taken from places where I have not been. How can it do that?"

"If it *is* a type of Fumi," Madam Blackwell said, "and I'm almost certain that it is, then it can become part of the air itself. My grandma told me that before London's air was so dirty, Fumis could shrink into a tight, thin band and shoot across the skies. Now they're too heavy with smoke and tallow grease. Our friend in here" – she tapped the box – "must be lighter and freer. And" – she gave it a harder tap – "not very discerning. It's taken all types of music from across London, even from the bones of old monks."

"And if it keeps taking music, the Domedary will keep coming for it," Marisee said. "That's what Effra said. It will track down what has awakened it."

Robert nodded. "And the more music it steals, the easier it is for the Domedary to sense…" To sense what?

"Its magical pull," Madam Blackwell said certainly.

"And now the Domedary's strong enough to come and find it," Marisee added.

Nannerl made a snorting noise and plucked the music box from Madam Blackwell's hand. Madam Blackwell gave her a look but stayed quiet.

"You say there's a magic air spirit in my music box?" Nannerl said. "Let me see."

Her finger flicked the lid. Madam Blackwell's hand banged down on Nannerl's, startling her.

"Let's not disturb it," Madam Blackwell said. "It's done enough damage."

"Yes, it has," Wolfgang said angrily. "It's your fault that the music has gone. You and your sound box!"

Nannerl stormed up to him. "You cannot blame me for something that I did not know!"

Madam Blackwell strode over and stood between them. "Stop it!" she said. "Both of you. It's nobody's fault. Somehow an air spirit has snuck away in your music box and it's taking the music…"

A bellow echoed through the streets beyond the crypt.

"And if the Domedary is following the magic," Robert said, "it's on its way here right now."

They all waited, listening. Its furious cry was closer now.

"It won't give up, will it?" Nannerl said, thrusting the music box towards Madam Blackwell. "If this is what it wants, give it to it!"

Madam Blackwell didn't take it. "Not if there's an air spirit inside. And we don't know if that will stop the monster anyway. It's well and truly awake now. We need to get the music back. But how?"

Robert suddenly remembered that there was more to tell. "We talked to the Dragon in the church on Cheapside," he said.

"That was very brave of you," Madam Blackwell said.

Robert felt a momentary glow of pride. He still wasn't used to praise.

"She said that the Thames is swollen," he explained. "Does that mean that the Domedary has woken the Magogs?"

"No," Madam Blackwell said. "If a Magog eyelid as much as twitches, we'd know about it. They have their spies, but we have ours too."

"Mr Cecil and Daisy?" Robert asked.

"And others like them," Madam Blackwell said. "Effra keeps eight eyes on things from across the river. And the Thames *is* full of poison from all the rubbish we throw into it. It barely has a life of its own."

"The Dragon said something else," Robert said. "A wind's blowing a ship towards London from the east. It's moving quicker than any ship that the Dragon's seen before."

"Moving quicker? That must mean a magic ship," Grandma said. "There is absolutely no reason for any magic ships to come to London. It can't be a coincidence. Who knows what extra trouble it's bringing?" She glared at the music box. "As if a rampaging chaos monster isn't enough."

Sally Fleet jumped up from her seat by the wall. "They're coming back, Madam Blackwell!"

She'd been so quiet that Robert had forgotten about

her. Silver threads crackled around her then wriggled, shaping themselves into a circle. The ground inside the circle disappeared. A hand reached up, then another, grabbing at the edges of the hole. Robert saw a tumble of braids held together with a shard of pottery.

"I'm too old for this," Turnmill said, as she clambered into the crypt. "Madam Blackwell, can you ask the Lord Mayor for a pipe so next time I can just flow in here?"

There was a snort below her and the Fleet Ditch boar leaped out. Wolfgang gave a little scream and ran over to Nannerl, hiding behind her back. The Ditch boar made a sound like a laugh and trotted over to Sally Fleet. She clicked her fingers and the door in the ground disappeared.

"Definitely an impresario," Turnmill said.

"Is the Domedary close?" Madam Blackwell asked.

"No," Turnmill said, "it's heading back to the Thames."

Marisee breathed out in relief. "That's good, isn't it?"

Turnmill's eyes met Madam Blackwell's.

"No," Madam Blackwell said. "It isn't, honey. The Domedary guards the Magogs. If it's returning to the Thames, that magical wind must be bringing a very dangerous ship indeed."

THE BOY WHO IS
BARELY THERE

Robert's thoughts were fighting each other. He wanted to stop the Domedary and whatever peril the ship was bringing, but even if he succeeded, what would change for *him*? Haakon, the capture-creature, would still be hunting him down. Or Steeple, or Benjamin, or others would still read the notices in the coffee houses and try to seize him in the street and claim their reward. Robert could stop London from being destroyed over and over again, but in the eyes of the law, he would always belong to Lord Pritchard or whoever Lord Pritchard chose to "sell" him to.

Robert's thoughts faded away and he felt like he was sinking into a heavy, warm blanket. He could smell old leather boot soles and the wet clay of secret tunnels. Sally Fleet was standing next to him. She touched his hand, leaving a silver mark that tingled then disappeared.

"Are you sad?" she asked. "We're all here to help you, Robert Strong. We'll never let anyone take you."

Robert gave her a little smile. In some ways, she was very old. Her human life had been filled with tragedy that had made her serious and wise. But in other ways, she was like a young girl. She believed what she was saying, but she was wrong. Above ground, he could never be free.

"That's settled," Madam Blackwell said. She jammed her hat on her head and crouched down to tighten the buckle on her boot.

"What's settled?" Robert asked.

Marisee looked sheepish. "Grandma and I are going to talk to the Panyer Boy." She saw Robert's confused look. "Don't you remember? Henry told us about him. He's supposed to know everything about London's ancient history. If that's true, he can tell us if there's another way to stop the Domedary."

"I'm coming too," Robert said.

How could they expect him to wait here doing nothing while everyone he knew and cared about was in danger?

Madam Blackwell shook her head. "It's not safe for you, Robert."

"It's not safe for you either, Madam Blackwell," Robert said.

"I know that," Madam Blackwell said. "But I would rather risk my freedom than yours." She blinked and rubbed her eyes. "Oh," she said. "Not now!"

The whole floor shone with silver, filling the crypt with dazzling flecks that made Robert's eyes sting. He blinked hard. When they'd cleared, Lady Walbrook was standing in front of them.

Robert stepped back from her. Lady Walbrook, the Chad riverhead, reminded Robert of an ancient statue that had come alive. Her skin was pale and Robert imagined strong currents pushing just beneath its surface. Her tunic was the same colour as her skin, flickering between grey, silver and brown. Her brow was wide and high, her nose bridge nicked, like chipped china. Her hair was sculpted into plaits that curled across the top of her head.

But it was Lady Walbrook's mouth that Robert watched. It was thin and turned down, but when it opened, she spat silver threads that looped around her prey. They stung human skin, but it was worse for Chads. The threads made them dissolve into dark, lifeless sand.

Her pale eyes glanced around the crypt and settled on Madam Blackwell. "You are summoned to the Court," she said. Her voice seemed to shift like the colours in her skin. Robert thought of ghostly bells pealing far beneath an old river.

Madam Blackwell raised her eyebrows. "Summoned?"

"You are the Well Keeper, are you not?" A silver streak glimmered across Lady Walbrook's cheeks, then faded. "It is your duty to protect us, Madam Blackwell. A well was smashed near Lincoln's Inn. The smaller streams have been flooded by the surge from Thames Rex. The Domedary prowls and is bent on destruction. So yes, Well Keeper, you are summoned." She cast a cool look at Turnmill, Sally Blake and the Fleet Ditch boar. "You will come too."

Madam Blackwell raised a hand in the air. "No, Lady Walbrook, I don't think—"

The floor shimmered silver again. Robert closed his eyes. When he opened them, Madam Blackwell and the Chads were gone.

Wolfgang scraped his foot along the floor where the silver had been. "London was not like this last time we came," he said.

Nannerl gave him a sharp look. "Perhaps it was. We just never noticed." She looked between Robert and Marisee. "So what do we do now?"

"I think you and Wolfgang should—" Marisee said.

"Come with you," Nannerl finished. "We are not staying in this cold … bony place. And it was me who brought the music box. It is me that should help fix it."

"Music box?" Wolfgang muttered. "Sound box, I say."

"Do you know where to find the Panyer Boy?" Robert asked. "Because I'm definitely coming with you."

Marisee gave him a little smile. "I think Panyer Alley would be a good place to start looking."

Robert trailed behind the others as they climbed the steps up from the crypt and passed through a passageway between two crooked cottages on to the street. According to Marisee, Panyer Alley was close to St Paul's Cathedral, so not too far. That didn't matter. As soon as Robert stepped on to the street, he was prey. He glanced up at the old St Bartholomew's gatehouse. He couldn't see anyone in there, but what if Haakon was lurking in the shadows, watching him? It would only take a few seconds for the capture-creature to seize him.

The houses beyond the gatehouse were tall and old.

Robert could smell the reek of dung and hear the croaky baas of sheep. Smithfield Market was close by, Newgate Prison too. The Red Guard Gang had often talked about the processions of condemned prisoners taken from the prison by cart to hang at the gallows in Tyburn.

"This is Giltspur Street," Marisee said. "We turn left at the end." She and the others hurried ahead.

"That little girl thinks she knows it all!" a high sing-song voice came from above Robert.

They were passing the Fortune of War tavern. Robert looked up towards the windows. He could see no humans, but a statue of a golden cherub was fixed to the wall. Robert stared at it. Its golden eyes stared back. It shook its wings and they clicked like scales.

"But *I* see you." The cherub giggled. "And I see what the wind blows into London. They're coming quickly. They want what's theirs."

Then it was perfectly still, staring over Robert's head as if it had never moved.

"Come on, Robert!" Marisee called back.

He ran on, glancing back at the cherub. It *had* spoken. "I see you." That's what the statue of the king had said to Robert when it stepped down from the steeple of St George's church, Bloomsbury, during the enchanted sleep. Did the statues only speak to him?

He would have to tell Marisee as soon as he had a chance. He caught up with the others; they'd paused at a junction by a church.

"Something just happ—" he started.

"Left here!" Marisee shouted and ran across the road, the others following.

Wolfgang stopped so suddenly that Robert bumped into him.

"Music!" Wolfgang looked towards the church. "A beautiful organ."

It did sound beautiful, but it only lasted for a very short moment. There was a rush of air, the smell of fried chicken and mashed malt, followed by a strange honking and wailing. The church door flew open and metal pipes tore through the air, clattering on to the road.

Wolfgang shook his head in shock. "The organ went..." He waved his hands.

"Exploded?" Robert asked.

Wolfgang nodded. "Bang." He glowered at Nannerl. "It's your sound box destroying everything. We should just throw it into the river for the monster to find."

"Didn't you hear my grandma?" Marisee said. "We can't do that because there's something inside it."

"Something that's causing us trouble," Wolfgang muttered. "Why should we care what happens to it?"

331

Robert had been thinking the same, especially if it was a Fumi. The air spirits may have rescued Robert from the capture-creature at Gripe's shop, but it was a favour with a high price.

"We should at least open the box and have another look inside," Robert said. "Now we know more about it. It might help us."

"We've looked already," Marisee said, impatiently. "We have to get to the Panyer Boy while the Domedary's distracted."

They hurried through a dank archway.

"What is this place?" Nannerl asked.

"It's Newgate Prison," Robert said.

It's like the Tower of London, Robert thought, *full of despair and fear threaded through with something else – fury.* He made himself breathe deeply. There was no taint of spoiled meat and ancient dust. No Haakon.

Still, he ran through the archway, looking neither right nor left. A flutter of wings made him look up towards the high prison wall. At first he thought it was the soot-covered statue of a bird. Then he realized that a raven was perched there. It cawed loudly then flew away.

Marisee had seen it as well. "The Goldsmith's spies," she said. "We have to be quick. Remember, we have to report back to him by sunset."

They ran along Newgate Street, Nannerl pulling Wolfgang behind her.

"This way!" Marisee puffed, turning into another alleyway.

Robert could see the dome of St Paul's ahead. He wondered if the Fumis were floating nearby watching them. He suspected they were. There was a restlessness to the air and the smoke from nearby chimneys wavered in a way that did not match the breeze. He wanted to shout out at them. *You asked us to do this, but you won't help us!*

"This must be it." Marisee was standing in front of a small stone pedestal. Above it, was a tablet with writing, then above that a carving of a small boy sitting astride what looked like a basket. The boy's hair was as curly as Robert's own. His face was worn down as if a giant thumb had smudged his nose and chin together.

Robert's mouth formed the sounds of the letters on the tablet. He still felt that joy; those strange scribbles that had seemed impossible to understand for so long now had meaning. His mother had warned him against learning to read and write. The plantation owners forbade people like Robert from learning.

"'When ye have sought the city round,'" he read, "'then still this is the highest ground.' What does that mean?"

Marisee sighed. "Another riddle…"

"No, it is advice," Nannerl said. "It means that you may look everywhere, but what you need is here in front of you."

"*I* think that it means there will be a flood," Wolfgang said. "And we must stay here. It is safest."

"How can we know what it means?" Marisee said loudly, staring at the stone carving. "Unless the Panyer Boy tells us himself. Will you help us?"

The figure didn't move.

"Are you sure this is the Panyer Boy?" Nannerl said. "Perhaps we should look for a real boy."

It's a statue, Robert thought. If it was true ... if he was the one that statues talked to, would the Panyer Boy answer him?

"Can you help?" Robert said quietly.

"Now that *you* ask, I will." The voice was like the rubbing of two stones together, but the carving didn't move. "But you must tell me something I *don't* know, Robert Strong."

"It talked!" Wolfgang said. He poked the Panyer Boy's arm.

"Ouch!" it shrieked.

Wolfgang jumped back.

"And I am not 'it'," it said. "I am 'he'. Please be polite enough to get that right."

Wolfgang hung his head. "Sorry."

"So everyone can hear you," Robert said. "Not just me."

"You're not *that* special," the Panyer Boy said. "Why would I want only you to hear my wisdom?"

This was one statue that Robert was beginning to wish he *couldn't* hear. Another thought struck him. "How do you know my name?"

The Panyer Boy sighed. A small cloud of dust puffed around his mouth. "I wouldn't be wise if I didn't, would I?"

"Please," Nannerl said. "Hurry and ask him your questions!"

"Um … Mr Panyer," Robert said, "if you know everything…"

"Nearly everything," the Panyer Boy interrupted. "There's always more to know. My basket of knowledge needs constant filling."

The monster bellowed in the distance.

"Oooh. That river monster is ready to fight." The Panyer Boy snickered.

"Fight what?" Marisee said. "Why isn't it still hunting for Nannerl's music box?"

The Panyer Boy was silent.

"You heard her?" Robert asked. "Can you answer?"

335

"No answers until you fill my basket of knowledge," the Panyer Boy said. "Tell me something I don't know."

"Who knows what he doesn't know?" Marisee yelled. "This is taking too long!"

"My name is Wolfgang Mozart!" Wolfgang announced. "I am…"

"Yes!" Robert said, eagerly. "And he's called a child genius."

"Of course I know that," the Panyer Boy said. "And his sister, Marie-Anna, also known as Nannerl, is even better than him."

Wolfgang gasped. Nannerl smiled widely.

"Your *sound* box still woke up the monster," Wolfgang muttered.

"It didn't," she muttered back.

"All the chatter is about the Mozarts," the Panyer Boy said. "People forget that I have ears. Try harder than that or we'll be here all day. Except that you haven't got all day. A ship blew past Tilbury Fort yesterday. It was so fast that those poor soldier boys didn't even have time to load their cannon." The Panyer Boy giggled. "And I'm giving you that for free."

Dust blew up around the pedestal in a whirl of grey and black smoke that stank of boiled animal fat and smouldering coal. A dark shape emerged. Its body was long and thin, its head square, circled with white smoke. It was one of the Council of Fumi Elders.

"Favour not repaid!" it squealed. "Favour not repaid!"

"It will be!" Marisee cried. "We haven't finished…"

"Favour not repaid! Favour not paid! You brought more danger! You brought more danger!"

"No!" Robert shouted. "That's not fair! This isn't our fault! We need a little more time to find the music. We know what happened. We just need to—"

"No more time!" it screeched. "You brought danger! Monster danger. Dragon danger. Outside danger from across the seas. What hunts you is close, Robert Strong. It is close." There was a short, cold blast of wind. "And now your scent blows towards it. It knows where you are."

The Fumi tightened into a coil then sprang open, lengthening into patches of floating smoke that suddenly disappeared.

Robert's body tensed; he was ready to run. He made himself sniff the air. *Was* Haakon close? He couldn't smell him. He had time to escape. There must be a well nearby.

But he couldn't leave yet. If he went, the Panyer Boy would not answer anyone else.

Robert stood squarely in front of the Panyer Boy. "Help us," he ordered.

"I will," the Panyer Boy said. "*When* you tell me something I don't know."

"Robert, you *must* know things that he doesn't," Marisee said. "Think!"

The Panyer Boy chuckled, but Marisee was right. Robert had been born far away from London. There must be so much about Barbados that the statue boy had never heard about. The problem was that there was so little that Robert wanted to remember.

"I have something," he said. "Hot chocolate comes from the seeds of the—"

The Panyer Boy chuckled louder. "The cocoa tree sometimes called cacao sometimes called the fruit of the gods. I can even furnish you with many recipes should you wish. The chocolate houses brew to different tastes but I have heard many. But do you have time to hear them?"

"No!" Nannerl cried. "We do not!"

There was a puff of dust from the pedestal. "The ship has reached its destination. The river monster's waiting for it. A battle will soon begin. The fighters are taking their places."

Robert heard the soft jangle of thousands of glass spikes. Five shard beasts raced past Robert, heading south towards the river.

"They go to protect the Magogs, their masters," the

Panyer Boy said. "But I am bored now. If you don't have knowledge, I'll return to my rest."

"Robert!" Marisee's voice was desperate. "Think of something!"

"I... I..." What could he remember? There must be something the Panyer Boy didn't know yet! Yes, there was! Even if Robert couldn't remember who told him the tale, he could remember the tale itself.

"My home country has water spirits too," Robert said. "Their queen is Mami Wata."

This time the Panyer Boy's face moved as his eyes widened into pebble-shapes. "Tell me more."

Robert opened his mouth, but Marisee nudged him aside. "No," she said. "Robert has done what you asked. You didn't know that. Now answer our questions before it's too late."

"Yes!" Robert said. "Answer our questions!"

The Panyer Boy sighed. "Ask me, then."

"Who's on the ship?" No! That wasn't what Robert meant to ask! He wanted to know how to stop the Domedary! But the Panyer Boy was already answering.

"An empress," he said in his grating voice. "She and the Sail Bloaters that have brought her here. They come for what has taken the music."

"Sail Bloaters?" Robert said. "Like Fumis?"

"Hapsburg Fumis. A little breeze told me that they've sent their top warriors." The Panyer Boy giggled. "Jaws built to huff and puff and blow a city down."

Nannerl took out the music box and stared at it. "All for this. Surely that's a good thing. London's music will not be taken any longer."

"But how long before the Domedary is soothed back to sleep?" Marisee said.

"If there's no more knowledge for me, there's no more answers for you," the Panyer Boy said. "So on that *note*, I will leave you." His eyes became shallow marks in the stone again.

"Wait," Robert said. "Can we stop the Domedary without music?"

"Tell me something I don't—"

"Mami Wata has the tail of a big fish and a snake coiled around her neck," Robert said, quickly.

The Panyer Boy opened his pebbly eyes again.

"Tell us how to make the Domedary sleep," Robert demanded.

The Panyer Boy gave a satisfied grunt. "Soothe it back to sleep with music. That's the only way."

"But Mr Dross has the only music!" Marisee cried.

A wind blew along the alleyway. Airy hands burst out of it and pushed Robert aside. He thought he saw a

Fumi, but the top of its head narrowed to a point and its jaw was large and square.

"Nannerl!" Wolfgang cried.

But his sister had been scooped into the air and was being borne away.

TRAPPED

Marisee should have moved quickly. She should have grabbed Nannerl when she'd felt that air blast down the alley and seen those murky hands shove Robert away. They should have run then, but they'd lingered. Now Nannerl was gone. The thing that had taken her looked like a Fumi, but not a London one. It must be one of the Hapsburg Fumis that the Panyer Boy mentioned.

"Please," Marisee whispered into the air. "Whatever you are, keep her safe."

"My sister," Wolfgang sobbed. "Where is she?"

Robert put an arm around the boy. "If they've

come for the music box," Robert said, "they'll take her to the empress. We'll find her ship." He looked at Marisee. "Won't we?"

"Yes." Marisee had to pull herself out of her despair. "We will."

There was the sound of beating wings. Marisee turned to see ravens, wing tip to wing tip, blocking the northern end of the alley, their small, hard eyes staring at her. Their beaks opened and they cawed, a harsh chorus like nails on stone.

"Will you?" the Goldsmith said. "I think not."

He was mounted on his horse behind them, the firebird clamped to his wrist. The Lord Mayor was on horseback next to him. He didn't look fully comfortable in the saddle.

"But it's not sunset!" Marisee said. "We've still got time!"

"You have done nothing but enrage the river beast," the Goldsmith said. "You have brought our city to near ruin." He looked towards the Lord Mayor. "We cannot allow them more time, can we?"

"No," the Lord Mayor said. "We can't."

Marisee was outraged. "But you thought the monster was a puppet, Lord Mayor! How come you believe that it's real now?"

The Lord Mayor looked confused. "Because…"

"Because the Lord Mayor accepts that I did not wish to spread terror across London before the facts were fully confirmed," the Goldsmith said smoothly.

"Exactly," the Lord Mayor said. "And Edward here…" He waved a gloved hand towards the Goldsmith. "Edward tells me that you know…" He half-swallowed the word "magic". "And summoned this fiend to destroy London. I will leave your punishment in Edward's hands." His horse whinnied and shook its head. "Are we nearly finished here, Edward?"

"Yes, sir." The Goldsmith gave them a satisfied smile. "With your permission, Lord Mayor, I will arrest the girl for plotting with her grandmother and those river Chads to rouse the monster and hold our city to ransom."

"If you say so," the Lord Mayor said.

"No, Lord Mayor!" Marisee was struggling to hold back her fury. "The Goldsmith didn't really want us to find out what had taken the music. He wanted us to blame the Fumis for the Domedary rising, so that the Dragons would punish them like they did the Squall's friend. Now he's trying to blame the Chads and make sure that there's no Well Keeper to protect them. He wants the Dragons to have all the power and…"

344

But the Lord Mayor wasn't even interested enough to look at Marisee.

The Goldsmith smirked at them. "And the runaway Pritchard boy will be returned to his owner," he said, as if Marisee hadn't spoken at all.

"Owner"? Now Marisee's fury did bubble over. No one owned Robert! No one should own anyone! She opened her mouth to shout it, but a man's voice boomed from the other end of Panyer Alley.

"And I am here to collect him, Lord Mayor!"

It was the same man who'd come for Robert at Grandma's house. The younger man next to him must be Benjamin, Lord Hibbert's groom.

The Domedary bellowed. They all looked towards the river.

"We have to stop it!" Marisee said. "People will be hurt!"

"No one will be hurt," the Goldsmith said. "Well, no one important. Our army and navy are the best in the world. They will kill the beast."

Steeple had thought the same. He'd been very wrong.

The Goldsmith gave Marisee another smirk. "And, of course, the Fumis will be punished for their role in inciting this beast."

"But they didn't…" Marisee started.

"They can blow music away," the Goldsmith said. "Can you honestly tell me that it wasn't the work of a Fumi?"

"It was, but…"

"There you have it," the Goldsmith said with certainty.

Why wouldn't he let Marisee talk? Why wouldn't the Lord Mayor listen? He was rearranging his gold chain to best catch the sunlight.

"And you and your grandmother," the Goldsmith continued, "have harboured a runaway. That is bad enough. But you are supposed to tend the rivers, and to know their secrets. I cannot believe that they didn't know that the Thames beast had woken."

He raised an eyebrow at Marisee. She stayed silent. Effra had known, but not long before the attack. She couldn't tell the Goldsmith or he'd twist everything that she said.

"All *I* want is my boy," Lord Pritchard said loudly, moving closer. "Undamaged if at all possible."

"You heard him, boy," the Goldsmith said. "Robert Pritchard, go to your master. Master Mozart, come this way. Queen Charlotte is most concerned about your welfare."

"My sister…" Wolfgang's voice shook. "I want my sister!"

"Yes," the Lord Mayor said. "Shouldn't you – we – try to save the girl?"

The Goldsmith grasped his reins tighter as his horse stamped and neighed. "The loss of Maria Anna Mozart is a tragic accident, but you will be a hero, Lord Mayor, for rescuing the prodigy from these felons."

"Of course," the Lord Mayor said. "A hero."

The Goldsmith raised his hands. The ravens rose in the air and settled closer to Marisee, Robert and Wolfgang. Marisee glanced behind her. Pritchard and Benjamin were moving closer too. There was nowhere to run in this narrow alley. She stared at the ground. If only a silver circle could appear and she could sink through. The ground remained muddy cobbles.

"Master Mozart," the Goldsmith said. "Walk towards me."

Wolfgang shook his head. "I want Nannerl."

"I am sorry about your sister," the Goldsmith said. "But wouldn't it be so painful for your mother and father if both of you came to harm?"

Wolfgang folded his arms. "I am not coming unless Nannerl is with me."

"That is not possible," the Goldsmith said. Marisee heard the anger beneath his words. "Is that not so, Lord Mayor?"

"It is not," the Lord Mayor said. "The loss of your sister is a tragic accident, but I've saved you from these felons and I will be a her—" He coughed when the Goldsmith glared at him.

"I am not coming with you!" Wolfgang backed away from the Lord Mayor, shoving himself between Marisee and Robert. "I am going to find Nannerl!"

"I'm afraid that you have no choice in the matter," the Goldsmith said.

He tapped his horse's flank with his boots. The horse took a step forward and stopped, its head cocked sideways as if listening to someone.

The Goldsmith pulled at the reins. "Move, beast!"

The horse lifted its leg then planted its hoof exactly where it had been before.

"Devil animal!" Lord Pritchard shouted from the other end of Panyer Alley.

As Lord Pritchard's horse bucked, he threw himself out of the saddle on to the ground, cursing loudly. Benjamin was clinging to his own halter as his horse tossed its head, trying to break free.

"Stop it, horse!" the Lord Mayor shrieked.

His horse reared, pivoting round on its hind legs. The Lord Mayor slid off the back and thumped on to the cobbles. Marisee supposed that his many layers of fine clothes would save him from serious injury.

The horses all calmed at the same time, nodding their heads towards St Paul's. Marisee knew why and smiled to herself. There must be a certain river spirit over by the chapterhouse using her skills in London Horse language. Turnmill would really have to teach Marisee how to talk to horses soon – it was very useful.

But not useful enough to save them now. The ravens were still surrounding them. Lord Pritchard and Benjamin were walking forward, hands on the hilts of their swords, grins on their faces. Marisee hoped that Turnmill had planned more to their rescue than whispering to the horses.

"There's nowhere for you to run," the Goldsmith said, approaching from the other end of the alley.

He flung his arm out. Thousands of tiny black and orange creatures cascaded down his sleeves on to the ground. More minute creatures joined the dark stream, hard flecks of burning orange and black spilling from the gaps between the cobbles, and the cracks in the wall.

"Dragon!" Marisee mouthed to Robert.

Benjamin gasped. "What the—"

"Ignore it!" Lord Pritchard barked. "This is not our business. The boy is. Take the boy."

Benjamin shook his head. "What use is six guineas if I don't live long enough to spend it?"

He jumped on his horse and galloped away.

"Marisee," Robert said, quietly, "how do we fight a real Dragon?"

It was still forming, but Marisee could already feel its heat and the air was heavy with its rancid smell.

"A Dragon?" Wolfgang said, eyes wide. "A real Dragon?"

The tiny creatures were locking into place like scales, the edges darker than the centre. The hazy shape became clearer – the arrowhead tail, the nubs along its ridged back, the heavy long snout.

"It won't hurt *you*, Master Mozart," the Goldsmith said, "*if* you're a good boy. But as Miss Blackwell and Master Pritchard know, Dragons do have a taste for human flesh."

Wolfgang whimpered and took a step towards the Goldsmith.

"Good boy," the Goldsmith said.

"And you!" Lord Pritchard made a grab for Robert. "You're mine!"

Robert dodged away, but Lord Pritchard just laughed. "Where will you go, boy? You're between the devil…" He nodded towards the Dragon. "And the deep blue sea. Or at least, my ship on the deep blue sea."

"I'd rather take the devil," Robert said.

The Dragon's body was nearly complete, hazy around the edges as the last creatures snapped in place. It was small, the size of a sheep, but as it opened its mouth, it revealed rows of dagger-like teeth. Its wings were pressed against its back, ready to spring open.

"Very impressive," Lord Pritchard said. "I heard rumours that the City had some *special* protections. You are truly a man of business, Goldsmith." He cast a thumb towards Robert. "And I have a lucrative line of business that may be of interest to you."

"Certainly, Lord Pritchard," the Goldsmith said. "We will speak when this wretched affair is over. Now claim your boy. And I recommend that you and your family repair to the country for a few days."

"Thank you, Edward, we will." Lord Pritchard raised his sword and advanced towards Robert. "No more games, boy."

Marisee looked from one end of the alley to the other. The Goldsmith shook his head at her and smiled, as if reading her mind. The ravens flapped their great wings and shook their heads too, seeming to agree with him. The Dragon opened its mouth. A forked tongue unfurled from inside a cloud of orange sparks.

"No!" Robert shouted. "I won't come with you!"

The tip of Lord Pritchard's sword poked Robert's chest. "You would rather die?"

"Yes," Robert said. "I would."

The ravens rose into the air, a blur of black, glossy feathers, beaks and claws. Marisee knew they were coming for her. How could she bear those claws tangling in her hair again? Or pinching her shoulders? She wished she could be as brave as Robert. She dropped to a crouch, her hands over her head, eyes closed.

The birds didn't land.

A wind rushed through the alley with such strength that it made the bricks tremble. The ravens screamed and the Goldsmith shouted in rage. Marisee opened her eyes. The Dragon was crumbling and forming again, crumbling and forming again, as the wind scythed through it.

Chalk dust swirled, coating everything it touched.

"The Squall!" Marisee cried. "And he's not alone!"

It was Henry! He charged at the Goldsmith, sharp teeth gleaming. The Goldsmith had no time to move out of his way. He was slammed forward on to the cobbles. He swore, scrambling to his feet.

"Goldsmith!" Lord Pritchard yelled. "Save my property or I will sue you!"

"Robert Strong is no one's property!" Henry roared.

He scooped up a bundle of ravens, hurling them at Lord Pritchard. The furious birds thrashed wildly, their claws scraping Lord Pritchard's head. Lord Pritchard's sword clattered to the cobbles.

Marisee felt a hand slip into her own. It was Wolfgang. "I'm frightened," he whispered. "I want Nannerl."

"I know," Marisee said gently. "Shall we go and find her?"

Robert took Wolfgang's other hand. Out towards the river, the Domedary bellowed long and hard.

Marisee, Robert and Wolfgang ran towards it without looking back.

A WARSHIP WITH
NO CANNON

As they ran towards the wharf, Robert knew that one hunter had not been in Panyer Alley. Haakon. He would come for Robert, there was no doubt about that. The question was when.

Wolfgang gasped for breath. "Where are we going?"

"Chapterhouse well!" Marisee shouted.

Yes, Robert thought. *Good idea.* They would be safe underground, at least for a moment.

Their feet pounded along Paternoster Row. St Paul's

loomed on their left. Robert imagined its gallery echoing with the whispers of the Fumis watching them run.

And doing nothing! he thought angrily. *Without a favour in return.*

"This way!" Marisee said, veering towards the churchyard.

There was the well and, leaning against it, was Haakon. Robert's heart thumped once and then settled. He'd known that the hunt wasn't yet over. But he hadn't got this far just to be caught.

The capture-creature looked less human now, like a rearing white bear crammed into human clothing. His snout twitched and he flexed his hand-paw, revealing thick, sharp claws.

The air above the well glowed behind the hunter. The Fleet Ditch boar shot out, followed by Sally Fleet. Her fingers wove silver threads that she flicked towards Haakon's ankles, looping around, binding them together.

"No!" Haakon tore them away. "Your magic will not work on me."

The boar grunted and charged towards him. Haakon crouched ready, hand-paws outstretched. The boar seemed to surge. He was no longer a boar. He was mud and stinking water and rotten fruit that burst in a filthy wave over Haakon's head.

Haakon staggered back from the well.

"Robert!" Marisee yelled. "You first!"

Would there be anyone to catch him? Please! Please!

Robert jumped. Silver threads darted back and forth around him until he was being carried in a silver cradle. Sally Fleet certainly had her own style, he thought. He jolted to a stop and the cradle dissolved. He tumbled on to the ground.

"Out of the way!" Marisee shouted.

Another silver cradle was hurtling towards Robert. He rolled out of the way just in time as Marisee and Wolfgang landed. He looked up.

"It can't follow," Madam Blackwell said. She was waiting in the tunnel. "No Chad will ever catch a creature like that. But hurry! We need to get to the dock!"

A small, high voice came from behind her. "Can we come back in now?"

It belonged to a childlike Chad that was so watery it could barely hold its shape. Robert could make out a ruff around its neck and a hymn book in its hand. As Madam Blackwell stepped aside, Robert saw many more crowded along the tunnel.

"Of course," Madam Blackwell said. "But keep us dry."

"Yes, Madam Blackwell."

The Chads dissolved, some holding their hymn books high as they became a stream. Their voices joined in a simple, pure tune as they flowed back into the well leaving a dry path in the middle for the humans.

"*They* still have their music!" Wolfgang cried.

"They do," Madam Blackwell said. "Perhaps whoever's taken it has stopped its antics."

"It's a perfect harmony," Wolfgang said. "I will try and remember it."

Madam Blackwell shook her head. "Please don't, Wolfgang. They haven't forgiven Handel for stealing their water music."

They hurried along the tunnels, going deeper and deeper underground. They emerged into a crater filled with a jumble of bricks. Some were scattered loose, all colours, all shapes. Others were piled into the remains of tumbledown walls. Sooty tiles balanced on smoke-stained columns. An arched window frame held just one shard of green glass. Fat wax candles in twisted metal holders burned among the ruins.

"It's all the St Paul's churches," Madam Blackwell said. "There's been one on this ground for at least a thousand years. This place holds memories of all of them."

Robert wished that there was a place that held his

memories, so he could go and find the ones of his brother that the tithe-master had taken.

The tunnel ahead took them uphill again to an iron gate. They emerged on to the Thames foreshore behind a wooden post holding up a jetty. The tide was out, leaving a strip of water between the shores.

"These quay doors aren't used much," Madam Blackwell said, closing the gate. "Chads aren't great at reading the tides. The last thing London's rivers need is Thames dirt flowing back into them."

A few feet away, a boat waited on the edge of the sand. The sailor wore a familiar dirty green tricorn.

"Mr Cecil!" Robert said.

Mr Cecil waved.

It was a tight squeeze, six of them in the boat, including Mr Cecil and Daisy and the bundle of poles, nets and oars in the bottom. Robert worried that the weight of them would push the boat deeper in the water, but it still sat just below the surface.

Robert could hear the Domedary in the distance, but the bend in the river hid it from sight. Part of him wished that no matter how quickly they rowed, they would never turn that bend.

"Are you sure Miss Turnmill Brook said that we should head *towards* the monster, Uncle Cecil?" Daisy asked.

"You were there as well as me," Uncle Cecil said. "You heard exactly what she said."

Heading towards the monster, he gripped the bench hard and tried to push his fear back down.

London Bridge stretched between the banks ahead of them. It was strange seeing it from below. Robert had once travelled across it, jammed between footmen at the back of Lady Hibbert's coach. One of the footmen had told him that the bridge used to have many small arches where the river rushed through. Some wherrymen would deliberately shoot their small boats through the arches to show off their skill. Not all had made it through alive. Now there was just one big arch in the middle and Mr Cecil's boat glided through with ease.

Hundreds of sailing ships crammed the water on the other side of the bridge, waiting to load and unload cargo, and pay their dues at the Custom House.

"It's too quiet," Daisy said. "I can't see no porters nor lightermen."

Something bumped their boat from beneath.

"Eyes open, Daisy," Mr Cecil said.

"Sorry, Uncle." Daisy grasped her oar in both hands. "There are so many of them!"

"So many what?" Wolfgang asked.

Daisy peered into the water. "Oysters, of course!

The usual ones are still amiss. I think the Domedary ate them when it crawled across the riverbed. Eat, rest, smash things. That's all that monster does. I hate it."

"So what are these new oysters like?" Robert asked and, he wondered, how big could they be if they bumped against a boat?

"They're not very happy," Daisy said. "That's what the new oysters are like."

"And big?" Robert ventured.

"That too," Daisy said.

"Those merchants can't be happy, neither," Madam Blackwell said. "Look what the Domedary's done to their ships."

Boat masts were snapped, their sails draped like sheets over the decks. A string of pennants trailed across a hull, tangled around the crow's nest still attached to the stub of broken mast.

Mr Cecil's boat was soon surrounded by barrels bobbing on the water, some whole, most shattered into ribs and nails. The smell hit Robert. Coffee, tea, spices and the sweet-sharp smell of oranges. His heart seemed to squeeze tight inside his chest. Oranges. They were important to him. His mother used to split them into juicy sections. And his brother... His brother... The memory was completely gone.

"Those children are not afraid," Wolfgang said, pointing.

The barrels were being washed up on to the foreshore. A group of ragged children had already gathered there to pick through the treasures.

"The Domedary is the least of their problems," Madam Blackwell said. "They face worse than that every day."

A barge hurtled past them, flying a white flag with a red cross.

"The Navy," Marisee said.

"There'll be soldiers too," Madam Blackwell said. "Not that it will do any good. If those soldiers start blasting the Domedary with cannon and guns, it will probably make it angrier."

Could it become any angrier? Robert wondered.

As they passed the Tower of London, Robert saw the yeomen streaming out. Some ran towards boats moored by the wharf, others were marching east. A troop on horseback was followed by carts bearing cannon. He held his breath as the Tower's smell enveloped him.

"It stinks, doesn't it?" Daisy said. "Me and Uncle…"

"Sssh!" Mr Cecil said quietly.

"You can shush me as much as you want," Daisy said, "but I'll never forget that stink."

The boat shook hard.

Wolfgang grabbed Robert's hand. "Is that the monster? Has it come for us?"

"No." Daisy squinted into the water. "It's the oysters. And they're now even more not happy."

A great sailing vessel anchored ahead of them tipped to the right, crashing into the ship next to it. There were shrieks from the deck as that ship fell into the next one. One by one the boats toppled over, smashing into their neighbours.

Madam Blackwell peered at the wreckage. Her voice was hushed. "Daisy, how exactly can oysters destroy boats?"

"Usual oysters won't," Daisy said. "But they've gone, and now the big ones are here. They should be far away, out in the deep sea, but the Domedary stirred them up and they've come close. I don't think they mean us any harm."

No harm? How could she say that? Robert had just seen huge sailing ships topple. He was in a small, fragile rowing boat, just thin planks of wood between him and them. What could they do to it – and all of them inside it?

"How big are these oysters?" he asked.

"I've heard stories that one of 'em swallowed a goat," Daisy said.

Robert tried to picture it, then tried not to. With the Domedary ahead of them and the oysters below them, it was all starting to feel hopeless.

A yellow tongue curled out of the river and grasped Mr Cecil's oar. Mr Cecil tried to hold on, but it was snatched away and disappeared into the water. A moment later, the broken halves bobbed to the surface.

Marisee hunched herself together, making sure no part of her hung over the water. "Are you sure they don't mean us any harm, Daisy?" She pointed to the floating oar blade. "It's hard to believe."

Daisy bent over the boat so that her face was flat against the water. When she sat up again, the water slid off her skin like glass.

"They don't like us rowing over their babies," she said.

The boat jolted. Robert's stomach jolted with it. The wide end of an oyster shell broke the surface as if it was balancing on its tip. It gaped open like a smile, then its tongue snaked out. It was thick and fleshy and covered in stiff, wire-like hairs. It scraped along the bow.

"Daisy?" Mr Cecil said. "Can you?"

"Yes, Uncle!"

Daisy stood up and made a little leap into the air without rocking the boat at all. As she leaped, she flipped upside down, holding her feet together like a tail. She plopped into the water with barely a ripple. All the time, her hat stayed jammed on her head.

Wolfgang looked from Robert to the river. "She … she…"

Before he could say anything else, Daisy reappeared.

"There's a path that doesn't take us over their beds," she said.

"Lead on," Mr Cecil said.

Daisy dived under again and bobbed up in front of the boat, or her hat did, slipping through the water ahead of them. Occasionally, her feet – and they *must* be feet because they wore shoes – flicked up behind her.

A few moments later, Daisy called out. "Brace, Uncle Cecil!"

Mr Cecil stood perfectly still with his oar upright in the water as if it was held by something just below the waterline. The boat remained steady. A hand clasped the side of the boat and Daisy hauled herself back in. She flopped down on top of the nets. Her clothes were soaked but it didn't seem to bother her.

"Why can't you jump back *into* the boat?" Wolfgang asked.

Daisy yanked out a spare oar that was caught beneath her feet. "Can *you*?"

"You know I can't," Wolfgang said. "But I suppose that you cannot compose a hornpipe."

"Braggart," Daisy muttered.

Wolfgang gave her a suspicious look. Robert supposed that it was an English word he hadn't heard before.

The river was becoming more crowded, and not with the usual cargo ships, boats and barges. A cluster of rowboats glided easily downstream against the current towards the peninsula. The navigators all stood in the bow like Mr Cecil, sweeping an oar through the muddy water. They wore greatcoats and hats.

"Shard beasts!" Robert said. "Look!"

Maybe everything wasn't as hopeless as it seemed.

A glass creature crouched in each boat. Robert could just hear the breeze tinkling through their glass quills.

"The Magogs's foot soldiers," Mr Cecil said. "Made from earth magic. Sometimes I wonder if the Magogs split the earth apart just to release them. I've never seen so many gathered, though."

"And I've never seen so many of our people gathered!" Daisy sounded excited.

"Sssh!" Mr Cecil said sharply. "Don't bring attention to it."

"The shard beasts haven't come to fight the Domedary," Robert said. "They both protect the Magogs, don't they? Who *have* they come to fight?"

"I think we're going to find out very soon," Madam Blackwell said.

Robert glanced towards the shore and drew in his breath. Madam Blackwell placed her hands over Wolfgang's eyes. They were passing a gibbet that held the remains of an executed pirate displayed in the cage as a warning to others. Robert hated the cruelty of it.

The boat seemed to speed up to pass it quickly, then on past the Breach. Robert could just see the masts of the three ships anchored in the middle of the lake. He wondered if the ravens had returned to their perches or if they were still fighting Henry. Up ahead were the windmills that lined Millbank. There was not even the slightest breeze and their sails were still.

"What is that smell?" Wolfgang said, pressing his nose into his palm.

Marisee groaned in disgust. "Yes! What is it?"

"That's Greenland Dock," Madam Blackwell said. "It's where the whaling boats anchor and the blubber is boiled."

"I wish I could curse any boat that killed our whale friends," Daisy said.

"And here we are," Madam Blackwell said quietly. "That must be the empress's ship."

It was anchored in the middle of the river. It was long and sleek, but sturdy too. It was fully rigged, every sail billowing as if filled with the strongest wind on such a still day. A black and yellow ensign rippled out from the highest mast.

"It's a frigate," Madam Blackwell said. "A warship. They definitely mean business."

Robert eyed the gun ports that lined the ship's hull. What business did they mean, though? It would take just one order from the captain and Mr Cecil's boat would be blown out of the water. But there were no cannon thrust out of those ports. Robert couldn't see anyone at all. It was like the ship had come as a warning – to show how powerful it could be if the owner didn't get their own way.

"My sister is on there?" Wolfgang asked uncertainly.

"She must be," Marisee said, too firmly, as if trying to convince herself. "Safe from the monster."

Wolfgang stared up at the ship, then across towards the river. "I think we will all be safe now. They have killed the monster!"

Half of the Domedary's legs were buried in the foreshore sand. The others were stuck out at strange angles, some stiff and straight like a giant's poker, others bent and folded like a fan. It was the first time that Robert had managed to count the legs. There were twelve. Its belly had started to split open so that the tips of the fangs poked out. It did look like a giant automaton when the clockwork had wound down mid-movement.

"Them foreign Fumis have power to hold down a beast like that!" Daisy said.

Mr Cecil grunted. "But what happens when they let it go?"

"We know the answer to that," Madam Blackwell said. "It'll be angrier than ever."

As the rowboat edged closer to the frigate, Robert felt the air moving so quickly his lungs barely had time to catch it.

"I can see them!" Wolfgang said.

"Hapsburg Fumis," Madam Blackwell said, shaking her head with admiration. "Air spirits, but *very* different from our own."

The Fumis whipped backwards and forwards between the boat and the Domedary. They were wider and longer than the London Fumis, their heads shaped like a triangle with the peak at the top. They were pale, though some were speckled with black as if they had been sprinkled with London's coal dust. Flashes of red wrapped across their thin bodies like a sash.

They twisted around the Domedary, whirls of air looping along its body and through its legs. Each time the Domedary tried to move, the Fumis pushed against it. A row of Fumis grasped the upper edges of its mouth and seemed to brace their thin bodies against the bottom edge to hold it in place so it could neither open nor close. Robert suddenly felt sorry for it. It hadn't asked to be woken up.

"They're preventing it from attacking the ship," Madam Blackwell said. "They'll release it when they have what they want."

"The music box?" Marisee asked.

"The stowaway Fumi inside it," Madam Blackwell said.

"And once the ship's safely away," Robert said, "the Domedary will be free again. But if the music thief has gone, the music will return, won't it?"

"Certainly," Madam Blackwell said. "But dribbles of music here and there all over London aren't going to soothe all that fury straight away. It needs something stronger and closer."

"Then we have to get on to that boat," Marisee said. "If the empress is there, surely she will help us. Perhaps her Fumis can keep the Domedary bound with air until the music has time to calm it."

Robert stared up at the frigate. "I can't see an empress," he said. "Or any sailors."

"Nannerl!" Wolfgang cried. "You said that she'll be on the ship!"

"We will find her, Wolfgang," Madam Blackwell said. "But wait. I think there are others with business with the boat."

The air became heavy with the smell of animal fat and coal smoke. A black cloud floated towards the frigate and split apart into individual Fumis.

"It's the Council of Elders," Marisee said.

"Turn from these shores!" a Fumi Elder screeched. "You did not seek permission to enter our air!"

The frigate's sails sunk as if the wind had fallen away. The Council shrieked as a gust hit them so hard that they were turned into streaks of darkness. They gathered back together, but kept their distance, bulging and wobbling, petals of colour scattering around them. It looked like they were having an argument in their own language.

An Elder drifted forward again. "We demand that you return the music. Then turn from these shores."

"We shall indeed turn from these shores," a woman's voice said. "Now that my warriors have found our stowaway. It is an … exuberant spirit that should not have left Salzburg. It cannot control its magic."

The woman was a small dark shape on the boat, not close enough for Robert to see properly. It must be Fumi magic blowing her voice so clearly towards them.

"It's the empress," Wolfgang whispered. "Empress Maria Theresa! I have played in her court!"

"London Fumis!"

Robert turned towards the new voice. It was the Goldsmith standing on the prow of his barge. It had slipped through the huddle of rowing boats while Robert had been staring at the empress. "Get over here, airheads!" he shouted. "Make sure that everyone can hear my voice!"

The Council wafted over to the Goldsmith's barge.

"You are responsible for waking a river monster!" the Goldsmith declared to the empress. "I order you to vanquish it!"

"Vanquish it?" Empress Maria Theresa laughed. "Me?"

"Yes! You! You have sailed in a warship. Use it to fight the beast."

The empress laughed again. "No man tells *me* what to do."

The Goldsmith drew himself up taller. "This man will!"

"Yes," came the Lord Mayor's voice from somewhere in the barge. "We will."

"Lord Mayor!" the Goldsmith said. "Give the order!"

The Lord Mayor stood. Robert noticed two servants standing behind to steady him. He lifted an arm into the air and there was the boom of a cannon from the riverbank. The aim was good, straight at the frigate. Robert tensed, expecting its gun ports to open, but they didn't. A whirl of pale shapes slashed with red darted around the hull. The cannon ball touched the wood, slowed, then stopped, hanging like a dark, solid bubble, before falling into the water.

Empress Maria Theresa flung her arms wide. "Take me to the man," she said.

She was lifted from the deck, her silky red skirts billowing around her as the Hapsburg Fumis wove themselves into a basket of air to hold her. They carried her to the front of the Goldsmith's barge, hovering just inches above the water. She was about the same age as Madam Blackwell, her white hair combed back and coiled down her neck.

The Lord Mayor pushed past the Goldsmith and stared at her.

"Such sumptuous fabrics, madam," he said.

"Are you the king of London?" she demanded.

"Well…" The Lord Mayor coughed. "In a manner of speaking."

The empress pointed towards the foreshore. "I advise you to call off your troops!"

The Goldsmith pushed his way to the front again. "Or what?"

Empress Maria Theresa whispered words into the air.

Hapsburg Fumis shot across the surface of the Thames making the water toss and roil before swerving towards the Isle of Dogs. The sails on the Millbank windmills spun faster and faster until they were just a blur. There was a loud crack as the sail flew from the nearest windmill. It sliced through the air, bounced off the embankment and dropped into the river. Another followed and another. The roofs of the windmills whined, turned slowly, then gathered speed, spinning as quickly as if a hundred millers were harnessed to the crank and chain that usually moved them.

"She's one we definitely want on our side," Madam Blackwell whispered.

But she's not on our side, Robert thought. The empress and the Goldsmith wanted to show off their power to each other and neither of them seemed to care that everyone else would be caught in the middle. The windmills went still. Robert breathed out. For a moment, there was silence, then the Lord Mayor raised his arm again and another cannon boomed out from the north

373

bank. A Hapsburg Fumi caught the cannon ball and hurled it back to shore. There was the crash of metal – the cannon ball had been thrown back at the cannon. A wave of Hapsburg Fumis swept through the troops. Guns, cannon and soldiers were lifted into the air. Robert heard cries for help then splash after splash as everything and everyone was dropped into the river. The Navy barge rowed towards the flailing men, trailed by a flotilla of soldiers in smaller boats.

The Goldsmith cleared his throat, but before he could speak, his barge began to rise.

"'Or what?' you ask," Empress Maria Theresa said, calmly. "Or this."

"Edward?" the Lord Mayor said. *His* voice was rising too. "Edward?"

A corkscrew of water was pushing the barge up and out of the river.

"Can our Fumis do that?" Marisee asked.

"They don't go near the river if they can help it," Madam Blackwell said. "But perhaps this is giving them ideas."

Empress Maria Theresa floated higher and higher, just in front of the barge's prow. "I rarely leave Austria because I never know who'll be sitting on my throne when I return. But this has definitely been worth the journey."

The empress and the Goldsmith stood face to face. The Goldsmith stretched out his hand. Robert heard the beating of wings and a big black bird landed silently on the Goldsmith's wrist. For a moment, the tips of its feathers glowed orange.

"You have a pet Dragon?" It sounded like the Hapsburg Fumis had made the Empress's voice even louder so all could hear her scorn. "Is *that* your best weapon? Because *I* know that giants sleep at the bottom of your river. *I* know how long they have been sleeping there, gathering their strength, waiting to rise again. They are not ready yet. I could order my warriors to strip away the tides and expose them. They would crumble."

"Then you would be doing me a favour, Empress." The Goldsmith's voice seemed louder too. "London does not need earth monsters."

Empress Maria Theresa looked surprised. Her voice was silky. "I am surprised that you dare speak ill of *earth monsters* in front of their soldiers."

She waved a hand towards the shard beasts and the Domedary.

The corkscrew of water dissolved. The barge plummeted then slammed back down on to the river, spraying Mr Cecil's boat and everyone in it. Once

Robert had wiped his eyes, he saw the Goldsmith's barge was surrounded by rowboats, each carrying a shard beast.

"They know that you wish their masters harm," Empress Maria Theresa said. "You had better prepare to fight, King of London!"

The Lord Mayor's whimper may have been quiet, but it echoed across the river.

As the empress was carried through the air back to her warship, her voice remained strong. "We have finished our business here. It's time for us to return."

"Empress!" Wolfgang shouted. "Where is my sister?"

"Of course," Empress Maria Theresa said. "I forgot."

A rowboat lifted out of the frigate. It was smaller than Mr Cecil's boat, with a solitary mast in the middle and a single sail. Robert could just see the Hapsburg Fumis bearing it. The boat hovered in the air before landing smoothly on the water.

Nannerl stood up, clinging to the mast. "Wolfgang!"

"Nannerl!" Wolfgang shouted back.

The sail filled with wind, buffeting Nannerl towards Mr Cecil's boat until they were bow to bow. Nannerl and Wolfgang reached out to each other until their fingertips touched. Robert felt a pang of jealousy. He would never see his sisters again or remember the brother who must have cared for him the same way that Nannerl cared for Wolfgang.

"I bid you farewell!" Empress Maria Theresa said.

The frigate's sails filled with air and the ship slowly turned. With one quick gust, it had passed the Greenwich Naval Hospital.

The Domedary's belly opened wide and it screamed in rage.

THE STOWAWAY

The Hapsburg Fumis huffed and puffed around the stowaway. They were furious with it, but secretly pleased too. Their warriors had displayed their strength to the empress who was very happy indeed. She would favour them well when they returned to Salzburg.

The stowaway tried to listen. It even tried to pretend it was sorry. It sulked on deck for a little while, swinging a hammock to and fro. And then it saw the music box. It had fallen next to a coil of rope. The lid was open and it looked like one of the hinges was broken. The poor ballerina lay on her back nearby, staring up at the sky.

The stowaway hadn't fixed anything. In fact, it had made things worse. It had tried so hard to stay still in that terrible man's house full of strange machines making music that the stowaway couldn't touch. But then the boy and girl started playing together. It had reminded him of Salzburg. It knew that it should have just listened. It had tried. But then it had been so sure that if it wafted just a little of the music into the box, everything would be fixed.

But it had broken the music again. And then, the monster had come.

The Elders had said that the music would return to London, but not quickly enough to stop the monster. Its fury would rage unchecked for a while yet. The stowaway shivered. What if one of its nasty feet flipped the girl's boat over? Or stomped right through the boat carrying the boy? Human Solids were delicate. It would be the stowaway's fault if they were broken like the music box.

The stowaway had definitely made everything worse.

But … but … perhaps there was a way to fix it.

The stowaway felt a salt crust in the air. The ship couldn't be far from the sea. If it was going to help the boy and the girl, it had to go now. It had never flown so far by itself. It wasn't even sure that those that it must speak to could hear it. But it would try.

It had to try.

The Sail Bloaters were busy powering the ship. Nobody would notice if it went away for a little while. It had learned in these last few days that it was fast. When it had felt the vibrations of human song and music, it had flitted between the columns of smoke and spiky steeples, hoping to blow that music back into the music box. It had sensed the London Fumis; it had been sure that they did not like strangers. It was young and not weighed down with centuries of dust and fumes. It moved too quickly for them to see.

It had to move quickly now before the boat was too far away for it to return and before the monster stormed out of the river and into the streets. It glanced around, checking that it was still alone.

It squeezed itself into a thin, long stripe of air and swooped away.

THE DOMEDARY
RISES AGAIN

Marisee watched the Domedary's legs buckle. As it tried to pull itself free from the heavy foreshore sand, it sank in even deeper. It paused, then the four legs at the front of its body stretched towards the quay. They pressed down on the hard surface and the Domedary started to lever itself up.

"We must leave," Grandma said. "We can't put Nannerl and Wolfgang in any more danger."

Wolfgang had crawled into the second rowing

boat to be with Nannerl. Daisy had lashed the two boats together, stern to bow, with a strip of netting, so that Mr Cecil could tug the other one behind.

Grandma was right. Nannerl and Wolfgang must be safe, but so should the children picking through the barrels – and every other child who wouldn't have time to hide from the furious monster as it crashed through London. The Goldsmith didn't think that they were important, but Marisee did.

"How long until it sleeps again?" she asked.

"I don't know," Grandma said. "Its strength has been growing. It must have returned to the riverbed to rest and feed after it attacked Vauxhall Pleasure Gardens. But it doesn't look very tired now, does it?"

"Because it ate all the usual oysters," Daisy said with fury.

Two of the back legs popped out of the wet sand, scattering chunks of brick and smashed barrel ribs. Marisee couldn't tear her eyes away as it tried to free the rest. "Please stay stuck!" she begged, quietly. "Please stay stuck!"

The air vibrated as a cannon discharged. The cannon ball thudded into the sand next to the Domedary. It bellowed so hard that the waves shuttled from foreshore to foreshore. Marisee rubbed her ears.

"Get away from me!" the Goldsmith shouted

towards the boats of shard beasts. He and his men – apart from the Lord Mayor – were standing, swords drawn on the barge. "Or I will break every unnatural spine on your unnatural body and grind them back to sand."

The shard beasts bristled. As one, the boat navigators lifted their hats and shook them out. A rope ladder fell out from inside each crown. The navigators flicked the ladders towards the barge where they stuck firm on the hull.

"Limpet ladders," Daisy said. "I hope they got the limpets' permission first."

The shard beasts started to crawl across the ladders. The Goldsmith's Dragon dived towards the closest, knocking it into the water. But it was only one. There were many more.

"Ravens!" the Goldsmith shouted.

The sky filled with the sound of the birds. They swooped towards the shard beasts. There was a rattle and a volley of glass quills.

"They're too clever to get spiked," Grandma said.

They were. The birds squawked and veered away.

A screechy voice came from above them. A Fumi Elder hovered above the Goldsmith's head. "We can help you," it said. "A favour for a favour."

The Goldsmith shouted words that Marisee hoped

Wolfgang would *never* understand the meaning of. The Dragon flew at it and the Fumi screeched and darted away.

There was a creak and clicking, then the slurping sound of wet sand filling a hole. Marisee's quiet pleas had been in vain. All the Domedary's legs were freed now. It slowly stretched out the two legs nearest to the shore, lifted them and struck. It easily cut through the wooden walls of the warehouses that lined the embankment. Sacks and bales spilled out of the gash. A crane tottered and fell.

Only one word was looping through Marisee's head – music. Music, music, music.

Surely somewhere a violinist must have taken up their bow, or a nursemaid sung a lullaby or mackerel-seller whistled a tune! Surely, London's music would flow soon and send the Domedary back to the riverbed! If not, this city that Marisee loved would be trampled into mud and brick dust.

The Domedary pulled itself on to the quay, the wooden planks cracking and creaking beneath it. Its cry made the Thames roll. Then it lumbered forward.

"We can't let it go!" Marisee cried,

"We need music!" Grandma said.

And suddenly there was music. The silvery notes of a clavichord drifted over from the Isle of Dogs.

"It's Mr Dross!" Robert said.

The animateur was driving a cart on to the foreshore, the pony picking its way carefully through the rubble. The back of the cart was filled with barrels, and Marisee could just make out a figure sitting on a stool, hunched over an instrument. It was the automaton that Nannerl had thought was her brother.

Mr Dross had attached great wooden cones to the cart, narrow at one end and widening out. They reminded her of big versions of ear trumpets. Marisee thought with a pang of the kind elderly man at the Pleasure Gardens, then of the crushed orchestra stand and the people lying on the grass injured or not moving at all. When the Domedary attacked, the destruction was quick.

Mr Dross had seen it too – and the way it had smashed through the houses in Soho and onwards to the river. Perhaps he understood that his revenge on the Goldsmith would hurt too many innocent people.

He clambered into the back of the cart and suddenly the barrels' lids flipped back. The porcelain heads sprung out and began to sing.

"The cones are like Fumis," Marisee said. "They make the music sound louder."

Even so, could just one choir of automata soothe the Domedary?

The Domedary's legs thudded back down to steady

itself. It was still, then one by one, the legs folded beneath it until it was just a giant shell in the sand.

"It's working!" Marisee cried. "The music's calming it down!"

"I think you've heard enough!" Mr Dross shouted.

The music stopped.

"No!" Marisee shouted. "What are you doing? Keep them singing! Please!"

The monster screamed and wobbled to its feet. One leg twitched, then its whole body trembled as if shaking itself awake. It took a few steps, staggered then started stomping towards the river.

"It's coming for us!" Daisy cried. "Uncle Cecil, we're in its path!"

"And we can't move out of it!" Mr Cecil said.

Their boat was trapped amongst the navigators' boats. The limpet ladders were still stuck to the Goldsmith's barge, the shard beasts gripping the rungs.

"They don't know what to do," Mr Cecil said. "They're not supposed to fight the Domedary, but what if the Domedary wants to fight them?"

The water swelled and rolled as the Domedary plunged through the river. A volley of glass quills shot towards it but bounced off its shell.

The music started again and the monster was still,

one leg raised. Mr Dross walked down to the edge of the water.

"Can you hear him?" Mr Cecil asked Daisy.

Daisy nodded. "He's asking if the Goldsmith is ready to pay him yet."

"The Goldsmith won't like that," Grandma said.

"Airheads!" the Goldsmith yelled. "Come here!"

The Fumi cloud didn't move. Then a voice squealed "a favour for a favour", though it sounded less certain than before.

"If you do not bring that man's voice to me this moment," the Goldsmith shouted, "I will command every Dragon in the City of London to hunt down and shred each and every one of you."

"Is he allowed to do that?" Marisee asked.

"The Whittington Articles state very clearly that he is not," Grandma said. "But the Lord Mayor isn't going to stop him."

The Lord Mayor was sitting in the middle of the barge, gripping the side, his eyes squeezed shut.

The Fumi cloud split into a dark stream. Some hovered by the Goldsmith; the rest floated towards Mr Dross.

"What is it worth to you, Goldsmith?" Mr Dross's voice was loud and clear. "I can stop the monster. I am the only one who can stop the monster! How much of your gold will you give me now?"

"I will pay you nothing!" the Goldsmith said. "Instead you will be hung in the Tower for treason and your body left in a gibbet in Covent Garden for everyone to see!"

"With this monster loose, do you think you'll live long enough to give the order, Goldsmith?" Mr Dross said. "Or that the Tower will remain standing?"

"Pay him!" the Lord Mayor squeaked. "Pay him! And then pay these glass things! Pay them all! Make them go away!"

"Ah," the Goldsmith said meekly. "Perhaps you are right, Lord Mayor. Mr Dross should be given everything that he deserves."

Marisee leaned towards Grandma. "He doesn't mean gold, does he?"

Grandma shook her head.

"Join me on the barge, Mr Dross," the Goldsmith said. "We will make a gentleman's agreement, witnessed by the Lord Mayor of London himself."

"You consider me a fool!" Mr Dross shouted. "You would imprison me and steal my creations. You have not even paid me for the firebird!"

"Forgive me," the Goldsmith said.

388

To Marisee, his words sounded blatantly false. He bent down, then raised his hands, brandishing a dark bird.

"Let me return it to you," he said. "You will see that I have made some improvements."

"Improvements?" Mr Dross laughed. "You could never improve on my perfection."

Marisee knew exactly what that bird was. She had no love for Mr Dross and his creepy machines. She knew that he would willingly destroy London to take revenge on the Goldsmith and others. But...

"We should warn him!" she said.

"He already thinks that everyone has betrayed him," Robert said. "If you tell him it's a Dragon, he'll stop the music straight away and let the monster do what it will."

The Goldsmith seemed to launch the bird towards the foreshore. It was too far away for Mr Dross to see that its body was made from something other than metal casing. It glowed as it flew, faster and faster.

"Goldsmith..." Mr Dross said uncertainly. "Goldsmith!"

The bird broke apart as it flew, dissolving into streaks of flame. The Fumis screeched and swooped away.

"Goldsmith!" Mr Dross screamed. "London will be ruined! Ruined!"

"Not at all," the Goldsmith said. "As you rightly

guessed, we will keep your musical creations and use your designs to make even more powerful ones. This demon beast of chaos will never wake again."

Mr Dross turned to race back to the cart, but the foreshore mud was thick and heavy. He stumbled and fell into a crater left by a boat. The ravens landed in a circle around him. In the air above Mr Dross, the Dragon was forming. There was no body, just a head. Its eyes smouldered and smoke curled from its nostrils. It opened its mouth and flames whirled around Mr Dross. The ravens lifted into the air, a blur of inky black, and flew away. Nannerl hugged her brother to her, shielding his eyes.

When the flames faded away, Mr Dross was gone. There was nothing left but the steam rising from the ruts in the mud.

Marisee swallowed hard. "They could have let him live," she said.

"Neither the Goldsmith nor Mr Dross would give up their power," Grandma said. "One of them had to win. At least the music is keeping the Domedary quiet for the moment."

The Domedary shuddered.

"Fumis!" the Goldsmith called out. "Make the music louder!"

The air spirits were nowhere to be seen.

Grandma shook her head. "The Dragon frightened them away."

Yes, Marisee thought. *They're probably huddling in the safety of the Whispering Gallery.* But they wouldn't be safe for long. The Domedary was stronger and more furious than ever. Its legs would swipe through St Paul's dome, cracking the gallery into pieces. Then onwards it would go, smashing and crushing everything around it. Surely, there was something that Marisee could do other than sit here and wait?

"Fumis!" the Goldsmith bellowed harder. "Where are you?"

The Lord Mayor stood up. "I think they went that way, Edward," he said.

"No, Lord Mayor!" the Goldsmith yelled. "Don't raise your arm—"

But it was too late. The Lord Mayor's arm was high in the air, pointing towards St Paul's. The soldiers on the shore saw the sign and primed their cannon. The first blast knocked the Domedary into the river. The second blasted Mr Dross's choir into fragments of porcelain and wood.

ORANGES AND LEMONS

Robert's nails dug into the sides of the boat as a wave of filthy water washed over him and Mr Cecil's boat was knocked into the boats around it.

"My breeches!" the Lord Mayor shrieked. "They are the best French silk! And my coat! You will pay for this, Goldsmith!"

The Goldsmith ignored him. Like Robert, his eyes were on the spot where the Domedary had fallen.

Robert felt the crackle of magic just before the Domedary's shell broke the surface. It wasn't near the boats now; it had moved upstream, closer to the centre of

London, closer to the poor children scavenging on the foreshore, closer to Garnet and the rest of the Red Guard Gang.

But maybe it wouldn't make it that far. Surely London's music should be strong enough to stop it soon. If only they could gather the music from across the city and bring it here! It would pour over the Domedary like hot water on ice and the thing would sink back into the Thames.

But … they didn't have to wait for the music to come to them, did they?

"We have to make the music ourselves!" he said. "As loud as we can! Straight away!"

"Of course!" Madam Blackwell said, smiling for the first time since leaving the shore. "Why didn't I think of that? Especially as we have the Mozart prodigies here to help us!"

"Nannerl!" Robert called to the other boat. "Wolfgang! Can you sing?"

"His voice won't be loud enough," Daisy said. "And it won't be London enough to make the Domedary go back. I reckon Dross's singing heads were made of porcelain from the Bow factories. They were properly London. That's why they worked so well."

"If I had a harpsichord," Wolfgang said. "Nannerl

and I could play together. That would be louder. Papa said—".

"We don't have a harpsichord!" Robert said shortly.

Wolfgang folded his arms. "I know that! But I was going to tell you that Papa said that Nannerl was so talented that she could make music out of anything."

"Oh," Robert said. "Sorry."

But what was there to make music from here? The river waves? The boats knocking against each other? A rhythm, but not music.

"I hear singing!" Nannerl said.

So could Robert. The voice was high and beautiful, childlike but old. High in the sky was a gold speck. It grew closer and closer. Wasn't it … surely it wasn't?

"It's the cherub from the Fortune of War!" Robert said. "On Giltspur Street."

How could it be flying towards them? As it came closer, Robert saw that its eyes were closed; its mouth shaped into a perfect O. Its wings were extended, but they didn't flutter as if flying. Something was holding it up. It was a Fumi, it must be, but Robert couldn't see the familiar dark smoke or smell candle fat and coal. But wasn't there a faint aroma of fried chicken and malt?

"I smell beckhendl!" Wolfgang shouted.

"And the Stiegl brewery!" Nannerl said. "Sometimes

394

the wind blows the smell across Salzburg." She sniffed. "This is the same."

"It must be the stowaway!" Madam Blackwell said. "It better not have come back to make trouble again, or I'll personally feed it to the Dragons!"

"Grandma!" Marisee sounded shocked.

Madam Blackwell didn't look sorry. "It's caused us all this chaos and whatever it's trying to do now isn't working," she said.

The Domedary paused as if listening to the song, then crouched ready to spring again.

"Then we need more music!" Robert said. "It has to be louder and stronger! Nannerl! What else can we use?"

"Them!" Nannerl said, pointing to the shard beasts. "They can help us!"

Marisee eyed them, frowning. "They're fighters, Nannerl, not musicians," she said.

"Yes, they are!" Daisy said. "They're London music."

"Daisy's right," Madam Blackwell said. "It wasn't a fancy orchestra that kept the Domedary asleep. It was the music of this city. Goldsmith!" she shouted.

The Goldsmith's eyes stayed on the shard beasts.

"You and your men must stand down," she said. "You must reassure the shard beasts that you mean no harm to the Magogs."

The Goldsmith squared his shoulders. "I will do no such thing."

"Lord Mayor!" Marisee shouted. "If the monster destroys London, it will be the Goldsmith's fault. But if you do as we say, you will be a hero!"

"Hero," the Lord Mayor echoed and glared at the Goldsmith.

For a moment, the Goldsmith glared back, then gave the order to stand down. He and the soldiers replaced their swords in their hilts.

The navigators pulled the limpet ladders from the Goldsmith's barge. They came away with a rhythmic pop, pop, pop, as the shard beasts scrambled back into the rowboats. The navigators started rowing back to shore. If they landed, Robert knew that the shard beasts would disappear back into the rookeries and alleys. London needed the shard beasts' music, but how could he stop them? They only answered to the Magogs; why would they listen to Robert?

Robert spotted a flash of red. Two of the shard beasts had red kerchiefs tied around the middle of their three legs, the same red kerchiefs worn by Spindrift and the gang.

Robert stood up. The boat wobbled; Mr Cecil steadied it.

"Shard beasts of St Giles!" he called. He felt his words being blown from his mouth across the river. In spite of what Madam Blackwell thought, the Fumi *was* helping. "We… No, your masters – the sleeping giants – need your help! The Domedary is like you. It protects your masters."

The navigators' boats were lined up on the north shore. The shard beasts were climbing out.

"If the Domedary doesn't return," Robert continued, "your masters will be unguarded." He cast a quick look at the Goldsmith. "You heard how this man spoke of the giants. *He* will not protect them, so you must."

The shard beasts turned as one, their quills tinkling. The Lord Mayor whimpered.

"Just remain a moment longer to help us," Robert said. "Until the Domedary is slumbering again."

A breeze, a waft of fried chicken and the shard beasts' quills began to hum.

"They must hold the music," Nannerl said. "No stopping."

"Your quills must keep humming!" Robert shouted. "Shiver or shake! Do what you must!"

Nannerl closed her eyes. "It must be louder!"

"Perhaps I can be of help." The boat swayed. A spiral of chalk dust flattened out then scattered into the air.

"It's the Squall!" Marisee said.

The air shimmered and the humming became louder. The Squall moved quickly between the shard beasts, sometimes tapping the quills, other times making them vibrate like piano strings. The cherub's voice faded and rose with the song.

"It sings in Latin," Nannerl said. "It is beautiful."

Daisy gave a little hop. The boat jiggled. "What about bells?" she said. "It's not London without the bells!"

"The Fumis could easily make them ring," Marisee said. "But I'm not going to ask them. I refuse to owe them another favour."

"But what if..." Robert said, the thoughts whirring through his head. "What if they owe *us* a favour?"

Marisee made a face. "I don't understand."

"London Fumis!" Robert shouted into the air. "The Goldsmith wanted to blame you for the Domedary rising, even though there was no proof that you had taken the music. The Lord Mayor listens to the Goldmith. He could still convince the mayor that all Fumis should be punished for what the stowaway Fumi has done. *You* know what happened to the Squall's friend. *You* know that the Dragons can kill you. *You* know that the Goldsmith wants the Dragons to be the most powerful elemental in London. So, *I* will offer *you* a favour for a favour. Help us now and

398

your innocence is assured." He turned to the barge. "Is that not so, Lord Mayor?"

"Yes!" the Lord Mayor shouted back quickly. "It is!"

The Goldsmith scowled and said nothing.

"Favour?" A Fumi Elder swooped down towards him. The swirl of white smoke around its head looked even more like a magistrate's wig now. "There is no favour. You still owe us a favour! You did not fulfil your task!"

"I owe you nothing!" Robert said. He couldn't hold back the fury in his voice. "You didn't let me fulfil the task. You forfeited my life before I could repay the favour. You broke the deal."

The Fumi darted up high again, joining a knot of dark smoke flecked with bright spots of colour. It was talking to the others. Robert waited, heart beating hard. He knew that he *was* right, but what mattered was if the Fumis agreed. He glanced downstream. There was a splash and a large wave engulfed the north bank as the Domedary sprung forward again.

Robert heard Marisee sigh. "Come on!" she urged. "Make up your minds!"

The Fumi returned. "What is your favour?" it screeched.

Marisee and Madam Blackwell breathed out with relief; Robert did the same.

"Make the church bells ring," he ordered.

The Fumi made a yappy, squealing sound, like laughter. "All the church bells, Solid human?"

"Ummm..." Robert said. "Nannerl?"

"We need bells that ring in harmony," she said. "They must play a song."

"A London song," Daisy said.

The Fumi Elder flew away. Up in the sky, a dark cloud moved quickly towards the city. Robert wasn't fully convinced that they'd help.

The Domedary crouched again, ready to leap.

"Boatmen!" Nannerl instructed. "Tap your oars!"

She clapped out a rhythm. The shard beasts' navigators took it up, a complicated tempo tapped on to the hull of their boats.

"Uncle Cecil..." Daisy said.

Mr Cecil sighed, adjusted his grasp on his oar and joined in.

The first church bell rang. Was that the Fumis or just a coincidence?

"It's the bells of St Clement's," Madam Blackwell said. "I'm sure of it."

More chimes responded. It was working! The Fumis were really ringing the church bells!

"That's St Martin's." Marisee grinned. "I know this

song! Oranges and lemons, say the bells of St Clement's. You owe me five farthings, say the bells of St Martin's!"

The Domedary straightened itself. Everyone held their breath. It took a tottering step towards the middle of the Thames then was still again.

"Is there more of the song?" Robert said. "What comes next?"

The bells rang. Marisee sang. "When will you pay me? Say the bells of Old Bailey!"

But it wasn't enough. The Domedary was calm, but it wasn't asleep. They still needed more London music.

"What about the ravens?" Nannerl said. "Perhaps they can flap their wings and…"

The Goldsmith gave her a cool look, then away again.

"You'll find no help there," Madam Blackwell said.

The Domedary took a few more steps. Its underbelly fell open, but it was slack, as if it didn't have the strength to keep it shut. Those fangs still looked sharp, though.

"When I grow rich, said the bells of Shoreditch!" the cherub trilled, accompanying the chiming. "When will that be?"

"Said the bells of Stepney!" Madam Blackwell came in on a deeper, less tuneful note.

"'I do not know!'" Marisee sang at the top of her

voice. "'Said the great bells of Bow!'" She grinned at Madam Blackwell. "And we saw them! Up in the belfry of St Mary-le-Bow!"

Robert imagined the Dragon giving them an extra-strong push.

It wasn't just the big bells that were chiming. Ships' bells were building layers of harmony. The music swept across the surface of the river. Robert imagined it sweeping across the whole of London, the notes lacing and interlacing as if by a weaver of music.

The song ended. There was silence, as if the music had played itself out. The Domedary's mouth snapped shut and it crouched once more – then sprang forward down the river.

"Again!" Nannerl shouted. "The song from the beginning!"

The bells chimed, the oars tapped, the glass quills rattled and hummed. The cherub sang. So did Marisee and Madam Blackwell.

Nannerl sighed. "It needs … it needs more."

"More London!" Daisy demanded. "Make it more London!"

"How?" Robert said. He felt desperate now. The shard beasts would grow restless soon and leave. And the stowaway had to return to the ship – Robert certainly didn't want the empress and the Hapsburg Fumis returning to look for it.

Nannerl held her hand to her ear. "Like that."

The voice was faint, but growing louder, a smooth baritone singing the last words of the song.

"Here comes a candle to light you to bed."

Then the music swept in. The fiddlers on the street corners *had* picked up their violins again. Sailors were hollering out shanties in the docks upstream. Porters were whistling as they lugged barrels and bales along the Strand towards Westminster. Robert wasn't sure if he could hear it or feel it. The music was being blown around him towards the Domedary.

It was joined by other voices – were they children's voices? One voice was higher and louder than the others.

Robert squinted towards the shore. There were five figures. One wearing a hat and long coat, tapped a staff against a pillion. It was Spindrift! And he could just see Emma, Turpin and Duval next to Spindrift. And Garnet was there too – it was her voice singing the loudest. All of them were like him, not born in London, but now a part of it. And all those parts were joining together – the human and the elemental; air, earth and water magic; metal, wood, glass and voices – to save this city.

"And here comes a chopper to chop off your head!" Garnet sang.

That wouldn't be Robert's choice of words for a lullaby. Madam Blackwell clasped his and Marisee's hands as the Domedary leaped again. It was coming back! Its clawed feet narrowly missed the top of their heads. It landed with a massive splash that rocked all their boats. Daisy muttered something rude. The Domedary wobbled and paused, then started walking downstream towards Blackwall Reach, shrinking as the water deepened around it.

"Chip chop, chip chop." Robert hadn't realized that he knew these words, but he was singing along.

As the Domedary turned the bend in the river, its legs folded into its body and it sank beneath the water.

The last words of the song poured through the air. "The last man's deeeeaad…"

The note hung in the air and the music of London rose around it – bells rang, glass hummed, oars tapped a final tattoo against the wooden hulls.

Robert saw a movement from the foreshore. It was the Fleet Ditch boar. He gave a little nod then disappeared beneath a jetty.

"Maybe that's why he always grunts," Madam Blackwell said, "because he's saving his voice for special occasions."

"Wheeeee!" The golden cherub squealed as it was borne away on a breeze.

"It *was* the stowaway," Marisee said. "Fixing what it had broken."

"Hmm," Madam Blackwell said. "I suppose so."

"Thank you!" Robert called into the air.

"Yes!" Nannerl and Wolfgang waved at it. "Thank you!"

"See you in Salzburg!" Wolfgang shouted.

A tiny pale hand unwrapped from the cherub and waved back at them. Then it was gone.

"Time to go home," Marisee said. "And this time, Robert, you will come home with us."

Could he be free at last? They'd helped save London again. There must be a way.

"Yes!" He grinned. "I will."

Marisee's face changed. "Rober—!" she started to scream.

But before Marisee had finished saying his name, strong arms grasped Robert around the middle and pulled him into the river.

SINKING, SINKING, SINKING

"Robert Strong, I have you now," Haakon growled.

As soon as Robert hit the water, he knew that he was going to fight this thing as hard as he could. He wanted to live – not only to live, but to live free. He closed his eyes and held his breath. He could feel fear twisting through his body. He had to press it down into a forgotten corner, or he'd be too frightened to think.

Robert had been held underwater before, when the plague monster in the Serpentine lake had trapped him in its tentacles. He'd survived that. What was different now? The plague monster hadn't needed to breathe. Robert was sure that Haakon did. They would have to surface at some point.

But it had to be soon. Robert's lungs were already begging for the air to be released. Haakon would most likely leave it as long as possible before surfacing, but he wouldn't want Robert to drown. It would be a poor victory for a hunter.

He had to stay calm. And he had to remember that he was not alone. There was a boat full of people above him on the Thames that would not let him die. But was he still near them? They might have no idea where he was.

But Robert couldn't hold his breath any longer. He slowly released the air from his lungs, watching the bubbles rise towards Haakon's head. He let his body go limp.

Instantly, Robert felt Haakon kick out with his legs and they began to rise, breaking the surface moments later.

"Take your breath quickly," Haakon said. "We go straight down again."

Robert snatched air into his lungs and opened his eyes. Shipyards, the reek from the Greenland Dock, warehouses. They hadn't swum that far.

"Where are you taking me?" he spluttered.

"To the place where I was made," he said. "The place that stinks of death and misery."

"The Tower of London?" His fear twisted free from its hidden corner. "Why?"

"Because I have masters who want boys like you," Haakon said. "Not the poor and the sick, but the healthy and the strong. You must be healthy and strong to survive their tasks. And then you will be like me. Stronger. Relentless. That weak human side of you will be gone forever."

No! Robert could not let himself become like Haakon. He grasped at any idea. "But what about Lord Pritchard?"

"My masters do the king's business, even if the king himself does not know about it," he said. "They want more who are powerful like me, to fight the battles to come."

"What battles?"

"Too many questions."

They plunged again. Robert's mouth filled with water. He clamped his throat shut and tried to spit it out without losing the precious air. He forced his eyes to stay open just in case something floated by that might help him escape.

A long yellow tongue whipped through the water,

looping around the middle of Haakon and Robert's bodies. It tightened. Robert felt the wiry hairs on the oyster's tongue piercing his skin. Haakon grunted and wriggled free. The oyster held on even tighter, drawing them both downward. The immense shell gaped open below, not just one, but hundreds of giant oysters with pearl-like lights gleaming from inside them.

Sinking.

Sinking.

Sinking.

The tongue slackened and Haakon shoved it away. They fell into the shell; the two sides, like pale walls, drew closer together. Haakon gripped Robert with one arm and bashed against the shell with the other, his legs twisting and kicking.

The shell continued to close.

Haakon grunted hard, air bubbles shooting from his snout. He bounced his feet violently off the curved inside of the shell. It was enough to lift himself upwards. He did it again, snatching at the top edge of the shell. He managed to grab it in one big paw-hand, the other still clasping Robert.

Robert glanced down. Something glowed in the centre below. A dark shadow was wrapped around it — the tongue, waiting to lash out again. Up above, the gap between the two halves of the shell was too small for them to crawl out through – and shrinking every moment. Only Haakon's grip stopped them falling inside.

Robert needed to breathe. His throat hurt. His chest heaved.

Hold on for just a little bit longer, he told himself.

Haakon braced his feet against the other side of the shell, trying to stop it from closing. Robert tried to help. It made no difference.

Soon there would be just darkness and water.

Robert must have air. Now.

The glowing light rose from the bottom of the oyster shell. The water fluttered as it floated towards Robert. It touched his foot; it was soft and slick and pulsed with life. He gasped and the air exploded out of him. He could hold it no longer.

"You down there?" a voice called from just above the water.

An oar blade slipped between the crack.

"No, no, new oysters," the voice said. "You do not eat people."

It was Daisy.

"If you do eat people," she said, "the humans will know about you, and they will come and eat you and your babies in pies. Though they'd have to be big pies."

410

The shell snapped open so quickly that Haakon was flung backwards, releasing his grip on Robert. Robert somersaulted up through the water.

"Hold on to this!" Daisy called.

He seized the oar with his hands and knees. Daisy, helped by Madam Blackwell lifted him out of the water. At last! Sky and air! Sweet air! He took a long breath in. He clutched the edges of the boat and shoved one leg over the edge. Marisee reached out to pull him in.

A hand-paw gripped his ankle.

"No!" Robert yelled and tried to kick it away.

But he knew the capture-creature's strength. A kick was nothing. Haakon surfaced, muddy water dripping from his white woollen cap and snout.

"We won't let you take him!" Madam Blackwell shouted.

Marisee tried to shunt Haakon away with an oar. It was like pushing at a rock with a toothpick.

Haakon shook his head. Droplets flew around him. "Are you ready for the Tower, boy?" he growled.

"He is not!" a new voice said. "And never will be!"

A figure was swimming towards them. The greatcoat that should have weighed it down floated around it. It seemed to be propelled by an invisible force, swimming but moving with the speed of a ship in full sail.

"You cannot stop me, traitor!" Haakon shouted, still clinging on tight to Robert's ankle.

"There must be no more like us," Henry said. "Leave him!"

"You cannot change what I am," Haakon said. "I was made to hunt."

"So was I," Henry said. "But now I will save the hunted."

Henry and Haakon were nose to nose in the water.

"Will you?" Haakon shifted his grip on Robert's ankle.

The moment the hold loosened, Robert kicked back hard. For a moment, he was free, but Haakon's arm lashed out, his claws grazing Robert's thigh. Then powdery air whirred round him, tossing and turning him on its current. His eyes stung with chalk dust.

A second later, he was dropped into a well. He kept his eyes closed as he fell. He'd fought to save London; now his friends had fought to save him. He wasn't scared. He let his body relax. Someone would catch him before he landed. He was sure of that now.

FOUR MONTHS LATER...

The supper room at the Vauxhall Pleasure Gardens was everything that Marisee wanted. The walls were covered with beautiful paintings of fields and woodlands. The table was spread with glittering silverware. The wax candles flickered in their sconces and beyond that, garlands of lamps splashed colour over the fashionable people parading up and down.

And best of all, she was sitting with Grandma on one side of her and Robert on the other. Who could have imagined this six months ago? Or before that, when she hadn't known where Robert was – and he hadn't dared walk the street in case he was kidnapped.

Grandma had said that this was the only time that she'd known Lord Mayor George Nelson to act quickly. He'd overseen the rebuilding of the Pleasure Gardens himself. Some said that he gave money from his own personal fortune to make it even more luxurious than before. But without Marisee and Robert, there might have been little of London left for a new Pleasure Gardens. Grandma was making sure that the Lord Mayor didn't forget it. She said that she mentioned it in every meeting, extra loudly if the Goldsmith was there.

It was a pity that the supper itself wasn't as sumptuous as the surroundings. Grandma held up a slice of ham. It was so thin that Marisee could see the candlelight on the other side. Turpin and Duval didn't seem to mind, though. They crammed their mouths with everything that was put in front of them – and Marisee was sure that their pockets were just as full. Garnet barely touched her food – she was too excited. Emma had given up trying to persuade her to eat.

Spindrift looked as if he would rather be anywhere else.

"He's worried that he'll see someone he might have … whose watch might have found itself in Spindrift's pocket," Robert explained.

After the pastries had been served, Spindrift

pushed back his chair. Turpin and Duval sprang up beside him. Marisee was impressed that they could move. Their bulging pockets must make them weigh double.

"It's late," Spindrift said. "It feels wrong being on this side of the river after the sun sets. It's too quiet."

"Well, you know where I am," Grandma said. "Very north of the river in Clerkenwell. If you need food or anything else..."

"Including medicinal water for your eyes," Marisee said.

"Come to us," Grandma finished.

Spindrift gave her a little bow. "Thank you."

Emma stood up last like she didn't really want to leave. "Are you sure you don't want to come back with us?" she asked Robert.

Maybe it was Marisee's imagination, but there was a little pause before Robert replied. He wasn't considering it, was he?

"Thank you," he said, with certainty. "I've never lived free before. I want to try."

Marisee smiled with relief, but Emma frowned. "You trust the Goldsmith?" she asked.

"I have a letter signed by him and the Lord Mayor," Robert said. "It says that in the eyes of the law, I am now a free man."

Grandma had secretly told Marisee that the Lord Mayor made the Goldsmith pay Lord Pritchard compensation for Robert's freedom. Marisee was furious. How could Pritchard be paid money to stop Robert being enslaved on his plantation? It was wrong and unfair. Grandma agreed, but it had been the only way to keep Robert safe.

Now, Grandma gave them all an innocent smile. "And just in case Hibbert or Pritchard try any tricks, every coffee house that still has notices offering a reward for Robert's capture has been flooded." Her smile faded. "Actually, every coffee house advertising rewards for any enslaved person has been flooded."

"The Lord Mayor even said 'sorry' to Grandma for arresting her," Marisee said.

"Only because we let him claim that *he* saved London," Grandma said. She kissed Marisee's forehead. "But it's a small price to pay for peace of mind."

"And what about the capture-creature?" Emma asked.

Robert looked serious. "I'm sure that he's still hunting me. Henry—"

"Our friend on the Isle of Dogs," Marisee said quickly. She wasn't sure how many magical beings Emma needed to know about.

"He knows the capture-creature," Robert said.

"He'll help me find a way to stop him."

Henry and the Squall had moved into another empty windmill on Millbank. The other millers chose to ignore the abandoned windmill's strange inhabitants because any time they called for a helpful breeze, their sails turned, no matter the weather in other parts of the Isle of Dogs.

"But it doesn't mean you're safe, Robert," Emma said. "If you come with us…"

Robert shook his head. "Even if it's just for a little while, I want to live free."

"It won't be for a little while!" Marisee said. "It will be for always."

So many bad things had happened to Robert, even before he'd come to London. Marisee and Grandma had sworn that he would never have no home or family again. They'd be his family from now on.

Robert smiled and nodded, but Marisee saw the fear behind his eyes. He didn't say it, but she knew – unless the capture-creature was stopped, Robert could never believe that it was "for always".

"Then you'd better have this back," Emma said.

She reached into the folds of her coat. She opened her hand. A gold box sat in the middle of her palm.

"I found it outside the back of Mr Dross's house," she said. "Steeple must have dropped it when he was running from the Domedary."

"Well, well, well," Grandma said. "I think it's come home." She took it from Emma and held it out to Robert. "Gold is always useful in this city," she said. "Sell it if you must."

They were the same words she'd used when she'd given it to him the first time.

Emma and the rest of the Red Guard Gang disappeared into the night. Marisee was pleased that Robert hadn't gone with them.

A waiter appeared. "Ladies and gentlemen, the performance is about to begin," he declared.

This time, Marisee didn't have to climb a tree. The supper room looked on to the orchestra stage.

She nudged Robert. "There's Nannerl!"

Nannerl was standing behind a harpsichord, Wolfgang by her side. The violinist raised his bow and they began to play.

"It's beautiful," Marisee said.

"It is," Robert agreed.

And of course, Marisee meant the music. And the fact that the Domedary was fast asleep. And that Robert had finally found a new family – her and Grandma.

And maybe, just maybe, he'd be by her side if there were more adventures to come.

KNOW YOUR ELEMENTALS!

THE AIR ELEMENTALS
AKA THE FUMIS

Who are they? Air spirits who are increasingly more smoke than air. They waft away the pollution – or are supposed to.

Realm: Across London, below the clouds.

Headquarters: The Whispering Gallery in St Paul's Cathedral.

Languages: Official language name has no accurate translation. The closest is Spots-Of-Colour-Carried-On-A-Gust. Weathervane is most Fumis' second language. Also speak London Sparrow, Traditional Chimney and Human English.

Powers: They can work up a hurricane and probably a tornado too, if forced. They move clouds and musical sound. They can boost a fire and put a fire out.

Weak spot: Being made from air, they absorb everything around them, including the stinking smoke billowing from London's chimneys.

Grudges: The Solid humans who insist on polluting London's air. The Dragons because ... well, let's just say that 1666 was revenge for something earlier. Fumis like to swap favours – and they will claim back their favour, or else!

THE FIRE ELEMENTALS
AKA THE DRAGONS

Who are they? Minute indestructible creatures that form the shape of dragons who guard the wealth of the City. They also eat humans.

Realm: The City of London, the walled financial quarter inside London. The cellar in the Lord Mayor of London's Mansion House. In the cracks in the walls of coffee houses and banks. Sometimes on top of church steeples overseeing their domain.

Headquarters: On top of The Monument to the Great Fire of London. It's lucky that they can make themselves small so that they can fit in.

Languages: Official language name translates as Click in human script, although it's a series of scuttles and smoulders in Dragon language. They are also fluent in the language of trade-dealing and money-making in any human tongue.

Powers: Sheer quantity. It takes over a million to make one full-size Dragon. They are telepathic so know how to fall apart and reform. Like bees, they all have all roles, which is especially important when they need to talk as a few thousand need to say the same thing at the same time to be heard. They presume they are indestructible. Oh – and not bad at riddling.

Weak spot: Smugness. They presume they're indestructible, so might not see their destruction coming… They will not, if they can ever help it, leave the City of London.

Grudges: A massive grudge against the Fumis for the incident of 1666. The Fumis blew the flames towards the flammable cargo by the river but never took the blame for the Great Fire of London. An enduring dislike of Richard Whittington for creating the Elemental Truce. Dragons should not have to follow Solid human rules. Everyone else is too inferior to have a grudge against.

THE WATER ELEMENTALS
AKA THE CHADS

Who are they? Shape-shifting water spirits. They usually take a solid(ish) shape that matches their location and its history.

Realm: The overground and underground springs and rivers of London. (Or waiting at the bottom of a well for Madam Blackwell or Marisee to drop in.) Also found guarding the plague monster of the Serpentine.

Headquarters: The Court Beneath the Wells, though Lady Walbrook may let chosen Chads into the Mithraeum, her personal domain.

Languages: Official language name translates as Fluenta in human script, although it's a series of splashes and surges in Chad language. They also speak Cockney River, London Horse and contemporary and historic human.

Powers: Have you seen the size of those stone watermill grinding wheels? Turnmill was pushing them for centuries. Chads can manipulate river water and also have a rather unnerving ability to trap their enemies in gloopy silver binding.

Weak spot: They presumed they were immortal, but pollution is defeating them. Can they survive being the city's waste disposal unit?

Grudges: The humans of Solid London for the nastiness being thrown into the rivers. The Magogs for losing the Freedom of London. The Dragons for guarding the merchants that build over the rivers to create new halls and mansions. The Fumis, just because they're airheads.

THE EARTH ELEMENTALS
AKA THE MAGOGS

Who are they? Gog and Magog, the giants that slumber at the bottom of the River Thames – or do they? No one knows for sure. They have a spy network all over London that keeps an eye on things.

Realm: The clay, gravel and mud foundations of London itself.

Headquarters: The spies are rumoured to meet in an old Roman amphitheatre beneath the Guildhall.

Languages: The language of the earth, a growling, rumbling, squirming noise that only Gog and Magog remember and speak. The spies are mostly fluent in London English and the other human languages of London.

Powers: Extreme patience. The power to move the earth and make London crumble into the ground.

Weak spot: Absence. Will the other elementals make secret plans against them?

Grudges: The rivers cut into the earth. The fires scorch it. The air drops soot across it. The humans push the foundations of their buildings deep into it and score their roads through it. Perhaps it's better to ask – against whom don't they hold a grudge?

ACKNOWLEDGEMENTS

School students often ask, "How do you make a book?" The truthful answer is: by being part of a great team of people.

Once more, domedary-sized thanks to everyone at Scholastic – Lauren Fortune, Sarah Dutton, Harriet Dunlea, Hannah Griffiths, Aimee Stewart, Andrew Biscomb, Cathy Liney – who enable my weird imagination to leak on to paper and out into the world. (And doing so through an office move too!)

Added thanks to the editing skills of Jenny Glencross and nerd-sister, Emma Roberts. I genuinely appreciate the logistics of lost music being discussed with great seriousness.

Paul Kellam, Marilyn Esther Chee and Luke Ashforth – thank you for the cover, chapter art and map, respectively. It's fabulous seeing my words transform into pictures.

Caroline Sheldon, my agent. I can never ever thank you enough for having belief in me all those years ago.

My wonderful friends who've helped me through the last few months – without you, I couldn't have written this. A special thanks to Karolina and Gary – your kindness and 'listening ear' means so much.

Caleb Parkin – little did you know that sharing your knowledge about a mollusc's radula would lead to genetically modified giant oysters. (Bivalves, I know, but I couldn't resist.)

Massive gratitude to London for your layers of history that are strewn around the rooftops and streets so frequently that we often don't see them. Your free museums and city churches are always a joy. Likewise the Spitalfields Life blog by The Gentle Author that inspires me with every post and every historian that continues to shout about the people from around the world that have shaped Britain for centuries.

And finally, a 'thank you' that's as tall as the Shard, as wide as the Greenwich 02 and as indestructible as the capture-creature, to librarians, festival organisers, teachers, family members and young people who read and share my books. Man, it's so appreciated.